Lorna versus Laura

Lorna & Tristan Series #1

Cynthia Hilston

Published by Cynthia Hilston

Cover design by Cynthia Hilston
Cover art from unsplash.com

To my writers group at North Ridgeville Library —thank you for your invaluable input. You make me a better writer. More than that, thank you for your friendship.

Subscribe to Cynthia Hilston's monthly newsletter to be the first to find out about new releases, cover reveals, special surprises, and more! Sign up at http://www.cynthiahilston.com.

Second edition author's note:
Writing is fluid. Therefore, with the publication of the third novel in the series in 2023 (*The Rock at the Bottom*), certain changes to Tristan's backstory were made in this edition. Also, slight modifications were made in some dialogue in sections that overlap between this novel and the third.

Chapter 1

My Bible was given to charity like a lot of other things I once owned when I packed what little I had left and sold the house I'd grown up in. For Christmas, I didn't celebrate with family or open presents. Rather, the last memory I now had of my childhood home was when I'd lit up a fire and burned all the old photographs. I drank a whole bottle of cheap wine and forced their faces out of my mind as the fire consumed their paper smiles.

That had all been three months ago.

Now, I sat in my new house gazing upon some sparrows as they spread seed over the hard earth. As I watched them in their messy eating from the picture window in my living room, I thought of the Bible and some vague scripture about sparrows, about God saying we're more valuable than those small birds. I idly twiddled with my wavy shoulder-length dark brown hair and remembered old Pastor Wilson's sermons on sparrows and the hairs on our heads being counted. I stopped playing with my hair and frowned at the sparrows. God had nothing important to say to me, not in nearly six years.

So I stopped speaking to him.

My thoughts and the sparrows fluttered away as my strange next-door neighbor walked into view. He was muttering under his breath, like he always did. I'd never spoken to him since moving here, but he hadn't bothered to come over and welcome me. Instead, the only time I ever saw him was when he made his trek on the narrow strip of green—well, on my side—between our houses and admired his rock garden. While it was odd for a thirty-something-year-old man to talk to himself outside, what was more unsettling was that his yard contained not a single living thing—no trees, no grass, no bushes, nothing. I assumed come spring, there would be no flowers. All he had were rocks, of all sizes and colors, but as for why, I had no idea.

Curiosity got the better of me that day as I stood from my only chair and approached the window. I turned the crank knob to open the window just enough to listen.

His lips moved vigorously, like he was delirious. His hands locked and unlocked in front of him. I leaned in closely to the cracked window and heard his voice for the first time.

"They need to take me away. They need to take me away. They need to take me away."

I quickly withdrew, shutting the window and pulling the curtains closed before he noticed. I nearly jumped out of my skin when the phone rang, as if its trill demanded to know what I'd been doing.

I ran into the kitchen and breathlessly answered the phone.

"Lorna, where are you?"

"Macy, what—?"

"It's four o'clock, darling. Or did you forget?"

"Sorry, sorry. I was just..." *Just spying on my neighbor who's probably got bodies buried in his basement.*

"Well, are you coming over or not?" Macy's voice rose in pitch by the end of her sentence.

"I'll be right over. You're sure you don't want me to bring anything?"

"Just yourself. You could use some company."

"See you in a few minutes."

I hung up and went to the fridge and rifled through it, hoping to come across a peace offering. I didn't think a half-eaten loaf of bread, a jar of mustard, or some week-old ham would do the job, so I closed the door and sighed. I wondered if a trip to the grocery store was in order after paying an overdue visit to Macy. Then I remembered that the grocery store would be closed.

I pulled on my Sunday coat over my house dress and dropped into the driver's seat of my ten-year-old Cadillac. While I fretted and fought with Ol' Bessie to start, I checked over my hair and smoothed it down. Looking like a fright show, I considered telling Macy I was practicing for Halloween, and my costume was a lonely old maid.

When I pulled into her driveway ten minutes later, Macy greeted me outside with a hug.

"How are you holding up?" she asked.

I tried not to scowl at my friend's concerned blond brow. Her green eyes shone with a hundred questions as I replied, "Fine."

"I thought maybe a walk since it's, you know, actually decent weather for late March in Cleveland."

"A walk's fine."

"So, have you heard from him?"

I kept my eyes trained on the pavement, the repetitive movement of my feet a nice distraction. "Not lately. It could be months."

"Laura, I'm—"

I stopped abruptly and glared at Macy. "It's *Lorna*."

"Sorry. It's just...you were Laura for a lot longer to me."

"That girl is dead." I felt Macy's stare but didn't acknowledge it. "Maybe a walk wasn't such a good idea."

"Lorna, come on. I feel like all I do is apologize to you anymore, but I shouldn't have to apologize for worrying about my best friend."

I gazed at Macy straight in the face. "I don't blame you. You have a family, a husband who loves you and two great children."

"I think you blame yourself."

"We're not talking about this."

"Then when are you gonna talk about it, darling? You can't live like this forever."

"I'm not. I just moved into a new house, remember? I'm starting over."

"Then when can I come over?"

I sighed and turned back toward Macy's house. The breeze was dancing with the almost bare branches above us. Macy's street was lined with what seemed like an endless number of hundred-year-old oaks and maples. Tiny buds of hope filled the branches, the promise of new life that came every spring. But I couldn't accept it. It was a gift that had been denied to me for the past six springs.

"The house isn't ready." *I'm not ready.*

Macy didn't need to see the physical manifestation of my solitude in a house so spartan that anyone breaking in to loot the place would question if anyone lived there. A bed, a table, my dad's old armchair, my two favorite books by bestselling author B.R. Stevenson, a few items of clothing, and a small radio were all I had, all I needed, all I wanted.

I didn't count the one photograph from my parents' wedding day that I couldn't burn.

"Then when? Maybe we could do some shopping? Decorate your new place?"

We arrived at Macy's driveway. Her husband, John, waved at us from the front yard while he played catch with his young son, and his baby daughter sat in her stroller, giggling and clapping. It was like some Norman Rockwell painting, and I was a black spot that marred it.

"I don't think so," I said. "Right now, I'm just making enough to cover my needs."

Macy didn't seem convinced. She grabbed me by the hand and yanked me toward her house like she used to when we were kids. "Maybe a walk wasn't the best idea, after all," she said, echoing my words from earlier. "Maybe some tea? Or something stronger?"

Remembering the elephant-ran-me-over headache I'd woken up with the day after Christmas from my drinking binge, I shook my head. "No, tea's fine. Just dandy."

Macy was already bustling about her small bungalow kitchen like the perfect hostess. With her back to me as she filled the teakettle, she asked, "Will you stay for dinner?"

"I-I don't know if..." I searched for an excuse. I had taken up a new hobby—ballroom dancing, still-life painting, figure skating, pottery—yes, pottery sounded interesting. "I have a pottery class this evening."

Macy set the kettle on the stove over the heat and turned around, her eyebrows raised. "I've known you since before either of us can remember, Lorna. We're like twins, and I know for a fact you don't have an artistic bone in your body. Besides, it's Sunday."

"Maybe part of my starting a new phase in my life involves exploring my creative side. Besides, maybe there's a private studio in someone's house that does pottery lessons, even on a Sunday."

Macy shook her head, her curls bouncing around her shoulders. "Speaking of Sunday, when's the last time you stepped in a church?"

My face must have darkened as my thoughts did.

"Okay, bad topic. Hair. When's the last time you went to the beautician's? I'm thinking of maybe going a little shorter."

"Your hair's beautiful," I said, annoyed at my own appearance. "I'll kill you if you chop it off."

"I didn't say that. I said a little."

"No, I don't think so. I'm fine right now."

The kettle whistled, ending our conversation for a minute while Macy poured two cups and placed two cubes of sugar in mine. She knew how I took my tea, how I was a creature of habit who didn't change her hair, and how I was as stubborn as an ox. She knew me too well, in fact.

Macy took the seat across the table and pushed my cup toward me.

"Thanks," I muttered, sipping the tea.

"Laura, look at me."

"I'm not—"

"But you are."

I sighed. Arguing with my best friend was getting me nowhere, except back at the beginning of the endless circle we kept running in. I half-wondered if I was running away from my past but really just forming a deeper trench in the mud as I ran that same circle, digging my plight lower into the ground.

"You are Laura Ashford. You were born February 29, 1916. You'll have your seventh leap birthday next year. And somewhere in there is the girl I knew for twenty years before she decided to try to become somebody else. You might think it's swell to pretend to play house with your new place and go to your job like we were kids again going through the motions, but, Laura, I know you better than that. You haven't talked, I mean really talked, to me in years. My goodness, this is the first time

I've seen you since you up and moved. Do you know how many times I've tried calling you?"

"Yes," I said in a tight voice. I could still hear the incessant ringing of the phone every evening at seven o'clock.

"You know what I think?"

"What's that? I'm sure you're going to tell me whether I want to hear it or not."

"All of this—selling your house, changing your name—it's just like when you refused to face what happened to your parents. You've been burying yourself for years, Lorna. You can't keep living like this. I'm really worried about you."

"Don't you bring that up. You couldn't know the first thing what it feels like, Macy. I showed up at that trial when I had to." My insides tightened, from my stomach to my throat. I thought I might stop breathing. Taking a deep breath, I forced myself to calm down.

"I'm sorry, darling. I didn't mean to go to that place, but the question still lingers: What are you going to do, Lorna?"

"Are you trying to make me angry, or have you taken up a new hobby?" I asked, making to stand. Enough was enough.

"You mean, like your supposed pottery?"

If there was one thing to be said about Macy Wells, it was she was twice as stubborn as me and ruthless, too.

"I should be getting to that class," I said dully.

Without a goodbye or any promise to see each other again soon, I walked out of Macy's house that late afternoon without looking back. I didn't know if her eyes were on me, if she was sad or angry or what, but I didn't care. At least that was what I told myself.

I humorlessly laughed as raindrops began pelting my windshield on the way home. How appropriate.

The pitter-patter drowned out in the background as my mind replayed a hundred memories of growing up with Macy by my side. We had taken countless walks down tree-lined streets in every season, our laughter echoing off the houses as we held hands. We'd skipped more than walked, actually. We'd jumped into piles of leaves by the road. We'd fallen to the ground in fits of giggles, sharing a secret joke. We'd blessed the neighbors' yards with angels in the snow. That had been Laura Ashford and Macy Grace, two little girls who'd grown into young women, whose lives had become so different. It was a small miracle they had remained tethered as long as they had.

I wiped a single tear from my cheek as I turned onto my street, careful to keep my other hand on the wheel. It wouldn't do to have an accident like my parents had.

As I was about to pull into my driveway, having almost slowed to a stop, I saw my neighbor again. He was standing in his rock garden at the front of his house, staring at the sky. He was soaked. Part of me wanted to yell at him to get a hobby, but then I wondered if the rocks and the freezing rain were his hobby. Just like mine was pottery.

One big lie.

Chapter 2

Monday morning dawned dreary and grey, the perfect companion to the mood that had settled inside me yesterday upon leaving Macy's house and hadn't left. My gloominess had invited itself into my house like an unwanted guest, but the way I clung to it, I half-wondered if I had invited it, after all.

Monday meant going back to work, and work meant going through my day pretending I was enthusiastic about molding the young minds of the next generation. Teaching wasn't a bad profession, but none of my students would ever mistake me for Miss Sunshine down the hall. Yes, there really was a Miss Sunshine teaching at Washington Elementary.

She was just like her name sounded. I, Miss Ashford, laughed little and had a darker sense of humor that wasn't appropriate for first graders.

After I dressed and did my best job to undo the Halloween costume version of me from yesterday, I made my coffee and picked at a bowl of cereal. I kept the chair in the living room, so there I sat, listening to the radio. News of the war didn't sit well with me, but I wanted to know what was going on overseas, nonetheless. I wondered how Chucky was holding up, a boy of only nineteen who should have been at home sleeping in the safety of his bed instead of firing bullets and having bullets fired at him.

∞ ∞ ∞

One year earlier...

The letter arrived three months after Pearl Harbor. Chucky had just celebrated his eighteenth birthday in January. He was a boy. Still in high school. The United States Army didn't seem to care a whit about any of that, however.

I had just come home from work. Upon entering, I found my brother, my only sibling, sitting at the kitchen table with a piece of paper in his smooth hands, his boyish face somewhere between breaking down in tears and utter shock.

"What is it?" I asked, rushing to his side, not even stopping to take off my coat or put my purse down.

Chucky handed the paper to me. As my eyes read every awful word, I hated this war even more. It wasn't enough that my brother and I had already suffered our own family tragedy, but the affairs of the world, first the Depression and now World War II, were our problems, too.

"They can't do this," I said.

"Lorna, don't let them take me away."

I wanted to run my hands through my little brother's dark curly hair like I had when he had actually been smaller than me. Now, he stood a head taller than me, and I often avoided looking him straight in the eyes, for that face, it was too unnerving. I saw only our father staring back at me, twenty or thirty years younger.

"It says you're to report in June. They're letting you finish school, at least."

My words did little to comfort either of us. My brother was being ripped away, the last member of our family torn from my grip.

"What's the point in going to school? Now my future's decided for me. I'll be shipped off to training and then to God knows where."

"God has nothing to do with this," I said firmly. "God couldn't care less about what's going on down here. Things just happen, and He lets them."

"Lorna, you can't blame God for what happened to them. There was someone to blame, but it wasn't God. It was St—"

"Chucky, listen," I hastily interrupted him, not wishing to hear more. Our words were too reminiscent of a conversation we'd had years ago. "I'll see what I can do. See if I can find a way to get you out of this. We have some time."

Chucky was already standing and leaving the room. I wanted to follow him and hug him like we used to do when we were younger. After our parents died, Chucky and I, we were all we had, just each other. But when the door to his bedroom slammed shut, I sighed and wandered into the living room. Our parents' smiles surrounded me, mocking me in that moment. I dropped into the ragged armchair, which my father had always called his own for years, and buried my face in my hands as I sobbed.

My tears meant nothing. There was nothing I could do to keep my brother safe. There was nothing I could do to rewind the past. More tears fell in June when my brother and I hugged for the last time, and he walked resolutely out the front door to step into the car that was here to take him away.

His eyes held betrayal as he stared out the back window at me as the car pulled away. Tears falling down my red cheeks, I stood there until the car disappeared around the corner. When I entered the house, I knew I could no longer stay in my childhood home. I went to the first framed picture I saw and took it down, placing my parents, a baby Chucky, and eight-year-old me face-down on the dining room table. One by one, the pictures all came down that day, every smile hidden, no longer able to stare at me as I sat and walked and slept in that house.

Alone. I was truly alone now.

The next day, all my mother's fine china went into boxes, wrapped in newspaper.

Next went my parents' clothes, still hanging in their closet. I stripped their bed, tossing the sheets in the trash.

For the next several weeks when I came home from work, I ate a quick dinner and spent the rest of the evening boxing my family's lives. By Thanksgiving, the house was nearly empty. I had donated, sold, and trashed nearly every belonging and piece of furniture besides my bedroom set.

I put the house up for sale in October, and it sold within two weeks to a young family. I couldn't look upon them without being reminded of my own childhood, but these walls meant nothing to me anymore. It had been the people dwelling within these walls that had made it memorable, that had once filled it with love. Now, the turn-of-the-century home was an entombed corpse.

Chucky was in Tunisia. After training in El Paso, he had been shipped off, as we had expected. Letters were sparse, but we wrote when we could. It had been two months since I'd heard from him. I didn't even know if he was alive.

By Christmas, I moved, and the rest was history. My history. A sad story without an ending.

∞ ∞ ∞

I went to the picture window out of curiosity but didn't see my strange neighbor. I wondered if he even had a car or worked, as I'd never actually seen him leave the house. Shaking my head to try to clear my thoughts, I pulled on my long everyday coat, went outside, and shivered in the wind, frowning that there was still too much winter in the air for spring.

I passed my neighbor's bungalow house as I drove, but from what I could tell, every window was dark. The curtains were pulled shut. Not that I'd stopped long enough to actually do a thorough investigation of his house or anything.

Fifteen minutes later, I parked my car in the lot outside the school and hoped it would start when I went to leave. The sputtering protests the engine made as I turned it off weren't promising.

Pulling my coat collar closer to my face as the wind whipped my hair, I was assaulted by the voice of the only male teacher at Washington.

"Good morning, Miss Ashford," Tom Darling said.

Yes, another unfortunate last name of a teacher at my place of employment. I always wondered if Mr. Darling took a special secret thrill in every female teacher calling him "darling," whether married or not. He made it clear in the staff room daily that he was single.

"Good morning," I muttered.

"Mind if I walk in with you?"

I inwardly sighed as my eyes surveyed him through my hair. Mr. Darling was about my age and attractive. I begrudgingly admitted that much to myself the first day he'd started teaching there back in the fall. The only problem was Mr. Darling knew he was darling with his wavy black hair and dark brown eyes. His olive skin, he said, was from his mother's side, a hail to his half-Italian status.

"Why would I mind?" I asked coolly, avoiding eye contact. I felt his eyes on me, however, and I was grateful for the coverage my coat provided. Even with the accentuation of my slim frame by my dress's shoulder pads, high waist, and A-line skirt, I didn't feel attractive.

"So, how was your weekend?"

Small talk. I detested it on principle. "Fine. Yours, Mr. Darling?"

He held the door for me, saying, "Call me Tom."

There it was. The invitation I hadn't invited. The line he used with all the girls. Well, one of his lines. Mr. Darling ought to start his own country called One-Liners and rule it. I almost told him so but chose instead to smile with all the plastic of Bakelite.

"Oh, you're too kind, but I'm old-fashioned, Mr. Darling. I'm afraid I was raised to be more formal than that until I actually get to know a person."

Every overly polite word should have been venom to his charms, but this man wasn't deterred. When we reached the end of the hall where I needed to turn right and he needed to turn left, he gently grabbed my hand.

Done with my charade, I withdrew my hand from his grasp like I'd been burned and scowled at him. I turned and proceeded to my classroom, only to be greeted by a horde of unruly children. The moment a few of them saw the no-nonsense look on my face, the pandemonium slowly died down, until every student dutifully went to their desk and sat.

"Good morning, class," I said.

"Good morning, Miss Ashford," came the chorus.

At the very least, my students knew what was expected of them, and I didn't often have problems with them. After the Pledge of Allegiance, I began the math lesson, followed by spelling. When lunch arrived, I'm not sure who was more relieved, the students or me, but we all hustled to the freedom the next hour afforded with enthusiasm.

My youthful exuberance fell flat when I saw Mr. Darling and Miss Sunshine flirting in the staff room. I opted to take my lunch outside by myself, imagining Darling Sunshines wandering the streets should they marry and procreate. The thought almost made me lose my appetite. Almost.

By the end of the day, I nearly kicked my car into gear. When it was running, I drove home as quickly, but carefully, as possible. My new habit of next-door neighbor-watching took full effect as I spotted Mr. Rock Garden in his yard.

Before I went inside, I walked to the corner of my identical house, where the driveway met the lawn. My front yard was small, but I hid behind an evergreen, watching and listening, my curiosity needing satiation.

"They need to take me away."

Wondering if those were the only words he knew, I was half-tempted to ask, "Who needs to take you away?"

But when his eyes seemed to fall on me, I withdrew and ran inside, mentally berating myself for acting like a schoolgirl with a morbid crush.

"If only you could see me now," I whispered to my invisible parents.

Chapter 3

For the next few weeks, I stopped spying on Mr. Rock Garden. My phone stopped ringing every evening at seven o'clock, the silence from my best and only friend deafening to ears that only seemed to hear the worst in people anymore. At work, I did what I needed to keep my job, but as the days warmed, I sought the comfort of the sunshine on my face while I took walks at lunch. At home, when I wasn't listening to the news on the radio, I reread *Forlorn for Love*, Stevenson's most recent book, for the fifth time in two years.

Easter came and went without any celebration on my part. The bells from the church down the street might as well have been tolling my doom. If God lived in churches, all the more reason to stay away, as if memory of my last visit to a church wasn't reason enough.

Sometimes I wished I hadn't burned all the pictures. I could've arranged them around my parents' old dining room table like a child playing with her dollhouse. I could make them say whatever I wanted and eat my invisible food. Their silence and imaginary presence would have made my Easter complete in its lack of promise to bring new hope.

The Monday after Easter, I received a letter from Chucky. It was the first good news I'd received in I'd forgotten how long.

Dear Lorna,

Sorry it's been so long. How was Christmas? The move? I still can't believe you sold our house. When I come back, it's going to take some getting used to being in a different house. It was the one thing that was familiar to me, the thought of coming home. All right, that's not really true. I miss you, Lorna. I could tell you about what's happening here, but I'm sure you've heard enough on the radio already. Just know that I've got friends in the squad. That makes it easier to keep going. We hold each other up. Hope you're holding up, Lorna. Write soon.

Love,

Chuck

Tears threatened to fall, and when they overwhelmed the rims of my eyes, I blinked until they tracked down my cheeks and dropped off. I wiped the remainder away and shook my head. Who did I have holding me up? Chucky was fighting on the battlefield, yet he was choosing hope, against all odds. I folded his letter like it was the only holy thing I had and kissed it, putting it in my shirt pocket right over my heart.

I went to the picture window, my companion in bird watching, and opened it to let the music and the sun in. I sat in my lone chair and closed my eyes, trying to go back to a simpler time.

When I opened my eyes, I was surprised to find over an hour had passed and realized I must have drifted off. I heard muttering and footsteps on the dirt and pebbles. My neighbor made his debut again after my absence from the window.

I couldn't help but study him. Unlike most men with their neat, trimmed hair, Mr. Rock Garden had a sandy mop that nearly touched his shoulders. His beard was equally unkempt, and his eyes and the parts of his face that weren't hidden by facial hair were obscured by large glasses.

I wondered what his story really was. Was he mentally unstable, or, like me, was he just sad and bitter? I'd spent so many years wallowing in my own torrents of turmoil, finally drowning myself in them after Chucky had left, that I had never given much thought to anyone else who might be in need of a life preserver.

Still, Mr. Rock Garden had his rocks. Maybe they were his friends, and if he were truly crazy, maybe they made him happy, even if it was all a lie. Then I remembered him standing in the rain, staring at the sky as if in supplication.

I was tempted to call Macy, to tell her how sorry I was, to let her know I'd finally heard from my brother, and to ask how she was doing.

Instead, my mind returned to the last thing I'd told her: about going to my phantom pottery class. I laughed at the irony. Making pottery was molding form, function, and life into something once seemingly useless. It was creating. I'd lied to Macy, and mostly myself, that buying this house was starting over, trying to recreate a life from a shattered pot. Nothing could be further from the truth, for I knew I was running away.

Tiring of the birds and my neighbor, I left the window and got into my car. I drove to the nearest shops and parked. I didn't know what had compelled me, but I entered an art shop. I listlessly walked up and down the aisles, idly toying with the idea of buying something. Or trying something new to force myself out of the dumps.

Ten minutes later, I left with three canvases of different sizes and a bag full of paint and paintbrushes. I had no idea what I was doing. I did know I had grown tired of my own company, and maybe I really did need a hobby. If nothing else, I could write about it to Chucky and provide him with free entertainment.

I could hear him now.

"You? Paint? Lorna, you can't even draw a stick figure!"

"Well," I'd defend myself, "I haven't tried painting since I was a kid. Who knows? I might be the next Van Gogh."

Chucky would laugh, smile, and shake his head at that, but he'd probably join me in my endeavor, if for nothing else than to humor me. And to be my support.

Upon returning, I laid out my treasures on the living room floor. Realizing I'd need something to protect the wooden floor from any drops of paint that were inevitable, I took the rattiest sheet from my small collection and stretched it across the room, filling it almost completely.

"See, Macy?" I murmured. "If I had furniture in my house, I wouldn't have room to create my own studio, and here you wanted to go shopping to decorate my place. Heck, maybe I'll hang my creations on these bare walls."

I briefly considered turning on the radio, but in the silence, I found peace.

Now it was time to see if I also found inspiration.

I picked my favorite color, green, and poured some of the paint onto some newspaper. Before I knew it, my largest canvas, a three-by-five-foot monstrosity, was covered with a mess of blues, greens, and yellows. The colors were the brightest thing in the room. For the next hour, my hand worked furiously with the brush. I used every color I had. I poured the paint. I dripped it. I smeared and blotted it. By the end, I stood back and marveled at my creation.

The red was splattered all over, including on me and the sheet. It looked like someone had been murdered, their blood sprayed on a grimy wall.

My clothes were ruined, but I didn't care. Maybe my painting would never sell for a nickel. Maybe it should've been burned. Maybe no one in their right mind would ever hang such a horrible thing in their house, but once it dried, I promised myself it would hang proudly on my wall.

It was my creation. The first thing I'd made in a long time.

∞ ∞ ∞

Twenty years earlier...

I ran home from school, nearly tripping over my feet because I couldn't contain my excitement. My painting was going to be displayed in the school art fair! Mrs. Manning, my first-grade teacher, glowed at my work, telling me that my kitty was "the best she'd ever seen, just ducky."

When I entered my house, Mom was busy in the kitchen. I blurted a hello to her before seeking out Daddy. Daddy was the one I really wanted to see. I found him in his chair in the living room, the newspaper in his strong hands, a pipe clenched between his lips as the smoke lazily swirled around his head.

"Daddy! I've got great news!" I bounded toward him, no longer able to contain myself. I nearly fell into his lap.

Chuckling, he folded the paper and set it aside. "All right, darling. What's this about?"

"I'm gonna have my painting in the art show at school!"

"Wow! That's wonderful, Laura. What did you make?"

I was too young back then to know he was likely humoring me, but Daddy always gave in to my whims.

"A kitty! A white one, just like I've always wanted."

"Well, we'll have to make sure we see this painting. As for the getting a cat, you may want to hold off on that. Mom has some news she'd like to share with you."

I frowned, curious, a bit deflated to have the subject changed. "What?"

Daddy laughed, a deep, rumbling sort that started in his belly and slowly rose through his chest and out his mouth. "You'll just have to wait and see at dinner."

As if perfectly cued, Mom announced dinner, and we were all in the tiny kitchen around the table a minute later. After our prayer, my parents took each other's hands, and Mom said, "Laura, you're gonna be a big sister."

My eyes felt like they would drop right out of their sockets. When I was able to recover, I squealed in delight. "Yay! Oh, Mom! Daddy! Is it a little brother or sister?"

My parents laughed.

"It'll be some time before we know that. The baby won't be born for several months, Laura," Mom said.

"Now, Laura, tell your mother what you shared with me."

"I've got good news, too. My painting from school is gonna be in the art show."

Mom smiled widely. "Wonderful, just wonderful. It seems like tonight is cause for celebration with all this good news."

A couple of weeks later, my parents went along with me to the school one evening to see my kitty painting. They told me how talented I was. Filled my head with tales of fame. Entertained a little girl's dreams.

Looking back, I realized every kid in the school had their artwork displayed. Maybe mine was nothing special, but my parents believing in me made it special. The truth was that painting hardly looked like a cat or anything resembling a living animal with four legs and pointy ears.

My painting dried by the next morning, and I hung it on the largest stretch of wall in my living room. As I stood there and admired/contemplated/scowled at it, I blinked away a stray tear for my old kitty painting.

With the photographs, I had burned it.

Somehow, now I wished I hadn't.

Chapter 4

Being on spring vacation the whole week after Easter didn't feel like a vacation at first, but then I took up my new hobby with vigor, losing myself in the paint and the canvases for hours in a way I never imagined. It was like dancing with a partner who never tired of me stepping on his feet. I molded perfectly into his sure hold on me, like two parts of a whole meant to be together.

I didn't tell all this romanticized version of my hobby to Chucky, though. In my usual self-deprecating manner, I wrote to him I'd painted the next masterpiece, sure to win us thousands in the next big New York art show, not that I had any plans of actually traveling to the Big Apple. I hoped it would put a smile on my brother's face, nonetheless. I read over my letter, then his letter once again, making sure I wasn't forgetting anything. I was half-tempted to tell him about Mr. Rock Garden, but then I thought I'd give my brother real reason to worry about me. Spying on my neighbor was an unfortunate habit, not a hobby. Well, that was what I told myself.

I noticed my brother had signed his letter as "Chuck" instead of "Chucky." I'd already written "Chucky." That was who he'd always be to me—my little brother—no matter how tall he grew or how old he got. As I folded my letter to him and placed it in an envelope, I inwardly shuddered, hoping that Chucky would have the chance to grow old. Every day fighting in this awful war, every day across a sea, every day away from home was a cruel reminder I was alone, my only family member hopefully alive.

If I dared to speak to God for just a few seconds, I might have prayed about how I was feeling, but all that nonsense about laying my troubles at God's feet, about Him taking on my worries, about His yoke being light, all that was more lies and a cruelty. Suddenly annoyed at even entertaining a speck of a thought of God, I addressed the letter and shoved it more roughly in my purse than I'd intended. Since the sun was out and it was pleasant, I decided to walk to the post office.

I had to go past my neighbor's house to get there. This was the first time I was walking instead of driving, and he was outside. While most people would have been working in their yards on a day like this, he was about his muttering and making merry with his loveable rocks.

I must have stopped just a little too long, for his mouth stopped moving, and he locked eyes with me. Unable to help myself, I stood there like the fool I probably was and stared back. Swallowing thickly, I tried to smile. I raised my right hand and gave a little wave, but he looked at me like I was the crazy one, turned, and walked toward the back of his house. Feeling like I really was the crazy one, my face heated with humiliation, and I resumed my walk.

What was his problem? The one time I tried to be nice to him, and what did he do but be rude?

I fumed on my walk, wishing I could take back my smile and my wave. I wasn't exactly doling out smiles and waves these days, so the extra effort I'd made had been more than I thought possible in the first place. And to have received nothing in return?

I posted the letter and left the post office in a rotten mood, my hands shoved in my coat pockets, my shoulders hunched, my gaze on the sidewalk. And nearly plowed over the one person in this world who, besides Chucky, actually gave a darn about cynical and twisted me.

"Lorna!"

I stopped abruptly, nearly tripping over my feet. The boots on them were too big to begin with, but Chucky's boots were the first thing I'd grabbed before going out the door that day. I'd taken to wearing them often, as if Chucky were strolling alongside me with every step.

When I finally met her eyes, I bit my lip and said, "Hi, Macy."

"Lorna, look at you." Macy was appraising me with her vivid green eyes.

My jagged nails dug into my palms, making crescent indents, the feeling a reminder of what and who I was: a nail-biting, unkempt hermit who spied on her odd neighbor and who pretended she was creating something worthwhile with her measly attempts at painting.

I scowled and stepped aside to let some people pass. We were standing directly in front of the entrance.

"You cut your hair," I said.

"So? Is that a crime?"

"We should move out of the way."

I took a few steps toward some bushes without waiting for Macy.

She gave a withering sigh and joined me. "I don't think what we really need to be discussing is my hair, but if you insist, you're overdue for a visit to the beautician's, darling."

I self-consciously pressed my matted hair down, silently agreeing. "So, where are the kids?"

"With John. He took a few days off during the break from school to spend time with the family."

"Wonderful. One big happy family."

"Oh, come on, Lorna. Don't be like that. I haven't seen you in weeks, and this is what you wanna talk about? There's a coffee shop just down the way. What do you say?"

I shook my head. "No, money's tight."

There was truth in that, although I guiltily knew it was due in large part to my new hobby.

"My treat." Macy, her short curls bobbing around her face, challenged me with every part of her expression: the firm-set mouth, the probing eyes, and the sharp set of her jaw.

My anger evaporating like water on a hot day, I gave a small sigh and nodded. "If you insist."

"I do."

Macy hooked her arm in mine, and together, we strolled to Joe's Joe. I smirked, able to appreciate the owner's use of his name. Joe Dylan had gone to high school with Macy and me and had always been nursing a cup of coffee every morning while he stood outside the school on the steps that led up to the main entrance. While he couldn't drink the beverage during school hours, whenever the kids gathered socially, he ordered his cup o' joe, while the rest of us drank our Cokes.

I didn't see much of Joe these days, so I was shocked to see that his hairline was already beginning to recede when we entered his shop. He was busy barking out orders to his employees. The place bustled with activity. The local businessmen tended to gather in coffee shops to conduct much of their business, although I half-imagined they did more gossiping like a gaggle of hennish women and imbibed more of the caffeinated beverage than was good for them.

Macy and I joined the chaotic fray. As we stood in line, she leaned toward me and muttered, "I'm glad I didn't stay with Joe. Time hasn't been exactly kind to him."

I studied Joe for a few seconds and had to agree, although I didn't think it nice to say so. Poor Joe had developed a small paunch to sport with his pate. I wondered if it was due to stress, but then again, I always thought he loved his coffee.

"You never were a good match anyway. Whatever happened?"

Macy giggled, her curls bouncing as she held a hand to her mouth like a schoolgirl with a juicy secret. "You really wanna know?" she asked.

"Of course."

"He was a bad kisser."

I couldn't help it. I laughed. For a few moments, it was like time had rewound, and we were ten years younger, Joe Dylan standing a few feet away on the school steps, drinking his joe while Macy belabored her recent break up with him.

"And his breath smelled. All the time."

My laughter doubled over. "Like coffee?"

Macy was in fits.

"May I help you?" the worker asked impatiently.

We stopped laughing.

"Just two coffees, please," Macy said.

"Any muffins? They're fresh."

Macy looked at me, askance. I shook my head, noticing Joe was staring us down. I wondered how much of a scene we must have made, but then decided I didn't care.

"No, just two coffees. Thanks," Macy said, handing off a dime to the lady working the register.

After we had our drinks and managed to squeeze into some seats among the men in suits who were pretending to work, I said, "Thank you. Maybe we should've left Joe a tip. Or at least said hi."

Macy briefly glanced at him and then looked back at me. "No, he's too busy bossing everyone else around to take a moment to say hello. Speaking of hellos, I'm glad I ran into you."

I sobered and smiled ruefully. "I am, too. Look, Mace, I'm sorry I've been such a wet blanket lately...well, more than lately. I guess it's been a long time."

Macy waved me off. "So, what have you been doing when you're not working? Are you really taking a pottery class?"

Her tone teased the truth out of me. "Well, not exactly."

Macy took a slow, deliberate sip and raised her eyebrows. "Well? Care to elaborate, or do I have to get Joe over here to breathe on you?"

"Ugh, that's disgusting." I groaned, chuckling. "All right. I give up. Don't laugh, but I've been painting. I mean, making paintings, not painting the walls."

"Really?" By the way Macy's eyebrows nearly shot off her forehead, I knew she didn't believe me.

"I'm not claiming to be an actual artist or anything, but it's keeping me busy. Maybe it's even helping me heal," I admitted softly.

Macy set her cup down and reached for my hands across the small table. She squeezed them, and I looked her straight in the face and saw tears brimming in her eyes, a tiny smile decorating her lips.

"Laura, that's wonderful."

"Please don't."

"I'm sorry, but I can't help it. You'll always be Laura to me. This Lorna girl you've been pretending to be isn't you. It's Laura who's painting, who's creating something from these ashes."

I sighed. "Maybe I shouldn't have mentioned it. It's nothing, really."

"Don't. Don't do that."

"What?"

"Don't deny. Stop the lies, darling. Hey, maybe I could see them when you're ready?"

I hesitated. "I-I don't know. They're not anything to brag about."

"But that isn't the point."

"Maybe someday, but not yet, okay?"

Macy nodded. "I understand. So, what else? Are you counting down the days before school ends?"

Grateful for the subject change, we talked for the next couple of hours like nothing had changed. We drank more coffee than Joe probably ever had in a day in high school. Afterward, I walked one way, and Macy went the other, our parting the antithesis of our previous one.

When I returned to my neighborhood, I slowed my pace, trying to relax the caffeine out of me. I was genuinely happy for the first time since I could remember. As I strolled past Mr. Rock Garden's house, he was standing in his usual spot. My hand and my mouth, whether compelled by the caffeine or by my elation, waved and smiled.

I stopped, not sure what miracle I was expecting.

Then it happened.

He waved, the most miniscule of waves, like a shy toddler whose mother tells him to say bye-bye. The smile could wait.

Chapter 5

My more positive outlook continued as green cascaded over the landscape around me, and flowers made their debut, unfolding from the winter's nap in the ground. Spring was infectious with its promises. For the first time in nearly six years, I felt a bit like Laura again. Despite the goodness being poured on me, I never fully embraced it. In the back of my mind, I knew the sixth anniversary of my parents' death was coming on June 21.

On the last day of school, Miss Sunshine announced in the staff room that she and Mr. Darling were engaged. Mr. Darling grinned, every bit the lovestruck fool, and added that he hoped Miss Sunshine would be Mrs. Darling before the next school year started. Applause broke out around me, and I joined in, actually happy for them. If nothing else, this news hopefully meant Mr. Darling would stop trying to woo anything with two legs and breasts.

As the teachers returned to their classrooms to finish packing away their things for the summer, Miss Sunshine stopped me as I made for the door. "Miss Ashford, do you have a minute?"

I gave her a small smile. "Yes, what is it, Miss Sunshine?"

Miss Sunshine was tall, blond, and had blue eyes, just like you'd expect with a name like that.

"It seems silly to keep calling each other by our last names, don't you think?"

I shrugged. "All right. Call me Lorna, then."

"And please call me Angela. Just think, I won't even be Miss Sunshine much longer. Mrs. Darling. Can you imagine?"

Miss Sunshine was beginning to give me a bit too much sunshine, so I took a step back and forced a smile. "Congratulations," I said, making to walk away.

Miss Sunshine grabbed me by the hand, the sudden movement taking me by surprise. When I frowned at her and retracted my hand, she gave me an apologetic smile.

"Sorry about that. It's just...well, this is embarrassing, but would you consider— Would you be one of my bridesmaids?"

I probably looked like a fish out of water, the way my mouth was gaping.

"But— What? Don't you have close friends, sisters, cousins?"

Miss Sunshine's countenance darkened, the sunshine covered by clouds. Storm clouds. "I don't talk to my family. I've only lived here for a year, so I haven't gotten to know many people. I grew up far away and cut all connections when I left."

Well, this was a new development.

"Really?" I couldn't help but blurt. At her hurt expression, I felt about as good as I'd feel at kicking a puppy. A puppy with begging eyes and a bow around its neck. "Sorry," I continued. "It's just... You always struck me as the type of girl who's got millions of friends following her everywhere."

Women like Angela Sunshine were the most popular girls in high school, the ones who every girl wanted to be and every boy wanted to date. I imagined her growing up rich and pampered, her family forging on through the Depression, their generations'-old money keeping them afloat. She was supposed to have visited Europe every summer and been spoon-fed delicacies by servants.

But the truth was I knew very little about the young woman who looked every bit a timid little girl asking for a lollipop at the candy shop, afraid the man behind the counter would bark his denial to grant her one simple wish.

Angela—that was who she'd quickly become to me—shook her head and asked, "Well, will you?"

"Angela, look, I'd feel better about this whole thing if we were actually friends."

"Oh, I get it." Angela turned, her eyes on her feet.

"Wait, that's not what I meant," I said, placing a hand on her shoulder and then awkwardly removing it. "I'm awful at this whole friendship thing. I only have one friend myself, and until recently, I nearly burned the bridge connecting us. We ought to try to get to know each other better. Then I'd feel like I could be the real McCoy to you."

Angela giggled. "'Real McCoy'? Lorna, you're out of practice. It's 1943."

I smiled ruefully. My slang was caught as much in the past as the rest of me. "Old habits die hard. So, are my terms acceptable?"

Angela's sunshine returned. "Oh, definitely." She clapped like the girl who had gotten her lollipop.

∞ ∞ ∞

When I returned home that day, I was grateful to have summer upon us. While I enjoyed the quietude of my house, I admitted that having a couple of friends would be a nice change of pace. Macy's constant presence in my otherwise lonely life was proof enough that she was the type of friend worth keeping. As for Angela, I was curious about her past but also ashamed for judging her all those months, not really knowing the person who hid behind all that put-on brightness.

When I didn't have human conversation, I had my paintings, which I'd hung throughout the house over the past several weeks. I'd slowed in my production of them, however, realizing I couldn't afford to keep up my newfound hobby at this rate. I still had to eat and pay for the roof over my head.

As the day wore on into late evening, I sat in my single chair by the picture window and listened to the birdsong. I sipped my herbal tea languidly as I drew to the conclusion of *Forlorn for Love*. Closing my tattered copy of the book, I wondered what the birds might sing if their voices allowed them words to speak their stories, but then I supposed they didn't really need to be like people to say what ran deeper than human understanding.

Something inside me that had been broken for a long time was on the mend. My painting, the birdsong, my stubborn best friend, the letters from Chucky, the potential of a new friend in Angela...these parts of the puzzle were creating something beautiful out of the mess my life had become.

When Mr. Rock Garden stepped into the flowerless place next door, for the first time, he seemed to be standing among tombstones. He was the only living thing. His back was to me as the orangey hue of dusk settled on his hunched shoulders. I watched carefully, leaving my chair to go to the window to get a better look. His shoulders shook erratically, and through the opening in the window, his desperate song of "They need to take me away" came with sobs. I gasped and recoiled. My right index finger came away from my cheek with the saltiness of a single tear. A single tear that would drown in Mr. Rock Garden's torrent of tears.

I closed the curtains, feeling I had intruded on a private funeral. While curiosity was my main culprit for watching my neighbor these past several weeks, I was beginning to wonder if I had developed some sort of unhealthy obsession with him. What was his story? Who was he really? What was his name?

As I walked through my desolate, pathetic house, I sadly marveled at how I could live mere feet away from another, yet he remained a perfect stranger. In my mind, I'd given him a name, mocked his rock garden, judged his physical appearance, and imagined any number of wild scenarios about his past.

I went into the bathroom and stared at my reflection, and for the first time, I realized how much my life could mirror his. We were riding in the same boat and standing at opposite ends, yet the boat was sinking just the same. We were going down with it if we continued to pretend the other didn't exist.

It was high time I saw Mr. Rock Garden as a real person and not just some caricature standing among a pile of dead things.

Heck, rocks weren't even dead. They'd never been alive.

But Mr. Rock Garden, he was alive. Very much, I hoped.

∞ ∞ ∞

It took me another week to work up my resolve to confront my neighbor. While waving and smiling were easy enough, what I was about to attempt was a whole new level of insanity. My concern for his well-being only increased as I continued to watch him. I couldn't seem to keep myself from my window. I was drawn to him like a moth to light, and whether that light would fry me or guide my way, I couldn't be sure.

As I stepped outside on the first day of summer, the warm breeze picked up around me. The gusts were coming fast, and I glanced at the sky to find dark clouds moving in. I'd just seen my neighbor in his usual spot in his yard, so before the storm drove him in, I planned to approach him and introduce myself.

His back was to me as I made the short trek across my lawn and onto his rocky ground. The crunching of the stones underfoot alerted him to my presence. He turned and gave a little start.

"Sorry," I blurted, holding up a hand. "I didn't mean to scare you."

I stopped about ten feet from him, the heat of the air adding to the heat from my embarrassment on my face. He scrutinized me for several seconds, relaxed, and shrugged.

"I-I'm Lorna Ashford, by the way," I said over the wind. "I meant to introduce myself to you sooner, but..." But what? The opportunity hadn't presented itself? The timing hadn't been right? I'd been too busy? My excuses fell, lame at my feet. Clearing my throat, I forged on. "But anyway, here I am now. Lorna. Hello."

He continued to stare. If I hadn't heard his mantra of "They need to take me away," I would have thought him dumb.

I stepped back. "I can see I've bothered you. I'm sorry. I'll—"

"Wait."

His soft voice barely carried over the breeze, but I was certain he had spoken. I turned back and blinked.

"Tristan Blake."

"What?"

"My name. It's Tristan Blake."

I smiled. This was more than I'd ever managed between us, and for Mr. Blake's part, he seemed as uncomfortable as me. "Hello, Mr. Blake. Anyway, I..."

The wind was whipping mercilessly around us now, my hair flaying my cheeks. Suddenly, something cracked, followed by a boom, louder than anything I'd ever heard. If the stones had ears, even they would've jumped. Stilled into silence, I looked around to see what had made such a noise and gazed in horror upon a large branch from an oak tree that had just smashed in my roof.

"Oh, my—" I started to say but couldn't finish.

Suddenly, Mr. Blake took my hand and pulled me roughly to him. "Tornado," he said, pointing at the sky.

My eyes followed his finger and connected with the funnel cloud not far off.

"Come on," he urged, yanking me farther into his yard. "In the cellar."

Without protest, I allowed him to lead the way. His strong arms quickly opened the cellar doors, and he pushed me in more forcefully than under normal circumstances would have been appropriate. Joining me on the stairs into darkness, he pulled the doors shut and secured them. He brushed past me, evidently searching for a light source. A minute later, he turned a small flashlight on, the light illuminating his hairy face. As the light beam moved around the room, a tiny, musty cellar was revealed. It was like some scene out of a horror film: end-of-the-world destruction outside and locked in total darkness with a stranger who was an ax murderer.

I forced such exaggerated thoughts from my mind and took a deep breath. Beyond the doors, the tornado was like a freight train going by right next to the house. Glass shattered. Branches cracked. Bits of wood and other debris hit the doors. Trees snapped to their demise.

I was about to approach Mr. Blake when he came to my side.

"Best we stay down here until it's over. Shouldn't be too long," he said in an unnervingly placid voice.

He smelled of sweat and dirt. Mr. Blake was entirely too close for comfort, yet given there was a tornado ripping apart our neighborhood just beyond a couple of shaking wooden doors, his presence was the only comfort I had.

"How can you be so calm?" I asked in a trembling whisper.

"I grew up in Kansas."

If we had more light, I probably would've seen a wry smile stretched across his bearded lips.

"You mean, like Dorothy? *The Wizard of Oz*?"

Mr. Blake chuckled. "Something like that, although I've never seen the movie."

I shook my head, but he couldn't see it, not with the flashlight's beam on the floor. While Mr. Blake didn't put his arm around me, his body heat wrapped around my back and shoulders as we huddled on the dank dirt floor in a space that felt like a tomb. The ends of his hair tickled my left cheek, his breath hot in my ear. I was frozen with fear, left at Mr. Blake's mercy. If ever there was a time for him to bring out an ax and do his work, now was the perfect opportunity, but Mr. Blake just sat there, silent and strong. In a few minutes, the noise beyond the doors lessened until the wind stopped completely.

Unable to contain myself any longer, I stood and took a step toward the exit. "Is it safe?"

"It should be, although you never know. Let me go first."

Mr. Blake opened the doors without effort and offered a hand. I took it, and he hoisted me up the stairs. When I stepped outside, the world around me was foreign. Thankfully, my house hadn't suffered any further damage, at least nothing immediately obvious. Of course, having a portion of my roof smashed in was already plenty serious. Tree branches littered every yard in sight, and like my house, there were others with trees lying on them. Broken windows, gutters half-off, siding strewn on the ground, the list went on... In the distance, sirens wailed into the otherwise harrowing silence.

"Oh, my goodness." I groaned.

"I've seen worse." Mr. Blake walked away and circled his house, inspecting it. When he returned, he said, "No damage to my place, believe it or not. Come on." He waved me toward his front door.

Part of me wanted to ask, "Are you serious?" Instead, I nodded and followed him.

He flicked the light switch upon entering, but when the lights remained off, Mr. Blake nodded. "Not surprising." He went to the phone next and picked it up. "Nope, nothing there either."

"I assume you're an expert on tornadoes?" I asked.

"I wouldn't exactly say that, but I've been through enough to know what to expect. We'll likely be without electricity for several days. No phone service either."

"What a mess," I said. "How am I going to get someone out here to fix my roof if I can't call? And I bet the roads are blocked, so I can't drive."

"You're breathing, aren't you?"

"What? Well, yes, of course."

"Then worry about everything else later. The important thing is you're okay."

"But my house… I've only lived there for six months. And— and —" Tears tracked down my cheeks. I had come into Mr. Blake's yard that day with the good intentions of finally meeting him, and, well, we'd met, all right.

"What's the matter?" he asked, scratching at the back of his shaggy head like an awkward teenage boy afraid to ask a pretty girl to the school dance.

"This has to be one big joke," I said.

Hiccupping, I wiped the tears out of my eyes and gazed in shock upon a picture on Mr. Blake's mantel. Blacked-out eyes stared back at me. My eyes shifted from one picture to the next, whether on the walls or on the tables. Black eyes everywhere. On every face.

My scream was silent, but as my eyes met Mr. Blake's, I expected him to bring out that ax after all.

Chapter 6

Behind the glasses and the beard, tears streaked down Mr. Blake's face. I gave a sharp intake of breath, and my hand flew to my heart. I wasn't sure whether I should step toward or away from him. Dare I offer comfort or leave him in peace? He reminded me of a dog that had been beaten, starved, and locked away in a cage. He might look melancholy and pathetic, but he might very well bite. Or he might warm to the right touch.

"Well, you've seen them," he whispered. For all his tears, his voice remained controlled, but it gave the slightest quiver.

"The pictures?" I asked just as softly.

He nodded. "My-my wife."

Mr. Blake turned so his face was in shadow, removed his glasses, and wiped at his eyes with the end of his sleeve. Sniffling, he returned his glasses to his face and turned back toward me.

"Sorry? I'm afraid I don't understand," I said.

"She's dead."

I glanced at the closest picture. A young, pretty woman with a heart-shaped face, a button nose, and a lovely smile looked back at me with phantom eyes. When I gazed at the next frame, then the next, and every one after that, I realized they all held the same woman. Mr. Blake was oddly absent from all of them.

"These pictures, they're all of your wife?" As I looked around the living room, the late Mrs. Blake's touch was everywhere. Unless Mr. Blake had a thing for feminine decorations, which I doubted by his own appearance, he hadn't taken anything down since her death. Vases with dry, brittle flowers; porcelain figurines of dancing ladies and little children; doilies; and Tiffany lamps sat on every surface, coated with a thick layer of dust. His house was like a forgotten slice of the past, and as my eyes finally traveled back to him, I realized he was just like the tomb in which he lived.

Mr. Blake nodded, dropping onto his worn floral sofa. He covered his face with his large hands, resting his elbows on his knees. For several seconds, he kept his face buried, until he finally gave a loud sniff and lifted his eyes toward me. "Sorry," he mumbled. "I don't talk about her. After everything that's happened, maybe it was too much...and then you showed up—"

"I'm sorry. I can go," I said.

"Don't go, please."

I took a step toward the door. "But I have to, Mr. Blake. I need to see the extent of the damage that has been done and maybe try to..." I stopped speaking. While my strange neighbor may have saved me from a tornado, I didn't know a thing about him except that his wife was supposedly dead. "Thanks for, you know... Well, I'll see you around."

Before he could protest, I made a hasty exit out his front door and dashed across his rocky ground and back into my own territory. As I stood in a front yard littered with branches of all sizes and other debris, I noticed the large branch had only smashed in a small part of my roof. I quickly walked around the exterior of the house, relieved to find no further damage. When I opened the front door, everything was as I had left it. The downstairs was unharmed, and like Mr. Blake's house, the electricity and phone were out.

I sighed, pacing. I then took the stairs, two at a time, and stopped on the landing. The upstairs housed a short hallway and two bedrooms that were unused. The ceiling was sagging with obvious water damage in one of the bedrooms. I had no experience in fixing houses, so my mind whirled as I tried to think of what to do next.

Macy. I needed to see Macy. I ran back downstairs, my heart thumping inside my chest. It seemed crazy that so much could change in an hour. If someone had told me today when I woke I'd deal with a tornado and would be thrown headfirst into an impossibly bizarre situation involving my half-insane neighbor, I think I would have stayed in bed.

I picked up the phone again, hoping for some ludicrous miracle it might work. I slammed the receiver down and groaned. Grabbing my purse, I checked the front door to ensure it was locked and then left through the side door, clicking the lock firmly in place. When I reached the end of my driveway, my fears that the road was blocked were confirmed. Several trees and branches were strewn over Stephens Street. People were beginning to flock into their yards to examine the extent of their own devastation, but I paid them no heed as I began my trek down the sidewalk. As I passed Mr. Blake's house, I frowned, half-expecting him to come outside and begin his usual murmurings among his blessed rocks. I shook my head and refocused on my task.

I reached the end of my street and turned right. After jogging a few more blocks, I was winded, so I had no other choice but to slow my pace. I'd never been athletic, but I blamed my fatigue more on my shoes. Yes. Had to be the shoes. Maybe Macy and I could go shoe shopping tomorrow.

In spite of myself and all that had transpired that day, I laughed. When I came to my senses, I gazed around me. Standing here, I never would have guessed that a tornado had ripped through the neighborhood just a few streets down. The trees were standing tall and unharmed, the houses intact.

A half-hour later, I arrived at Macy's house. Sure enough, every street I passed as I continued was in perfect condition. Well, maybe not perfect condition. There was always the rogue neighbor who let their house go unpainted for too long or left their grass unmowed. On my street, I was that neighbor, so the tornado had done me the favor of making the other houses blend in more with mine.

As I knocked, I wondered if I had gone temporarily insane. My thought patterns were off more than usual, but perhaps being forced into a dark cellar with an odd fellow would do that to a poor, unsuspecting girl.

When Macy answered, I stepped inside and pulled her into a bone-crushing hug. "Oh, thank goodness," I said into her shoulder.

Macy returned the hug and released me, although I was still holding onto her. "Darling? What's happened? You've got a death grip on me, but a girl needs to breathe, Lorna."

I let go and took a step back. "Sorry."

"You're crying. Laura, what's the matter?"

"Am I?" I touched my cheek, surprised to find it wet. "I've had the worst day, Macy."

"Well, let's sit down with a cup of tea...or something stronger if that's your preference, and tell me all about it."

I nodded, following Macy into the kitchen, where the kids were just finishing lunch. Little Annie sat in her highchair, her chubby cheeks covered in baby food. Johnny smiled and waved at me, a milk mustache on his upper lip. I held back as Macy cleared the plates, unsure what I could do to help. She seemed to have everything under control, whereas I was a mess.

"Miss Lorna, will you play ball with me?" Johnny asked.

"Not now, dear," Macy told her son. "Miss Lorna and I need to talk. It's a nice day now that the rain's passed. Go outside and find someone to play with."

Johnny didn't need to be told twice. He was out the door before I could say goodbye. As Macy held Annie, she said, "Let me just put her down for a nap. Darling, please sit. You look like a rabbit who's been running from a fox and just managed to escape with its life."

"I feel like one," I said quietly, dropping into a seat at the table.

While Macy was away, I gazed around her homey kitchen. The Wells family wasn't rich in money, but they were wealthy in their love for each other. Johnny's artwork decorated the fridge. Several plates I knew belonged to Macy's mother were displayed on shelves running along the wall near the ceiling. Macy's recipe box and cookbook rested next to her stove. My heart gave a small lurch as a moment of sadness crept inside.

Macy's return ushered me back to the present. As she pulled out the tea bags and cups, I stood. "I should've done that— "

"Nonsense. Sit, darling. Now, tell me what's got you all in a tizzy."

"You wouldn't believe it by looking at your street, but mine was hit hard by a tornado just a little while ago, and— and a huge branch fell on my house."

Macy set the cups down and turned. "Oh, my...well, thank the dear Lord you're okay!"

"That's what Mr. Blake said. Well, not quite in those words, but —"

"Who's Mr. Blake?"

"That's the other part, Mace. I have this neighbor...living right next to me. He's a single man, and —"

"Oh, single?" Macy smiled teasingly.

"Not like that." My face heated. "He's probably crazy. I don't know, but the thing is, I went to introduce myself to him, and that's when the tornado struck. He took me down into his cellar. It was awful, Mace! I thought I was gonna die, but then he was just so...so off. Anyway, my house is a mess. I have no idea where to start or what I'm gonna do."

Macy placed the kettle on the stove and joined me. "One step at a time, darling. You can spend the night here. Is your house even safe?"

"I think so, from what I can tell. My room's on the first floor."

"Hmm, I'd know that if you ever invited me over." Macy winked.

"I'm sorry. I should've had you over by now."

Macy waved me off. "That's not important, Lorna. What you need is a good night's sleep."

"But it's the middle of the day. I should be doing something useful back home."

"If John weren't at work, I'd have him drive you as close to your street as possible and park and go with you to help out, but with the kids here and no car..."

"You don't have to do that, Mace. If you don't mind, I'd like to stay here with you. I don't think I want to be alone right now. On top of all this, you know this is the anniversary of my parents' death."

Macy nodded, frowning a little. She stood as the kettle whistled and filled our cups. "Drink up, darling. And I don't mind a bit. I offered for you to stay, remember? Anyway, the tea may not be as good as your mom's, but it's the best I can do."

I smiled sadly. "No one could make a cup of tea as good as Mom."

I cradled the cup in my hands like a precious treasure, allowing the warmth to soothe me. If I closed my eyes, I might be able to imagine I was ten years younger and sitting in my childhood home's kitchen. Mom would be whipping together one of her culinary masterpieces, and Dad would be in the living room smoking his pipe as he read the paper. Chucky would come running in the side door, demanding to know when dinner would be ready.

But that was Laura's life. I didn't close my eyes, because really, what good would it do to run away from dealing with my current situation?

I smiled ruefully at Macy across the small table.

"You look a million miles away, Lorna."

"Maybe I am, Mace. But I'm here with you, and that's what matters. Thank you for just...you know."

Macy smiled, reached across the table, and squeezed my hand. "You're welcome. Now, drink up before it goes cold, and we'll see about getting the cot out for you and some linens."

∞ ∞ ∞

The next morning, John and I got in his car ten minutes earlier than he normally would when he left for work.

"Are you sure you want to return home?" he asked after a short drive.

I sighed, a little exasperated. "Yes, John. You sound like Macy."

John chuckled. "Guilty as charged."

I got out of the car. John was parked in the five-and-dime lot. We'd driven as close to my street as we could get, but the road was still blocked. "I need to at least work on getting my yard cleared. Maybe the city will have the road cleared later today."

"I wouldn't count on it. Any government-run group is the least efficient sort out there."

"Maybe the grand city of Cleveland will prove you wrong."

John snorted. "Doubt it. But don't be a stranger, Lorna. You're welcome to return tonight."

"Thank you, but you've already been kind hosts to me. I don't want to hold you up. I'll see you later."

John waved and was on his way. I gazed at the blue sky. What a contrast from yesterday. My walk home only took ten minutes. I pondered how I would go about undoing all the damage and stopped abruptly when I reached my house.

Tristan Blake was outside, but he wasn't in his yard. He was swinging an ax in my yard. His motions were sure and strong, his stance and back taut and steady.

Shaking my head, I tried to sort out my thoughts. As if it weren't enough that a tornado had ripped apart my neighborhood and inflicted costly damage on my house, my neighbor was literally among the mess.

"What are you doing?" I asked when I reached his side.

He stopped mid-swing and lowered the axe, standing straight as he wiped sweat from his brow. His face was flushed from the heat as he turned toward me.

"What's it look like?"

"Cutting branches."

"That's right. Already got the biggest one down off your roof and chopped it up." He nodded toward the pile of wood ten feet away.

I stared, dumbfounded. "How long have you been—? How did you—? Never mind. Why are you doing this? This is my yard."

"I didn't see you out here working."

"That's not your concern. Thank you, but I'm fine."

He raised his right eyebrow. "You can get me a drink of water."

"Excuse me?" The nerve! "I'm not your servant, Mr. Blake, and while I appreciate the effort, it's not needed. It's my house, my mess, my responsibility. I'll fix it on my own."

Mr. Blake laughed. Yes, actually laughed. "How do you propose to do that?"

"Then let me help, at least. Where can I find an ax?"

"Get me that glass of water first, and I might tell you."

I scowled at him and went inside. I was half-tempted to let the man sweat and die of thirst, but as I watched him work out what seemed to be his own frustrations on those branches, I sighed and filled a cup with water.

When I returned to my neighbor with my peace offering, Mr. Blake grunted what might have been "thanks" and drank the water in a few gulps. He handed the glass back to me, but when I didn't move, he asked, "Now what?"

"I said I wanted to help. That ax?"

He scowled, then shrugged. "If you're serious, go to my backyard and get the smaller ax out of the shed. You should be able to manage that."

I glared at him. "You're about to find out what I can manage." If he thought me a weakling, I'd show him. I marched away, careful to pick my way over fallen limbs and other debris. When I reached the shed, I undid the broken, rusty lock and pulled open the creaky door. I coughed from the dirt and dust as I looked for another ax. There was nothing remarkable about the shed with its garden tools, although when I remembered that Mr. Blake's yard had no garden, I couldn't help but wonder if it had at one time. When my eyes fell on the rake, I tried to picture him raking leaves, maybe his wife joining him and sitting among the piles like a pair of children. I shook my head, refocusing on the task as I found a small ax and left the shed. Who knew if he'd ever had a wife?

When I returned, Mr. Blake didn't stop working. I searched for a limb that would be suitable for the size ax I held and began to swing. Together, we chopped, sweat pouring down our brows. For the next several hours, we worked in silence, the only sound the chopping of the wood. By the time we were done, Mr. Blake found some rope in his shed to tie the smaller pieces of branches off and placed the bundles by the side of the road.

I was shocked to see the sun almost setting as we finished. I dropped onto the grass, sitting cross-legged, and said, "I'm exhausted. I can't believe we worked all day."

"Makes the time fly, doesn't it?"

I heard the rustling of clothing and looked up at him, surprised to find him shirtless. He was mopping his forehead with the bunched-up shirt. I couldn't help but stare at his physique. He wasn't overly muscular, but he was nicely toned, from his chest to his stomach to his back. I blushed and looked away.

"About your roof, how are you gonna pay for it?"

"What?" Any brief warmth I might have had for him evaporated at his bluntness.

"Your roof. It's pretty banged up."

I glowered at him. "That's not your concern."

"I didn't mean it like that."

"Then what did you mean?"

"It's a simple question."

I stood and stepped up to Mr. Blake. He towered over me. I wasn't sure if it was the fact that it was late and I hadn't eaten all day, that I was emotionally and physically exhausted, that my roof had been destroyed, or that the man in front of me was impossibly, infuriatingly, intoxicatingly getting under my skin like a disease and a remedy all at once, but I was done. Just done.

He exhaled loudly through his nose, his mouth kept firmly shut, and stalked away. Left standing there, wondering what he was up to now, I wanted nothing more than to go inside my house and lock the door. Instead, I stood rooted to the spot as he returned with a plate bearing a sandwich. He thrusted it into my unwilling hands.

"What's this?" I asked.

"What's it look like?" he growled.

"Th-thank you," I said, losing my fight. I sat in the overgrown grass again, picking up the sandwich like a little girl who's been scolded to finish her dinner.

Mr. Blake dropped unceremoniously onto the grass a few feet away and sighed. He was still topless, but as the sunlight faded, he appeared as a silhouette.

"Are you going to eat?" I asked.

"Not hungry."

"Sorry about before. You know, with the roof—"

He waved me off. "Forget it."

I took a few more bites. "You didn't need to clean up my yard, but thanks."

"It's nothing."

"But it's not," I said, setting the dish aside. "I feel like we got off on the wrong foot."

"Don't worry about your roof. I've got it."

"What do you mean?"

"Let me pay for it. I can fix it myself to save on the cost of labor. Materials aren't that expensive."

"I can't let you do that. It's too much—"

"Can you pay for it?"

"Well, not exactly, but—"

"Then it's settled." His tone brooked no room for argument. "Besides," Mr. Blake added softly, "it's the least I can do."

"Call me Lorna."

"All right, Lorna. Then I guess I'm Tristan."

Tristan. Mr. Blake. Mr. Rock Garden. Who are you?

Chapter 7

I slept in my own bed that night, and the roof didn't cave in on me. Not that I thought it would.

I woke to the sounds of trucks and chainsaws. Rubbing at my eyes, I stood and went to the window, pushing back the curtain. The city workers were busy clearing the road.

As much as I wanted to go back to sleep, the noise was too loud, and my back, shoulders, and arms were sore. I went into the kitchen and tried the lights and the phone, disappointed to find they were still out. A cup of coffee would've been just the thing, but I made do with water and some flake cereal.

Just as I was about to throw away the food that had gone bad, someone knocked at my door. I was still wearing my nightgown, so I ran back to my bedroom to change clothes. "I'll be right there!" I called.

The flower pattern on my blouse clashed with the stripes on my skirt, and I wasn't wearing a girdle or hose. Sure my hair was a fright, I answered the door and immediately wished I hadn't. I'd expected to find a city worker there, maybe telling me the street was clear. Instead, Tristan Blake stood on my stoop, shifting his weight from one leg to the other.

"Good morning," he said.

"Hi. Uh, sorry about the—" I pointed toward my hair and then my outfit. Tristan didn't seem to care about my appearance, for he raised an eyebrow.

"I thought maybe I could take a look at your roof."

"Oh. Of course." I stepped aside, letting him in. What was I doing? "You know, you really don't have to—" I followed him as he walked through my house like he owned it. "Uh, excuse me, but—"

"An art gallery," Tristan remarked as he came into my living room.

That comment stopped me in my tracks. My eccentric neighbor was in my house, and he was interested in my paintings? "Not really. You're the first person to see them."

"They're fascinating." Tristan stepped closer to my first and largest painting and studied it. He didn't say anything, and I stood there, anticipating his critique.

This was ridiculous. What did I care if he liked my paintings or not? His presence unnerved me, yet a not completely unwelcome feeling of gratitude for his attention toward my artwork filled me. "I burned all my pictures," I blurted. My, my, I really had lost my head. "You don't have to fix my roof, I mean. It might be for the best if—"

Tristan turned toward me, his brow furrowed. "What?"

"The roof. I can get someone else to come out and look at it. With the roads almost cleared, I'm sure it won't be a problem."

"It might be weeks before you get someone out here. In case you didn't notice, your house isn't the only one that suffered damage from that tornado."

I frowned. Why was he so insistent he fix my roof? "Maybe, but it's my house. I don't know if—" *If I feel comfortable with you here.*

Tristan stared at me. "I scare you."

"No, you don't." I placed my hands on my hips and did my best impression of an intimidating short, thin woman.

He chuckled. "I can see why I might, but all I'm offering is help. But I wasn't asking about the roof before when I said 'what.' I meant what you said about burning your pictures. Must've been quite the fire."

"I shouldn't have told you that, but fine, since I opened that nasty can of worms, I'll enlighten you. That's why I don't have anything else hanging on the walls. When I moved, I burned everything. I couldn't— I couldn't bear to see their faces, all happy and smiling. My parents are dead, you see." As I spoke, I slowly lost my own fire. I sighed and then met his eyes. "That doesn't matter, though."

I wasn't completely sure why I was baring my soul to this almost -stranger. As I continued to stare at him, the thought flitted through my mind that maybe I was telling Tristan this secret because he found my paintings fascinating.

"You probably are wondering about the blackened eyes," Tristan finally said. "It was my way of dealing with losing her. I could never burn her pictures, but neither could I have her looking at me."

There it was again—talk of his dead wife. Maybe he was delusional and only thought he'd been married, or maybe he made up the story with the full knowledge that he was having me on. Reminding myself to breathe, I shook my head. Tristan's back was to me. His breathing was loud and slow, like he was trying to calm himself. I spoke not a word and instead stared at the picture window, where I'd watched him for weeks on end.

"The roof," he said gruffly. "Where are the stairs?"

"Through here," I said softly, walking toward the door that led upstairs.

Tristan walked past me like I didn't exist, his boots stomping on the steps, echoing through the stark house. When he reached the second floor, he muttered under his breath. I joined him.

"No damage to the ceiling from the impact, but there's water damage." He pointed toward the ceiling. "That will all need to be replaced."

"Yeah, I know. I looked at it already. How much will it cost?"

"Hard to say. I won't know until I can get in there and see the damage." Tristan began pulling the ruined ceiling apart with his hands. "Can you get me something to stand on?"

I ran downstairs and grabbed a stool. When I returned, Tristan stepped up onto it.

"I don't suppose you have a ladder?" he asked, his head now up in the rafters.

"Sorry, no. I have only a few pieces of furniture. A couple of books— "

"I'll need a flashlight," he said. "I can't really make heads or tails of much of anything up there, although I clearly see the hole in your roof."

"Okay." I stood there, biting my lip. "Um, I don't have a flashlight either. Sorry."

Tristan sighed loudly and withdrew from the ceiling, stepping back onto the floor. He scowled at me and said, "I'll be back in a minute."

As he left, I muttered, "Aren't you just a ray of sunshine?"

This man's personality was a prickly as a porcupine. As much as I tried to be understanding, my patience was wearing thin.

Tristan returned with his flashlight, the same one he'd used in the cellar, and poked his head back up into my attic. A few minutes later, dusty and smelling of wet wood, Tristan joined me on the floor. "It's not as bad as it could be. Before you ask, I've done work like this before."

"Kansas?"

"Some, although quite a lot when I was a young man."

"You aren't old."

Tristan's lips quirked in what might pass as a smile. "Thanks, I think. Anyway, we should see if the roads are cleared. I have a truck that can carry the materials."

We returned downstairs.

"Just give me a minute. Do you mind waiting outside?"

"I'll be at my truck." Tristan trudged through my house and slammed the door upon his exit.

I went into the bathroom and ran a brush through my unruly hair. I checked myself over in the mirror and frowned as I pulled my hair back into a ponytail. What was the matter with me? Never had I met a man who stirred such conflicted emotions within me. For a man I hardly knew, something about him continued to draw me to him. Logic told me to stay away, but I'd spent months watching him out my window. If it wasn't obvious already that I couldn't stay away, I didn't know what was. Tristan Blake was the last sort of man I ought to have any feelings for. Angry with myself, I left the bathroom. Once outside, I found the man of my mixed thoughts standing next to his pickup truck.

"Let's go," I said curtly, strolling past him in much the same manner he often did with me.

Tristan and I piled into his rusty truck. His garage held an assortment of car parts and many objects I couldn't name. Luckily, our street had been cleared enough to drive down it, and when we made our first turn, the next road was also safe. We drove on in silence, me staring out the window at the white clouds in the distance.

We picked up what we needed and headed back, the way unhindered. I watched in amazement as Tristan hauled the wood, shingles, and other materials into my yard. While I helped where I could, his determination seemed to drive him.

You might think fixing a roof would be dull work, especially since we hardly said ten words to each other the rest of that day and into the next. However, I proved a quick study, an able student, a quality worker, following his instruction. The work kept me busy.

Chapter 8

Well into our second day of roof repair, I heard the unmistakable trill of my kitchen phone. By the time I was able to answer it, whoever had been on the other end had hung up. I flipped the switch in the kitchen and was pleased to see the overhead light turn on.

"Hey, get me some water while you're down there," Tristan called down.

"Sure," I yelled.

I considered calling Macy. She'd probably been the one trying to reach me, but knowing Tristan wouldn't take kindly to being kept waiting, I filled two cups with water and joined him.

"We're making good progress," I said, finishing my water with a refreshed sigh.

Tristan gulped his water down and wiped the excess water from the hair around his lips. He nodded and resumed hammering a nail into a shingle, his beard and hair hanging in his face.

"You know," I remarked, "it might be more comfortable to shave."

Tristan stopped hammering and gave me a fierce glare. "Maybe I like my beard."

"It looks like it would make you hot. Your hair, too."

"It's none of your concern," he muttered, returning to his task.

I shrugged. This was exactly why we hardly talked. My efforts nearly always fell as flat as a pancake rolled over by a steamroller. We resumed our silence and our work. The afternoon wore on, and just as I was about to get us more water, a voice called up.

"Lorna, is that you up there?"

Shocked, I set aside my hammer and nail and carefully made my way to the lowest part of the roof, spotting Macy standing in my driveway beside her car.

"Oh, my Lord!" she exclaimed. "It really is you! I was getting worried when I didn't hear more from you."

"I'm fine," I said. "I've just been...busy. I'll be right down."

I glanced at Tristan, who continued to work, so I left him to it and made my way down to ground level. Macy was upon me the instant I stepped off the ladder, crushing me in her arms.

"Whoa, Mace, a girl needs to breathe," I said, echoing her sentiment from a couple of days ago. I returned the hug.

Macy released me and smiled as she leaned into me. "Are you aware of the big, strong man up there?"

I tried not to laugh. "Oh, that's Tristan, uh, Mr. Blake, the neighbor I told you about."

"Ah, now I understand why I didn't hear further from you. You've been taken care of already."

"What? Oh, please," I said. "Sure, Tristan's been great with helping me get my roof fixed and my yard cleared, but his personality could use a few repairs of its own."

Macy continued to eye Tristan up and down. "You know, with a body like that, I'd say that compensates for other lacking qualities."

"Don't say it. Tristan and I are, uh, just friends. Maybe not even that."

Macy frowned. "I'd say any man who's done all that for a woman is more than just a friend, Lorna. Don't look now, but someone's got his peepers on you."

I turned and looked up, and sure enough, Tristan was gazing at us.

"Hello, Tristan!" Macy called, waving. "Why don't you come down and introduce yourself properly?"

"Uh, that's probably not— I mean, he's kinda shy."

Tristan withdrew from the roof's edge, and I wondered if he was going to return to hammering. I was surprised to find him coming down the ladder seconds later, crossing my small yard.

"What's going on?" he asked.

"Tristan, this is my best friend, Macy. Macy, Tristan."

Tristan gave her a nod and said, "I'd shake your hand, but, well —" He held up his dirty hands and shrugged.

"Pleased to meet you, Tristan," Macy said kindly. "Lorna told me about you the other day."

I glared at Macy, afraid to look at Tristan.

"I see," Tristan said, turning and walking away.

When I finally met Macy's eyes, her eyebrows were even higher. I was beginning to wonder if they'd disappear into her hairline completely.

"Handy, ruggedly attractive, but you're right—his personality could use some work," she murmured.

"There's nothing between us. Like I said, we're just neighbors, and Tristan was kind enough to help me out. He didn't have to, especially since all he does is stay inside and mourn his—" Realizing I'd said too much, I stopped.

Macy had already bitten the line I'd swung tantalizingly over her head, however. "Mourn his—?"

"Oh, okay. His wife. Supposedly." I kept my voice low, not wanting Tristan to overhear. I was completely certain he wouldn't approve of me telling Macy this information.

Macy's expression changed from disapproving to downright sorrow. "Aw, but that's so sad."

"Shh, keep your voice down."

"Sorry, but it is. No wonder he's the way he is." She paused, then added, "He's a tragic hero, Lorna. You must be torn—"

"Please. We're done talking about this. Macy, thank you for checking up on me, but I'm fine. Just fine."

Macy smiled as her eyes traveled up to the roof at Tristan. "Oh, I'd say you're more than fine, darling. I'll leave you to your boyfriend's capable hands."

"He's not my boyfriend."

"Whatever you say, darling," Macy sang as she waltzed to her car. "Ta-ta."

I waved, watching as she pulled out of my driveway and didn't go back to the roof until she turned off my street. I slowly climbed the ladder, my stomach fluttering with every step as my cluttered thoughts made my head spin. When I finally reached the roof, I made my way back to where I'd been working and resumed hammering.

For the next half-hour, we worked in silence.

"We should be able to finish with the shingles today," Tristan said.

"Good. That's good." I set my hammer aside and wiped the sweat from my brow. "I'm sorry about Macy."

"It's fine."

Everything about Tristan's shortness of his words spoke the opposite of what he uttered. I sighed, not wishing to argue. Instead, I left and returned with another glass of water. Tristan drank it down in his usual quick manner and handed the cup to me.

"Listen, I was thinking I'd make something for dinner since the power's back on and all," I said. "I can just run to the store around the corner, pick up a few things, and have supper ready in a jiffy."

"You don't have to do that."

"But I want to," I said, and I meant it. "Please."

"Very well. Are you a good cook?"

I smirked. "I'll let you be the judge."

∞ ∞ ∞

After returning home, I prepared spaghetti with tomato sauce and made a bowl of salad with lettuce and cucumbers from my little victory garden. When the meal was ready, I went outside and called up to Tristan. He joined me a moment later on the grass.

"The roof's fixed. Now I just need to repair the damage on the inside."

"That's great. Thank you."

"It's not a good idea to stand downwind of me. I'm a sweaty mess. I should wash up first. Give me five minutes, and I'll be back."

"Okay."

Tristan came back in a fresh shirt, his hair tamed, and his hands and face clean. As I watched his sturdy frame lumber toward me, I felt a blush surface on my cheeks when I recalled Macy's comments about Tristan's rugged handsomeness.

"Hopefully dinner hasn't gone cold," I said.

He didn't remark but simply followed me into the kitchen. When we reached the table, I remembered something that should have been obvious.

"I'm an idiot," I groaned, shaking my head. "I only have one chair."

"You're not an idiot. You just don't have an extra chair. It's an easy fix. Do you have any reservations about us sitting on the floor?"

I laughed. "Well, if that's okay with you."

"I don't mind."

I smiled as we filled our plates and took seats in the living room. There was more space in there than the kitchen, so we could spread out as much as we wished.

"This works well," Tristan said. "We can look at your paintings."

I scoffed. "They're hardly much to look at."

"Why do you do that?"

"Do what?"

"Put yourself down."

"It's just, I know I'm not talented, okay? Art isn't my strong suit."

"I still hold to my original thought that they're fascinating."

"Why? They're just paint on canvases, splattered, sprayed, smudged. They don't resemble anything real."

Tristan ate for a little while, a contemplative look on his face. His eyes roamed the room, tracking my paintings, and finally settling on me.

"What they say is more real than anything," he said quietly.

I stopped breathing, as if I'd forgotten how, the deepest part of my being exposed for Tristan to see in some messy painting rendering a messed-up life on a canvas. A two-dimensional representation of a three-dimensional person, of dimensions that we couldn't even see that transcended what we showed to the world. Except through art. Except to those like Tristan who seemed to sing the same song.

"That's probably the nicest thing someone's said to me in a long time."

Tristan smiled slightly. "It's true."

Was it crazy that I wanted to hug this man right now? Instead, I picked at my food, my emotions too heightened to concentrate on eating.

Seeing Tristan's empty plate, I said, "I'll clean up."

"I'll help."

After we washed the dishes and put everything away, I stood at the kitchen window for a moment, watching some sparrows in the yard. Beyond the rooftops, the sun was lowering quickly.

"I can't believe how late it got," I said. "These past couple of days have flown by, yet they feel like much more time has passed."

"Keeping busy will do that," Tristan replied.

I turned to face him, my back against the edge of the sink. Tristan didn't move, but he stared directly into my eyes. Unnerved, I blinked and lowered my gaze.

"You have the darkest eyes I've ever seen," he said.

"My brother has the same eyes. We got them from my father." Even mentioning my father made my aching heart beat faster.

Tristan seemed to wince. "We should go outside," he suggested. "It's a comfortable evening."

Anything was better than staying in that stuffy kitchen. I readily agreed and followed him out the side door. We aimlessly roamed toward the backyard. My flowers were in full bloom and overgrown, a stark contrast to Tristan's yard a few feet away. The long grass tickled my bare feet and halfway up my calves.

"It's like a jungle back here. I guess I ought to get a lawnmower," I said.

"You can have mine. Better off, I'll cut your grass if you'll cook me another dinner like that."

"So, you're saying you liked it? It passed your test?"

"It was delicious."

"About the mower, thank you, but you've already done so much. I don't really feel like my attempts at cooking would do your kindness justice."

Tristan's face was mostly hidden by the shadows, but the dim glow of the sunset leaked in. What wasn't obscured by his hair, beard, and glasses was hard to discern, but I could have sworn I saw a thoughtful sadness there.

"It's not kindness," he said.

Not wanting to push him, I asked, "Do you mind telling me why you have a mower if, well, you don't have any grass?"

Tristan's bearded lips smiled wistfully as he dropped onto the ground and sat cross-legged. I joined him, the unspoken invitation there as he watched me.

"My yard wasn't always filled with rocks."

"I'm sure it's easier to manage than all these plants," I joked lightly.

Tristan didn't reply. Maybe he shrugged, but I hadn't seen his reaction. My eyes were too occupied watching the sky change color. The last bit of the sun disappeared beyond the horizon, blinking out for another night. I'd never been able to sit in silence with someone for so long like I could with Tristan.

We hadn't talked much since meeting. What we had shared, however, were glimpses into each other's soul—or so I believed. The man sitting six inches from me was every bit a mystery, and whenever I tried to read him, I came away with more questions. And yet, somehow, I felt I knew him, like he'd been a part of my life much longer.

The leftover oranges and reds from the sunset faded to blues and purples, and eventually, the western horizon darkened to the velvety blackness that filled the rest of the sky. Stars opened their eyes and stared at us from farther away than I could comprehend.

"It sounds overdone, but I've always enjoyed watching the stars," I whispered.

"Me, too," Tristan murmured.

"My father had a telescope. He was an amateur, but he loved it. He taught me how to read the night sky."

There I went, talking about my late father again. Father. It sounded so formal, so distant, so unlike the relationship we'd had. He'd been Daddy. But he was distant now, more distant than those constellations he taught me the names of.

"Tell me about them," Tristan said.

For a second, I thought he meant my parents, and my heart leapt—not in a good way. I nearly stood, and he must have sensed my unease, for he amended, "The stars. Tell me about the stars."

"Oh, of course," I said, relieved. Pointing toward the sky, I said, "There's Cancer, the current zodiac sign. Gemini is just to the west, and Leo is to the east."

"I've been told I'm a Capricorn."

"I'm a Pisces, not that I believe in that stuff."

Tristan snorted. "Me, neither. My wife was an Aquarius."

"Oh, um... So, she was born in February, or late January?"

In the near-darkness, I barely saw Tristan's nod. He fell silent again, and I sighed softly, deflated.

He abruptly stood and said, "I should be going home."

"Oh, okay. If you're sure —"

"I'm sure."

He was already trudging across the grass, and before I could say goodbye, the crunching of the stones under his feet filled my ears.

"See you tomorrow," I said, but I didn't think he would hear me.

Even if he did, he might as well have crunched my heart under his feet.

Chapter 9

Tristan showed up at my house the next morning at eight o'clock. I had just finished breakfast and was cleaning up when his knock came from the side door. When I opened it, he looked like a man who had gotten next to no sleep. Dark circles surrounded his eyes, and his hair was sticking up in every direction. As he slumped inside, I stepped aside and closed the door.

"I should be able to finish up today," he said, his voice dull.

"Oh, that's good," I replied with false cheer.

He nodded and walked out of the kitchen, no doubt ready to begin repairing the ceiling and be done as soon as possible. I wondered if he would return after today. Sure, he'd offered to mow my lawn if I'd cook for him, but that was before mention of his wife had surfaced. The more time we spent together, the more I was certain he really was a widower.

I sighed, wishing I could figure him out. Was I merely fooling myself any time I thought I understood him? Then again, what did three days amount to? We'd hardly said much to each other in that time, but the exchanges we had shared had been meaningful, at least to me.

I finished cleaning up in the kitchen and went to my usual spot by the picture window, pulling up my chair. The man who had been Mr. Rock Garden much longer than Tristan Blake was now in my house instead of among his sacred rocks. His actions were undoubtedly selfless, and sometimes he came across as gentle and kind. But he could turn into Mr. Hyde in a second with the smallest unintended provocation. Were the two versions of him really two sides of the same coin I kept flipping in my hand, never knowing whether I'd get heads or tails? I sure couldn't make heads or tails of Tristan.

I stayed out of the way for the next couple of hours, inwardly remarking how ironic it was to be unwanted in my own house. At least that was how I felt. Annoyed by this thought, I abruptly stood and marched upstairs to check on the progress.

When I reached the top of the stairs, Tristan was stepping down from his ladder and brushing his hands on his jeans. "Looks like I'm done here," he said.

"It's perfect," I said reluctantly, eyeing his flawless work on my ceiling.

Tristan shifted from one foot to the other and met my eyes after a long silence. "Is something wrong?" he asked.

Men! "Seriously?" I asked. "Do you honestly not know?"

"I can't read your mind, Lorna."

Deflating some, I sighed. "I just never know what to expect with you, and it's-it's infuriating. You're not an easy man to get to know, Tristan Blake."

Of all the ridiculous things, he smiled. Actually smiled. More like smirked. The nerve!

"And you're an easy woman to get to know, Lorna Ashford?"

"Well, well—" I sputtered. In a huff, I crossed my arms over my chest and did my best glare to appear intimidating. Tristan was a full head taller than me, however, so my tactics quickly fell short. Short. Ha.

Tristan was laughing. "Okay, what's this about?"

I sighed. "Maybe we should go downstairs and talk?"

He shrugged. "Fine with me."

As Tristan followed me down the steps, I suppressed rolling my eyes.

When we reached the living room, he said, "We can sit here. Another chance to look at your paintings."

He didn't sound sarcastic, so I obliged him and dropped onto the wooden floor. "I should probably invest in a rug," I said. "This floor is too hard for my taste."

"Or a sofa or a couple of chairs," Tristan said, that smirk back in place as he joined me.

I couldn't help the smile that spread across my lips. "You're hard to stay mad at."

"I didn't realize you were."

"Okay, maybe not mad, but I'm tired of walking on eggshells around you."

"Is this about last night?"

"Yes. I thought we were having a nice time just talking, but then you just...left."

I was really beginning to detest the tiresome blush that kept appearing on my face whenever I was around Tristan. I was putting myself out on a limb here, and I was half-worried Tristan might sever that branch with his ax.

But Tristan's face softened. "The truth is, I've been used to no one's company but my own for so long that maybe I've forgotten what it's like to have a conversation. For what it's worth, I'd like to keep talking with you."

My heart leapt, but I tried to play it calm and collected. "I'm glad, but about the eggshells?"

"Fair enough. Any talk of my wife is off the table unless I bring it up."

"You brought her up last night."

"Okay, you're right. I'm sorry for my reaction. It's a sore spot for me."

"And we don't talk about my parents," I said, "unless, you know, the same rules apply—I mention them first. I don't talk to anyone about them, even my best friend. So, I guess I'm like you there. But about friends, you said you hadn't really talked with anyone in, what, how long?"

An unreadable expression passed over Tristan's face before he recovered. "I speak to people on an as-needed basis. I go to the store when I need to, have dealings with my agent over the phone—"

"Your agent?"

Tristan must have realized what he'd said too late, for he exhaled through his nose, irritated.

"Oh, come on. Your agent isn't your, you know...your wife." I paused, afraid I'd just heard an invisible eggshell crunch under my foot.

He sighed. "Oh, all right. I have a literary agent. He takes care of everything for me, so I don't have to."

"You're a writer?"

"Yes."

"What have you written?"

"Nothing you've read, I'm sure."

"That's your job, then?"

"Yes."

"You must be pretty successful. That's great."

"What about you? You like to read, I take it?"

"I love to read, although I've been rereading two books for a few years now. *Forlorn for Love* and *A Travesty of Torn Souls*. Maybe you've heard of them?"

"No, haven't read them."

"Do you read anything?" I asked.

"I've always enjoyed reading. Kinda goes hand in hand with writing, don't you think?"

I shrugged. "I wouldn't know. The extent of my writing involves letters to my brother and teaching first graders how to actually write, as in their letters and numbers. I never really had a creative bone in my body. Macy would tell you that."

"Refresh my memory. The woman who came by yesterday?"

"That's Macy, all right." I smiled thoughtfully. "We've been friends since we were babies. We grew up next door to each other and were inseparable. Of course, our lives took different directions after high school. I went to college, and she got married. She's home with her two kids."

Tristan's eyebrows were raised behind his glasses. "I doubt I'll see her again."

"Why do you say that?"

Tristan was visibly uncomfortable as he began shifting like he had something in his pants. "This whole friendship thing—" He stopped and sighed. "I'm no better at it than I am at much. Writing takes me away from this world and lets me forget it exists, which is all the better in most cases if you ask me."

He sounded broken and bitter, but I wanted to encourage him to keep talking. "So, when did you start writing?" I asked instead.

"I was just a kid. I'd make up stories all the time. My father mostly left me to my own whims."

"And your mother?"

His gaze was on his lap. "She died giving birth to me."

"Oh." Lorna's voice was small. "I'm so sorry."

"It doesn't matter. I never knew her."

Unsure what to say, I paused, then asked, "I'd love to hear what your first story was about."

"I don't even know where it is anymore, but it was about a squirrel named Robbie. We had squirrels in our backyard, but there was always one who was by himself. He tried to join the others, but they ran away from him. This squirrel became Robbie in my story, and he decided he didn't need the other squirrels anymore."

"That's so sad. What happened?"

"A duck named Sammy came along one day—in the story, of course—and befriended him. Robbie didn't care that his only friend was a duck or that the other squirrels laughed at him for it. Sammy knew how Robbie felt, so they walked away and found their own home in the forest, away from the yard. The end. Happily ever after. It was a dumb story."

"No, it wasn't. You may have just been a kid, but it seems to me you understood something most didn't. I'm a teacher. I've seen how mean kids are toward each other."

Tristan looked like he was going to say something, but he kept quiet for a long time. Together, we sat in my ersatz art gallery, his eyes on my paintings, my eyes mostly on him. Beyond these walls, a whole world waited to be explored, lived in. Tristan and I had been doing a lot of living within walls for years, the ones of our houses and the ones we'd erected in our minds.

"We should go outside," I said.

"If you like."

"It's early, not even lunch yet. When was the last time you had lunch somewhere?"

Tristan stood but didn't make to move. "No."

"Have you got somewhere else to be?"

"It's not— Oh, fine."

I smiled in victory. Getting this man to leave his cozy, locked-from-the-inside cell was no easy feat.

"I'm not sure why you're so eager for my company," he said.

"Why not? Are you hiding a dead body in your basement or something?"

Tristan smiled slightly. "At least let me go home and change into something cleaner than this."

"All right. See you in a few minutes?"

Ten minutes later, we were sitting in my Cadillac. I tried to start the car up, but as usual, Bessie gave me trouble. "She's old and moody," I explained. "She almost always protests to having to do any work."

"I could take a look—" Tristan started to say, but I cut him off.

"You can fix cars, too? Forget what you said earlier about not being good at much. You fixed my house, and now you're offering to fix my car?"

"Whoa, there. I don't have to. Is this a sore point for you as well?"

I sighed, annoyed more at myself than anything. "Sorry. It's just frustrating that so much has to fall apart all the time. The maintenance... This house is my first that's really mine. I lived in my childhood home until last December. No one told me it was gonna be so much work being on my own."

"You're right; no one tells you that, except maybe your parents. Sorry, I didn't mean to bring up—"

"It's fine." I cast a rueful smile in Tristan's general direction. "It's the eggshells all over again."

Tristan nodded.

Ol' Bessie finally managed to start sometime during our exchange, and I backed out of the driveway.

"Where did you have in mind?" Tristan asked.

"There's a little cafe about five minutes from here where Mace and I have met a few times. Tina's. They have the best chocolate milkshakes."

"I'm allergic to chocolate."

I tried to keep my eyes on the road as I replied incredulously, "No one's allergic to chocolate."

"Well, I am."

"You're serious?"

"As always."

"I've never heard of such a thing. Well, they have other flavors and plenty of other food to boot."

"I'll go on your recommendation since I haven't eaten out since 1937."

"You really ought to get out more," I teased.

We pulled into the parking lot a short while later. Tina's Cafe was nothing to brag about, but the food was cheap and good, and the company was pleasant. We entered the small establishment, nestled between a bar and a laundromat, a minute later and seated ourselves. We were just picking up our menus to peruse the selections when an unexpected voice said, "Lorna, is that you?"

I looked up and smiled in bemusement at Angela Sunshine. "Angela, hello...and Mr. Darling."

"Miss Ashford," Tom Darling returned, taking off his hat.

I was glad to see his eyes on Angela, her arms wrapped around his right bicep like she'd just won the prize for best in show for a pig at the county fair. When both of their gazes shifted toward Tristan, I cleared my throat awkwardly and said, "This is Tristan Blake, my neighbor."

"Hello, Mr. Blake," Angela said, polite as ever.

"Just neighbors?" Mr. Darling inquired smoothly, grinning back at me.

"Just friends," I said firmly.

Tristan simply gave each of them a nod. After a pregnant pause, I asked, "Are you here for lunch?"

"We just walked in, so yes," Angela said. "Would you mind—?"

Feeling guilty that I hadn't yet spent time with Angela after the end of school, even if my excuses about a tornado and the aftermath wouldn't have been exaggerated, I nodded and patted the booth seat beside me. "Please."

Angela giggled and said, "Oh, thank you, Lorna. This will be just perfect."

"Perfect" was probably among the bottom ten words I'd use to describe the situation as I watched Tristan's face change from discomfort to reserved annoyance upon Mr. Darling's bottom joining his in the booth. Tristan scooted toward the window, away from this intruder of his personal space. With the little room the booth seat provided for two grown men, he might have managed increasing the distance all of an inch between them. The contrast between them would have been laughable under different circumstances, Tristan with his disheveled clothes and shaggy hair and Mr. Darling with his impeccable attire and clean-cut features.

"So, what are you thinking?" Angela asked.

I blinked, my thoughts almost startled out of me. "W-what?"

"What are you going to have to eat?"

"Oh." I chuckled weakly. "What I always get—the grilled cheese."

Angela's button nose scrunched up like a toddler being fed Brussels sprouts. "Grilled cheese? My mom used to make that for me when I was growing up."

"So did mine," I said softly, my eyes on my hands as they twiddled in my lap. When I looked up and locked gazes with Tristan, his eyes echoed back a sad understanding. "I'm a creature of habit."

"I was telling Angela that we could go any place for lunch," Mr. Darling said. "We could have tried La Petite Ville over on Chestnut. They're open for lunch now on select weekdays, but—"

"But I said here was just peachy," Angela said brightly, although her eyes held steel in them.

"Yes, well," Mr. Darling resumed, clearing his throat, "what do you do for a living, Mr. Blake?"

"Something more exciting than teaching, surely," Angela said. "Mr. Blake, we all work together at the school."

"I write," Tristan muttered.

I felt his eyes on me, but the waitress saved us by arriving. We placed our orders, Tristan copying me with my no-frills grilled cheese. Angela opted for a salad, and Mr. Darling took his chances with getting a steak. If he was expecting filet mignon quality at Tina's, he would come away sorely disappointed. The food was good, but the steak could use some work.

"Ooo, are you published?" Angela was acting every bit the adoring fan, even though she had no idea what Tristan wrote. Then again, neither did I.

"Yes."

"Let me guess. You write about the hopeless romantic," Angela said. "You seem just the type because, well, you come across as the opposite."

"You know," I cut in as brightly as Angela's sunshine, "how are wedding plans coming along, you two? Angela, you must be so excited."

I painted on a smile worthy of my bright counterpart, and she took the bait like a starved fish about to be lured in.

"Oh, I thought you'd never ask," Angela said. "I've picked the colors, a gentle pink, of course, and roses— cliché, I know—for the flowers. Tom, darling"—here, Angela giggled at her own joke—"why don't you share the date?"

"August 21. We've secured the church and got a hall booked."

"You're getting a hall?" I asked. "This must be a big affair."

"It is," Mr. Darling said self-importantly. "I have a large family."

Angela slumped back into the booth ever so slightly, like a balloon slowly losing its air. I remembered what she'd said about being estranged from her family. As my eyes traced back to her fiancé, I wondered if the Darling family was footing the bill. Angela was the type of girl who had dreams of marrying her prince, yet when I studied her face, her eyes betrayed every ounce of optimism she exuded. I knew right then and there that it was decided.

"I'll be your bridesmaid, Angela," I said.

The storm clouds left Angela's face as the sun returned. "Thank you, Lorna!" Turning toward Tristan, she explained, "I'd asked Lorna to be one of my bridesmaids at the end of the school year, but, you see, we're just getting better acquainted. She's already a great friend."

Tristan smiled slightly. "She is a good friend."

Under such unexpected and foreign praise, I wished I could have disappeared into the wooden bench or slid under the table, but the waitress saved us once more by arriving with our food. While we ate, Angela took most of the time to regale us with plans for a honeymoon to Florida, to return just in time for the start of the new school year, when she'd be Mrs. Darling.

By the end of lunch, I was relieved that the meal had gone as well as it had. After promises to get together with Angela soon and farewells with the happy couple, Tristan and I rode home in my moody Cadillac.

"You have interesting friends," he remarked, "although both Macy and Angela seem quite—I don't know—different from you."

I raised my eyebrows, glancing briefly at him and then back at the road. "What's that supposed to mean?"

"You seem much more grounded and realistic. They're the type who seem to have their heads in the clouds."

"Dreamers?" I asked wryly. "Well, maybe, but it all balances out. Who's to say I don't have a few dreams of my own?"

"Nothing wrong with dreams."

When we pulled into the driveway, the mailman was just walking up to deliver my mail. As I stepped out of the car, I hailed him down and thanked him as he handed me a couple of bills. While rifling through the envelopes, I said, "Sorry about them showing up and joining us like—"

"Excuse me, ma'am?" came a voice that wasn't Tristan's.

My index finger stopped, the envelope for my electric bill half-torn. I looked up into the face of a Western Union boy on a bicycle.

"Yes?" I asked, my heart lodged in my throat.

"Are you Miss Laura Ashford?"

I could sense Tristan as he moved to stand beside me, but all I could do was stare past the boy as he got off his bike and walked toward me.

"I am."

"I'm sorry, Miss Ashford." His gaze was on the ground as he offered me a telegram and something clutched in his hand.

His words made no sense. My hands moved of their own volition, trembling as I took the telegram and the item, a dog tag. "What?"

"Miss Ashford, your brother, Charles, was killed while serving his country, the highest honor—"

"Stop," I whispered, the telegram falling to the grass. I clutched the dog tag in a hard fist to my heart. Then I turned away from Tristan and this stranger who thought he knew some truth about Chucky that I didn't and went into my house, my tomb.

Chapter 10

If a person could feel what being dead was like while still living, the first word that would come to mind would be numb. All my higher brain functions stopped working, my mind unable to process what I'd just heard. I stopped walking when I came to the largest canvas in my living room. And stared. Just stared. My vision blurred until I couldn't discern one color from the other, one form or shape from its neighbor.

Somewhere a door opened and closed. Somehow, someone was standing next to me.

"Lorna—"

That voice. A whisper. A plea.

I swallowed thick saliva that did little to quench my thirst for an answer to all this— this impossibility.

"Maybe, you should...read it."

The telegram. A hand was holding it in front of me like a supplication.

"No," I said hollowly.

"But it might... Maybe it would give you some..."

"Answers?" I barked, anger flooding me like a furnace that had suddenly been turned up.

"I just thought—"

The telegram disappeared from view, and my rage died with my brother.

"It's just—" My breath hitched, and the words died, too.

I sobbed, and when two strong arms pulled me to an earthy-scented shirt, I crumpled into Tristan like a ragdoll, worn and misused for years. Every seam torn. My insides falling out, exposed for the world to see every weakness. Every surface stained and dirty.

He didn't try to say anything or offer any platitudes of false comfort. Instead, Tristan was my rock. The only sure thing I had in that moment. The only real hope I had.

When I could finally manage to speak as the tears slowed, I whispered into his shirt, "It can't be."

His arms squeezed gently and didn't let go.

"It has to be a mistake. A lie."

But I knew the truth. Knowing and accepting were two different things, though.

"I'm sorry." Tristan finally released me and took a step back.

Shaking my head, I said, "If read that telegram, it'll be confirmation of it. I can't do that."

"I'll leave it here until you're ready," Tristan said quietly, setting the telegram on my lonely chair.

"What if—?" *What if I'll never be ready?*

"I can go if you like."

"No. Stay." I crossed the small room and reached for his hand. "Stay." *If you go, I'll truly be alone.*

"Okay."

"I need— the backyard."

Tristan let me pull him where I needed. Among overgrown grass and a jungle of flowers, we sat. I didn't glance at Tristan to see what he was doing at my side but kept my eyes glued to the clouds as they lazily drifted overhead, indifferent to my pain and all the other troubles of the world. At some point during the afternoon, I lay down, folding into the grass as it embraced me, the blades caressing my arms and legs.

I hadn't realized I'd fallen asleep until I opened my eyes to find the sun much lower in the sky. Shocked, I bolted up, wondering if my brother's death had just been a horrible dream. But when I saw Tristan's frown and the sorrow coating his vivid blue eyes, I knew Chucky was as gone as my parents. Dead.

"You've been here this whole time?" I asked.

Tristan nodded. "You asked me to stay."

"You didn't have to stay this long. It must've been hours. Why—?"

"You asked me to stay. So I did."

His words, so simple, spoke more when any well-rehearsed speech could hope.

"Thank you."

I could have said more, but exhaustion overtook me. Had we really eaten lunch with Angela Sunshine and Tom Darling that same day? It seemed a couple of weeks ago now.

"I can stay as long as you need."

"You don't have to do that." I smiled weakly. "I guess the question is—what next?"

"One day at a time. I think we both know something about this."

I rested my hands in my lap, locking and unlocking my fingers. My mom's old wedding ring was nestled on my left index finger with its chewed-down nail, my hands smaller than hers. One of the few things of theirs I hadn't departed with. I examined the simple gold band, so plain and ordinary. It went months at a time, there on my finger, the feeling of it forgotten because it had become as much a part of me as my skin. With my other hand, I reached into my pocket and withdrew Chucky's dog tag.

"I want to put this on a chain," I said, "and wear it."

Tristan nodded.

"But yeah, I know too much about this." I waved my hand in the air, as if that explained everything. All the heartache that didn't go away. All the memories that half-plagued me and I half-longed for like an addict does a drug, an alcoholic his liquor. Every remembrance of my dad's laughter or my mom's strawberry pies, the horsey-back rides through piles of fallen leaves, Mom's quiet voice reading a bedtime story—my balm and my wound, my cure and my disease, my comfort and my pain.

Now Chucky's giggles as he snorted milk up his nose with a straw, his excitement the first time he rode a bike by himself, the smile that never left his face on the day he went to prom with the most popular girl in school, and the haunted look in his eyes as he said goodbye...all memory. All past. All dead.

"You should eat something," Tristan said.

"I don't think I could eat if I tried."

"Maybe you should still try. Come to my house."

I walked beside Tristan, the long grass giving way to stones crunching underfoot. We entered his place through the side door and went into the kitchen, where I sat and stared ahead. This was my first time back in his home since the tornado, which seemed months ago.

A few minutes later, a plate with a sandwich was placed in front of me. As I mechanically chewed, the bread stuck to the roof of my mouth, too thick to swallow. Eating was a mindless enough task, so I managed to consume half of the sandwich before I set it on the plate and shoved it away. I drank my glass of water like I'd been dying of thirst for days in a desert.

"Sorry," I said, "but I can't eat another bite."

Tristan laughed softly as he took the plate away. "I don't claim to be a French chef or anything."

I finally turned my gaze to him and said, "Did you eat?"

"Yes. You were somewhere else, so I just let you be."

The crumbs on the counter were proof that Tristan had stood there. I offered to help clean up, but Tristan just shook his head.

"You need to sleep. I'll walk you home."

As much as I dreaded being alone, I wasn't about to ask anything else of Tristan. He'd already done more for me in the past few days than most people had done for me in a lifetime. My feeble thanks seemed pathetic by comparison, but as he dropped me off on my side stoop, I leaned in and hugged him. He hesitated for a second, but then roped his arms around me, the feeling of being in his embrace natural.

"Good night," I said, trying to smile.

"Good night. Please, try to sleep. I'll see you tomorrow."

"Tomorrow..."

I stepped inside, watched him retreat, and then closed the door. With nothing left to do and feeling drained beyond comprehension, I went to bed. As I lay in the comfort of one of the few familiar pieces of furniture I owned, my eyelids grew heavy, and I dreamed of better days.

∞ ∞ ∞

Six years earlier...

Drops were still falling, even though the rain had stopped a while ago. The water dripped from the hundred-year-old maple trees lining Emerson Street like a dog shaking itself dry after a bath. From our front porch, I watched for him. I sat in a rocking chair that was rickety with three generations of Miller and Ashford women making good use of it. The left side was slightly lower than the right, giving it a unique feel as the well-worn rockers moved back and forth over the wooden planks.

I had just finished another year of college, arriving home an hour ago on a bus. One year away from becoming a teacher. I smiled to myself, counting myself fortunate and blessed to have the opportunity most didn't, especially women during the Depression. My parents had always been smart with their money. My dad had never trusted placing too much in the banks, much to his friends' amusement—until the Crash eight years ago. My parents were both the only offspring to survive into adulthood in their families and inherited whatever money their parents left before I'd been born.

My thoughts snapped away as I saw my little brother bounding down the sidewalk, laughing with the carefree spirit of a thirteen-year-old boy. His two best friends, Teddy and Elliot, flanked him. The boys playfully shoved and hit each other as they made their way down the street.

Chucky waved goodbye to Teddy five houses down and then to Elliot three houses away. When he saw me on the porch, he raced the rest of the way home. He stopped at the foot of the driveway, looked both ways, and ran to me. We hugged.

When we released each other, I said with a wry smile, "Didn't want your friends seeing you hugging your big sister?"

Chucky blushed. "Well, it's not exactly—"

"No need to explain," I said. "It's good to see you, Chucky. How was your last day?"

"The best day of the whole year."

"Why's that?"

"Because it was my last!"

"You silly little—"

"We can't all be smart like you, Laura." He stuck his tongue out at me in jest. "I'm parched. I'm gonna get a drink, but you gotta tell me all about the big league later...after dinner, okay?"

"Of course. You'll probably fall asleep from boredom anyway. College isn't as exciting as you might imagine."

"It's better than livin' here with our parents. You get the freedom of being on your own. D'you think I'll get to go to college?"

"If you want."

Chucky's brown eyes shone with youthful hope. He dashed into the house, leaving the door almost slamming in my face. Chuckling softly, I checked the time. I could already hear my brother regaling our mom in the kitchen with tales of his last day of school. Making my way to the phone on the rolltop desk in the living room, I took a seat and dialed Macy. Even though it had been two years since she'd married, it was still strange to call her when I needed to talk to her instead of just going next door and knocking on the door.

After two rings, Macy picked up. When she heard who it was, she exclaimed, "Laura! It's about time I heard from you! Back home for the summer after another year at that bigwig school?"

I shook my head, smiling. "Ohio State isn't that bigwig, Mace. It's not like I'm at Harvard or Stanford."

"Still, look at you, Miss Smarty Pants. Only you would consider it fun to study Greek and Latin with your free time while we were still in high school."

"You know the requirements—" My eyes landed on my algebra textbook that I'd had since high school, stacked with several others, on the coffee table.

"Well, not really. I'm just a housewife and a mother, Laura. What do I know about higher education?"

"Don't say that, Mace. You're a great mom to Johnny and a loving wife to John. I don't know how you do it, honestly. I couldn't imagine having a kid yet."

Macy laughed. "Well, they don't come with an instruction manual; that's for sure."

"You might think that having books to learn is like an instruction manual to college, Macy, but it's not like that. I do have to think, use my brain."

"Okay, Miss Brainy, when are we getting together? I haven't seen you since Easter."

"I have no plans, so whenever...tomorrow?"

"I have a meeting at the church...Sunday school committee. Hey, maybe you could come?"

"You think I should teach Sunday school?"

"Well, you're studying to be a teacher. It might be good practice."

"Look, Macy, I know I go to church when I'm home and all, but—"

"You haven't found a church near the college?" The disapproval and shock mixed in Macy's voice.

"Well, no...sorry. I mean, sure, there are churches nearby—plenty, in fact. It's just Sunday morning is more time to study. I think God understands that. I never got much out of old Pastor Wilson's sermons. They were a good naptime." I laughed.

"They were pretty bad, weren't they?" Macy joined me in chuckling. She sobered, and there was a long pause. "Well, tomorrow after the meeting, why don't we meet up? Come to my place, and we'll figure out what we're doing from there."

"It's on my calendar," I replied. "Good night, Mace. It's been great talking with you again."

After I hung up the phone, I took my books up to my room. Mom wouldn't appreciate having them on her coffee table, especially when she would have the ladies over for tea and Bible study. As I found spots on my already-crowded desk for my books, I smiled wryly to myself. Mom's weekly Bible studies were more gossip sessions for the women of Emerson Street than anything. What would the esteemed ladies make of algebra and classic literature? I supposed I could joke that they were new decorations for the living room, that all the ladies who knew anything about the latest styles were leaving stacks of cumbersome books on their coffee tables, but I didn't imagine that would go over well with Mom.

I tidied up my room, the bed smelling of fresh sheets Mom must have laundered earlier that day. My dresser and desk had been dusted, and the floor had been swept. Taking a seat in my chair, I thought of the care my mom had always taken with the house, including my bedroom. Being away for a few months at a time gave me a whole new appreciation for everything she did.

Satisfied, I left my room and went to the kitchen, finding my mom standing at the sink as she peeled potatoes. I kissed her on the cheek and took the potato from her hand.

"Let me do that," I said.

Stunned, Mom handed me the peeler and went to the oven to check on the roast.

"What's brought this on?" she asked.

"Well, Chucky isn't helping," I said.

Mom laughed. "I chased him out of the kitchen, that rascal. He kept trying to stick his nose in everything I was cooking or preparing for dinner."

"It smells wonderful, Mom."

Mom shrugged. "It's a special occasion with you being home from college and it being Chucky's last day of seventh grade. I thought it would be nice to celebrate."

"It's like Christmas or Easter. A roast, Mom? How much has that set you and Dad back?"

Mom waved me off. "It's not your job to worry about money yet, Laura."

As I peeled, I lifted my eyes to my mom and smiled. Of everyone in the family, she was the only redhead. Her fair skin was freckled on her nose and cheeks. Her light green eyes creased as she returned the smile.

"I'm surprised you're not reading," she said.

"Even I need to take a break sometimes."

"Peeling potatoes is a break?"

I shrugged, laughing a little. "Maybe. Hey, are you still tutoring kids after school?"

"I was when school was in session."

I finished peeling the last potato and added it to the pot. Turning to face my mom, I asked, "Did you ever think of being a teacher?"

Mom smiled, but it didn't reach her eyes. "Few women did any sort of profession in my day."

"You're smart. You could have."

Mom shrugged me off, grabbed the pot of potatoes, and set it on the stove. "Go check the garden. See if the strawberries are ready for picking yet."

Knowing when I was being dismissed, I grabbed a basket as I left the kitchen and went outside, only to find my brother already in the garden. Chucky was picking strawberries, all right, but every plump fruit's existence was short in his fingers as he popped it into his mouth.

"Working hard, I see," I said, coming from behind.

Chucky gave a little start and stood, turning on the spot like a thief caught in the act. "Oh, it's just you," he said with a sigh.

Joining him, I knelt on the sodden earth and began plucking strawberries from the plants and filling my basket.

"Looks like a good yield this year," I said.

"Then Mom won't miss a few." Chucky sat back down.

"A few? It looks like a flock of birds picked some of these plants over, Chucky. How long have you been out here?"

He shrugged and added the berry in his reddened fingers to my basket. "I was getting hungry."

"You're always hungry."

"Hey, I'm still growing! Just you wait, Laura, one day I'll be taller than you."

I smiled. "I should hope so."

"Almost all the girls are taller than me right now," Chucky complained.

I chuckled. "It's a whole different ballgame in high school."

"I'd love to play football in high school. If I went to college, d'you think I could play?"

"You have to be really good to play in college. Not that I'm an expert on sports."

"I've played for years with the kids on our street."

I loved Chucky's innocent enthusiasm and didn't wish to be the rain that put out his fire, but the realist in me wanted to give him a clear picture. "Are you really serious about this going to college bit?"

"Yes!"

"Well, it's more than how well you can play football, little brother. You'll have to work extra hard, do a lot of studying outside of what they teach you in high school. It's not easy to get in, but if that's what you want, then you should go for it."

"Really? You mean that?" Chucky's eyes gleamed like it was Christmas morning.

"Of course. I can help you."

He threw the last of the strawberries into the load, and as I stood, I was careful not to spill the overflowing basket.

"Is Mom gonna make a pie with these?"

Chucky was speaking a mile a minute, and his happiness infected me as we strode back to the house.

"She always does. Let's get back inside and wash these off. Dad will be home soon."

"And that means dinner."

I rolled my eyes playfully. "Yes, that means dinner, you poor starving child."

We laughed and entered to the smell of Mom's roast coming out of the oven.

∞ ∞ ∞

When I woke, dim sunlight filtered in through the opening in the curtains of my bedroom window. I groaned and sat up, blinking, stretching, and trying to shake the cobwebs from my brain. For half a second, I'd forgotten about my brother, until I felt the slight weight of his dog tag on its chain on my chest. I clutched the tag as fresh tears fell.

"Damn You," I muttered, glaring at the ceiling.

I dashed the tears away and stood. It wasn't like I wasn't already well-acquainted with unexpected death. Two words. *Damn You.* That was all God was getting from me. As I marched to the bathroom to shower, I knew God was nowhere closer to me in this tragedy than he had been six years ago, so I forced myself to go about my day like none of it mattered—faith, life, God. None of it was important. All that mattered was to keep going, whatever that meant. I could do little else.

A few minutes later, I stepped out of the shower, dressed, and left my hair to dry. As I picked at my breakfast, I sighed and stood, leaving my oatmeal mostly uneaten. I walked through the house with my small cup of coffee and opened a few of the windows. When I reached the picture window, I stopped, stunned to find Tristan standing among his rocks. I could see his mouth moving, and I knew what he was saying. I frowned, stepping back and sitting in my chair.

Watching his lips quiver soundlessly through the closed window, anyone watching us would have thought nothing was different from a few weeks ago. Here I was, locked away in my prison, spying on my neighbor, who was equally in his own cell.

Only everything had changed.

Chapter 11

I returned to the kitchen and poured the already-cold coffee into the sink. Like much else in my life, it belonged down the drain, irreversibly removed from me. The side door banged behind me as I marched out, crossed my front yard, and came to an abrupt halt between the houses. Tristan stopped pacing and blinked at me.

"Who? Who needs to take you away?" I asked.

Tristan frowned. "Good morning, Lorna."

I stomped across the stones, kicking them with gusto out of my way. When I was a foot or less from Tristan, I glared at him and demanded, "Who needs to take you away?"

"You heard that, did you?" His voice was grim, his mouth a firm line. But those eyes—my goodness—they shone.

"Every word," I whispered. "For-for weeks."

"It doesn't matter."

"But it does!" I reached for his hands and squeezed them like a child desperate to make her daddy listen as she tells her deepest secrets.

"You shouldn't have listened."

"Maybe not, but I couldn't help it. There you were, right there—and I was right there." I jerked my head toward my window. "No one needs to take you away. Do you hear me? No one. You can't—"

And then those damning tears were back in full force, but I didn't try to stop them. Tristan pulled me to him like he had yesterday, and he eased me into his house. Once inside, he sat next to me on the floral sofa and let me cry.

"If I keep this up, I'm going to dehydrate," I joked weakly.

Tristan laughed softly, the deep rumble in his chest an agonizing reminder of my dad's laughter.

"You hide behind all that hair and those glasses," I said. "Your eyes are beautiful."

He stopped laughing. "Lorna, you've been through hell."

"Yes, and you're my light right now. Perhaps I'm being too open saying this, but, Tristan, you've been like a candle in the darkness the past several days, and now, more than ever, I-I need you."

"No one is going to take me away if that's what you're worried about."

"Then why do you keep saying it?"

Tristan sighed. "You're persistent, you know that?"

Just when I thought he was avoiding the question again, he continued, "The angels, God, whoever's up there." He pointed toward a crack in his ceiling. "After she died, I wanted nothing more than to die, too. I wanted them to take me away."

If my already-broken heart could have shattered more, it would have. My breath caught in my throat as my tears stilled. A buried woe surfaced inside as I placed my left hand, the one with my mother's ring, on Tristan's rough cheek. Those impossibly bright blue eyes gazed at me like a lost child looking for answers. So empty. So full. A contradiction with every breath.

"I am sorry," I whispered.

Tristan took a small breath and pulled away from my touch. His eyes were everywhere but on me as he replied, "It was a long time ago. I should've let it—*her*—go years ago."

"I have no more accepted what happened to my parents so long ago," I said. "I understand. You don't have to—"

"But I do. Your brother. That's fresh. This other stuff, those we've been mourning for six years, that's old wounds. Not your brother, though. You have every reason to be as angry or as sad as you wish. In your shoes, I would be."

I shook my head. "I don't know where to start."

"Have you called Macy?"

"No, I haven't told anyone. Only you know."

"Call her. She would want to know, and I'll be right here, Lorna. I promise. I'm not going anywhere."

I wanted to tell Tristan to not make promises he couldn't keep. No one was guaranteed another day. Death and I were close acquaintances, and if I knew anything about death, it was that it knocked and invited itself in whenever it felt like it.

"Maybe I'll call her now," I said. "There's no point in waiting."

"Take as long as you need. Call whoever you need. When you're ready, I'll be here."

I nodded and murmured my thanks, leaving Tristan's house to return to my own. When I entered, the kitchen seemed to stare back at me, unchanging. I saw dirty dishes in the sink and on the table, but my eyes fell on the phone hanging on the kitchen wall. Going to it, I picked up the receiver and dialed Macy's number.

Much later that day, I lay on my bed, my arms crossed behind my head as I stared at the ceiling. A crack quite like the one in Tristan's house above his armchair made its presence known among the otherwise white ceiling.

Macy had been every bit as shocked as expected. Of course, she'd offered to come over, had invited me to stay with them, had insisted on making me something to eat, but I'd declined all her well-meaning attempts at consolation. After a long, painful conversation with Macy, I'd called Angela. That conversation had been much shorter. As my other friend expressed her sorrow and platitudes, I'd been unable to handle much more, so I'd politely said good night.

For a while after that, I'd stared at the phone, half-contemplating whether it was worth trying to call distant relatives I hadn't seen since I was a kid. My parents had a few cousins, but many lived outside of the area, and their children, although second cousins to me, might as well have been perfect strangers. Chucky had been born later than any of them, and I couldn't say if they'd ever met him.

I was used to having next to no family. Now I truly had no family.

At least not blood family. Macy was the sister I'd never had, and even though she'd give an arm or a leg to me if I lost mine, she had her own family. I couldn't ask her to forsake her lifestyle for my benefit. Angela was too new, barely a friend, and I'd likely just scare her off if I leaned on her too much.

Coworkers were just that—people I worked with. They had no bearing on my personal life.

And then there was Tristan. If anyone could be family besides Macy, it was him. I hadn't planned on it. I hadn't expected it, but here we were, mere days after being thrown together by a tornado, and Tristan Blake mattered to me.

But who was I kidding? His heart belonged to his wife. How could I possibly expect anything more than friendship?

I stopped my thoughts.

When had I started thinking of Tristan as more than just a friend?

The thought unsettled me.

I sat up, unable to sleep. I half-wondered if I should bother Tristan again that day. Maybe I'd been spending too much time around him. Maybe we'd both been so starved of human affection that we'd latched onto the other like a leech sucking blood.

Was it healthy for me to be in Tristan's company like this? I reconsidered how little I knew of him, how little he knew of me—at least in facts.

I could tell you Macy's favorite color, about every birthday party she'd had as a kid, about the time we'd pulled the fire alarm at school in eighth grade, and even about the first time she'd gotten her period. Those types of details weren't common knowledge about a person, but did knowing facts really add up to actually *knowing* someone?

I'd never forget the day Macy called me, sobbing as she miscarried, or the time she'd broken her arm when we'd been fooling around, trying to climb the drainpipe outside my childhood home, and she'd cried in my arms until her mother came.

And the time she'd held me like the mother I'd just lost six years ago. She hadn't tried to explain the reason why. She hadn't told me how to feel. She had just been there. Like Tristan.

I ruefully smiled. How would Tristan react if I told him he was akin to my best girlfriend? Shaking my head as I stood, I murmured, "Only I want more than just a best friend." I already had one of those.

Too much of the day remained for my liking, so I lay back down, and sleep claimed me.

∞ ∞ ∞

Several hours later, the ringing of the phone was my alarm. When I first opened my eyes, I thought I'd been dreaming, but realization dawned, and I dashed to the kitchen. A man from the Army spoke on the other end, filling me in on the details. My brother's body, like many of the soldiers, had been buried overseas. The man claimed that these cemeteries were temporary and that when the war was over, the bodies of our soldiers could be returned to American soil if the loved ones wished. Still, a memorial service would be held to honor Chucky, and this officer wished to meet with me to make the arrangements. I stoically listened and took down the information, my emotions regarding Chucky's death past the point of coherence.

When I hung up the phone, I read over the notes I'd taken and set them aside. Unsure if my lack of tears at the moment was due to denial or acceptance, I walked into the living room to close the picture window. It was evening, and the breeze coming in was unseasonably cold. A quick look outside confirmed no presence of Tristan in his rock garden.

Then my eyes fell on the telegram. There it sat, undisturbed on the chair.

With shaking hands, I picked it up. I tried to calm my breathing as I closed my eyes and inhaled deeply. I could do this. I *had* to do this.

To know the truth. To know how Chucky died.

I opened my eyes, and they fell on the telegram. My hands continued to fumble like an alcoholic trying to unscrew the cap from his flask.

I read.

In war-torn Tunisia, Chucky had died while trying to save one of his fallen comrades from a building that was about to cave in. He had been too late.

So he hadn't been shot by the Germans.

That was no comfort. I folded the telegram in half and set it down, unsure if I wished I had read it.

I inspected my artwork. The mess on each canvas should have been a battlefield, the splattered paint the blood. I considered taking my creations down, but what would replace them? These monstrosities might have been fascinating to Tristan, but to me, they had replaced my family.

What I wouldn't give for a picture of Chucky's smile on my wall right now.

Unable to spend another minute in that house—yes, that house, not my house—I left and hoped Tristan wouldn't mind my intrusion.

He answered the door within seconds. "You don't have to knock," he said as he let me in.

"I should just come in without letting you know I'm here?"

"I wouldn't expect anyone else, so yes."

"I couldn't stand my own company anymore, but I don't know what to do, to say. I'm afraid I'm still going to be miserable company."

"Your company is never miserable."

"Stop being so kind," I muttered, walking past Tristan into his house like I owned it. I dropped into the armchair and continued, "I read the telegram."

Tristan nodded. "Did it...help?" He frowned, then added, "I'm sorry; that was a stupid question."

"It's not stupid. I know you're just trying to be a friend, but can we, I don't know, just drive somewhere?"

"Where did you have in mind?"

"Let's go to the beach. We live a few miles from the lake, and I can't tell you the last time I went there. It's pathetic."

Tristan smiled, the strip of light from beyond the window illuminating his face. "I think the last time I went to the beach was when Julie was still alive."

His words caught me off guard. Mouth agape, I closed it and swallowed. "Julie? Your wife?"

Tristan extended his hand toward me, and I took it. He led me to a bookshelf in a dusty, dark corner of the living room and pulled out an album.

"I want to show you something," he said, motioning toward the sofa.

I silently took a seat as Tristan fell in place at my side. His face was as unreadable as always in the dim light that filtered past his mostly closed curtains, hidden behind his mask of hair and glasses. His hand stroked the front of the photo album almost reverently.

Then he opened it. He flipped through pages too quickly for me to see much of anything, but then he stopped and pointed to one of the pictures. "That's the last time I went to the beach," he whispered.

I leaned in closely. Blinking past darkness and dust, I saw her. A young woman sat on a towel with an umbrella perched in the sand behind her. The style swimsuit she wore hailed from about a decade ago. Julie smiled at me with friendly eyes, not the blackened version I had seen on display everywhere else in Tristan's house.

"She's beautiful," I said.

Tristan closed the album and set it aside. "Yes, she was, but she's gone. It's about time I realized that."

"Why are you telling me this?"

"Because, like I said, your brother's death is fresh. Seeing your pain right now makes me realize how ridiculous I've been all these years."

"It's no more ridiculous than how I've felt about losing my parents." I thought how our words echoed what we'd said yesterday. Saying it again, I wondered if I was moving on, giving myself permission to bury the hurt that had lived with me for the past six years.

Tristan shifted, moving away from me a bit. "I'm sorry. I told you when we first met that I'm no good at offering comfort. I'm being selfish—"

I laughed softly. "No more than I'm being. I seem to recall a conversation about eggshells. Truth is, if there's anyone I'd talk to about any of this, it's you."

Tristan's brow furrowed. "Why me?"

"It makes little sense to explain it. I don't even think I can. It just feels right."

"Lorna, maybe you should—"

"Should what?" I asked, something sinking inside.

"We should take that drive. Let's go to the beach."

I stood with hesitation. What had Tristan been about to say? Not wishing to push him, I nodded and asked, "Who's driving?"

∞ ∞ ∞

A few hours later, we were still sitting on the beach. The wet sand squished between my toes, my shoes long ago thrown off to the side somewhere. The gentle crashing of the waves as I watched the sunset reflecting on the ripples lulled me toward peace. The delighted screams of thrill-seekers going down the biggest hill of the appropriately named Thriller roller coaster echoed in the distance.

"My parents used to take us to Euclid Beach Park when I was growing up," I said, my eyes on the rainbow-hued sky.

"We didn't have anything like that where I grew up in rural Kansas, but when the fair happened every August, that was a big deal. I think the smell of the food was exciting enough for me. I always got sick on the rides."

I couldn't stop the giggle that bubbled up inside my throat. "Really?" When Tristan just stared blankly at me, I continued, "My goodness, it feels good to laugh."

"Glad I could provide a source of entertainment," he said wryly.

"I'd like to take you to Euclid Beach just to see your reaction. The Flying Turns and the Rotor are sure to be favorites."

"I'm glad to see you smiling."

I sobered as the wind picked up and whipped my hair about my head. I turned my gaze to Tristan to find him unfazed by the wind's dance with his own locks. "Chucky was always so much younger than me. I remember complaining about having to go through the kiddie section so he could go on the rides for his age. One time, while we waited for the carousel, the line was so long that poor Chucky peed himself. I was more upset than he was. Now, what I wouldn't give to have just a minute of that part of my life back—my family together again."

"It sounds like you had a lot of good memories."

"They were great memories," I said as my voice broke. "And now that's all they are, all my family, just memories."

"You're lucky to have had the family you did. You must have been really close."

I wiped a couple of errant tears away and blinked against the wind. "What about your family?"

"My father moved our family to Cleveland for a better opportunity. He worked for the Ford plant. The auto industry was booming back then. I was the youngest."

"You never said you had siblings," I said.

"Because we aren't on good terms. I wasn't exactly planned, being born so much later than my brothers and sisters, and everyone made that clear my whole life. I was the black sheep, the disappointment to my family."

"I'm sorry. We don't have to talk about it if you don't want."

"Probably for the best."

"Still, I think it's an awful thing what they did to you, how they mistreated you." My hackles rose against a faceless group of people who had no bearing on my life.

Tristan shrugged. "It was a long time ago."

We lapsed into silence for the next several minutes. The moon now hung low in the sky, full and bright over the waves as they calmed to the dying wind's lullaby. A chill went through me as I stood.

"We should go home," I said.

Tristan joined me and pulled me close to his side. Surprised by his gesture, I looked up at him.

"You seemed cold."

As we got into his truck, I said, "The Army called today to go over the details of everything."

As Tristan started the ignition, he said, "From what I hear, they will be a lot of help—not that anything is easy about—"

"I know," I whispered, my hand resting over his as he made to grab the shifter.

Understanding passed between us, unspoken, but its presence in our eyes.

Chapter 12

Two weeks later, I stood outside the old Methodist church my family had gone to most of my life. From the bottom of the steps to the main entrance, I stared at those large, wooden doors, closed for the moment. Closed to me.

The service wouldn't be for another three hours. In the July heat, I baked under the sun and felt like an overripe melon about to burst. A glance up and down the street showed that I was still alone.

Driving through my old neighborhood to come here had been an odd mixture of fond nostalgia and broken-heartedness. I'd avoided my childhood home.

I withdrew into the shade of a tree, fanning myself with the service bulletin that old Pastor Wilson had given to me yesterday while going over the details for Chucky's memorial service. That was a conversation I wished to relegate to the deepest recesses of my mind, lock up tight, and throw away the key.

"Laura," Pastor Wilson greeted me, "it's been too long. I'm sorry it's under these circumstances I'm finally seeing you again."

"Pastor," I replied coldly.

Pastor Wilson hadn't changed much in the past six years. His hair had gone from grey to white, but his facial features had long been lost in wrinkles. A lifetime bachelor as far as I knew, he never had any idea what family life was like firsthand.

I took a seat across from him at a little table in the parlor, the eyes of previous pastors glaring down at me from their high spots in frames on the walls.

"Laura, I am sorry—"

"Let's just discuss what I came here for."

Maybe sadness crossed his expression, but I kept my eyes averted on the tabletop. While he went over the elements of the service, I remained quiet, only supplying answers when needed.

When we finished, Pastor Wilson said, "Laura, how have you been holding up?"

"It's Lorna."

"Of course. My apologies. I'd forgotten you'd changed your name after—"

"Are we here to discuss my name or Chucky's service? I thought it was the latter, and it seemed like we were done. If that is all, Pastor—"

"Child, I simply wanted to ask after your welfare. You've been dealt another unfortunate blow, and it's times like these when our trust and faith in God can really waver. But that is when we need to turn to Him the most."

"God and I have nothing to say to each other."

"I would humbly disagree, Lorna. God is always speaking."

"I didn't come here for a sermon."

"Of course. I'll see you tomorrow, then."

With those parting words, I exited the parlor as quickly as my legs would carry me.

Now I was back, and I wanted nothing more than to turn around and walk the other direction. As my eyes wandered down the street, I caught Macy rushing toward me, her heels clickety-clacking on the pavement.

"Be careful. Don't fall on my account," I said.

"Oh, darling. Don't fret." Macy enveloped me in a hug, the vanilla scent of her hair wafting up my nose. "Do you need anything?"

"I still have plenty of food. You've been feeding me like I'm an army." I frowned.

"Is Tristan here? You two have been practically attached at the hip. You're together every time I see you."

"Not every time." Deny. Deny. Deny.

Macy released me enough to survey my face. My earlier unease as I stood in the church's shadow dissolved as Macy gifted me with one of her skeptical smiles.

"I was there at least every other day for the past two weeks, darling. You can't tell me you weren't with your ruggedly handsome man every time. He was either working in your yard, helping you move in furniture—which, it's about time you got some!—or standing about looking every bit the moody, dark hero."

I rolled my eyes. "Tristan and I are just friends."

"Like I haven't heard *that* before. Lamest excuse in the books."

"He offered to help me get my house in order."

Macy harrumphed. "Yeah, and you needed it, Lorna. You really did." Her voice softened, as did her eyes. "Seriously, how are you doing today?"

I inhaled deeply and released my breath. "I've had time to come to terms with things. And okay, Tristan has been a godsend." After a pause, I hastily added, "And you, of course. You've been an angel."

"A godsend? An angel? Laura, darling, has standing this close to a church infected you?"

I glared. "Not that again. First the pastor and now you—"

Just then, Tristan joined us. When I say, "Joined us," I mean he was awkwardly standing ten feet off to the side, engaged in his usual shifting from one foot to the other.

My heart filled with warmth as I went to him. He was dressed more formally than I'd ever seen him. No ratty shirt and jeans today. He was wearing a suit and had tamed his hair and maybe even trimmed his beard.

"Good morning," he said. His eyes briefly fell on Macy as he gave her a nod.

"Good morning," I replied, longing to reach for his hand. "You came."

"Of course I came."

"Macy just got here. I've been here for a while."

I didn't want to admit I'd been pacing in front of the church the past hour on my own. Somehow, Tristan seemed to know I was having a hard time finding my words, like searching for a treasure with the wrong map.

Macy, bold as ever, came to my side and said, "Hello, Tristan."

"Mrs. Wells," he replied, his voice guarded.

With all the times my two friends had come across each other lately, I'd have thought Tristan would have felt he could open up more around Macy—not that I expected him to share his every secret, but why was I the only one he could relax around?

"You may call me Macy."

Macy seemed to be reading my mind, but I'd always been an open book to her.

"Very well, Mrs.—Macy."

I tried not to chuckle as Tristan's tongue tripped over Macy's name as if walking on uneven pavement. Having them there was keeping me afloat, and I watched as more people, many of whom I didn't know, gathered around the church and went inside.

"Has there been a mistake?" I asked. "I recognize the man who works at the drugstore and the woman from the library, but they're practically strangers."

"Your brother served his country," Macy said. "I expect you'll see lots of people from the community here. They'll want to show their respect."

Tears welled in my eyes, and I failed to find my voice as my mouth gaped. I closed it and looked from Macy to Tristan.

Macy kissed my cheek, squeezed my hand, and walked away as her own family approached. A moment later, Tristan took my hand. In his steady, calming presence, he stayed at my side every step up those imposing church stairs. The task was not so insurmountable with him there.

We entered.

The next couple of hours for the calling was a blur. I politely thanked all those well-meaning strangers who expressed their condolences, but my smile was beginning to hurt as we took our seats in the uncomfortable pews. Unsurprised to find none of my distant relatives in attendance, I kept my eyes on the altar. An empty casket with the flag draped over it rested at the front of the sanctuary.

Beside me, Tristan murmured, "Are you sure I should be sitting in the front row? Isn't this for family? Where's Macy?"

"Macy's with her family. Her kids are little, so she wanted to be able to step out if need be." I gestured toward the back. "As for you, you're more family than anyone but Macy," I said. "My family, at least what remains, is like yours."

"Ah. Well, if you're sure."

"I am."

I squeezed his callused hand, staring at the dark sleeve of his suit jacket that covered his wrist. As Mr. Darling and Angela walked past, I gave them the smallest of nods, while Angela murmured her apologies for being late. I thought I recognized a few of Chucky's old friends and some of the folks from our childhood neighborhood.

As people took their seats, I forced my thoughts away from the sadness that threatened my outlook with every breath.

The organ music started. As Pastor Wilson took his place behind the pulpit, I half-listened to the ritualistic words. When the time came for the eulogy, I gave him my full attention. I owed it to my brother to hear every syllable spoken about his short life, even though I already knew everything the pastor uttered.

"Charles Patrick Ashford was born in January 1924 here in Cleveland. His older sister, Lorna, survives him. His parents, Charles and Elaine, entered eternity in 1937...too soon, my friends, too soon...just as Charles has left us too soon. Charles loved basketball, his mother's strawberry pies, and his sister. They were very close in the years before he was drafted to serve in the war..."

After the church service was over, I numbly followed the military pallbearers down the aisle and outside to the small cemetery next door. When we reached our places, the heat of the sun bore down on us. It didn't take more than a minute for the sweat to begin beading on my forehead. Of all the ridiculous thoughts, I wondered how the military personnel could stand to wear their uniforms in this stifling heat.

Once everyone was outside, a chaplain from the Army began the military component of Chucky's service. Seven Army men lined up and aimed their guns toward the sky, firing off rounds. Another man played "Taps." Prayers. More words. Prayers and prayers. Finally, the soldiers surrounded the casket and lifted the flag from it, folding it into a triangle. At the end, an officer approached with the flag and held it out to me.

I took it, the silent tears tracking down my cheeks. As I pulled the American flag to my chest, it pressed against Chucky's dog tag hanging around my neck. I felt Tristan's arm wrap around me as I fell into his grasp.

A few minutes later, the service was done. People slowly withdrew, their murmurs and the rustling of the branches the only sound. If Macy, Angela, or anyone else tried talking to me, I didn't remember it. I came away with a vague impression of the Army offering me their respects on behalf of my brother, but it was like I was underwater, every sound muffled. And if I stayed under too long, I would drown.

But for Tristan keeping me afloat.

When Tristan and I were the last, he remained a silent comfort at my side. He took my hand. I leaned into him as he held me close. My gaze was on the plot as the birds sang around us.

"You know," I choked out, "there's a verse in the Bible that talks about groanings too deep for words. I guess those are prayers when words fail us, for moments like this."

He squeezed my hand.

"But, Tristan, I'm not sure if I believe that." I turned in his arms and looked into his eyes.

He kept his gaze locked on mine, but a sadness showed in his voice when he spoke. "I'm afraid I'm the wrong person to ask when it comes to questions of faith."

"Why does God allow bad things to happen? Why take Chucky after He already took my parents?"

"God...didn't take your parents from you." He hesitated, on the verge of saying something more, but stopped.

I sighed, closed my eyes, and said, "I want today to be over. I'm spent, Tristan. I can't think about moment."

"Then let's go home."

∞ ∞ ∞

Later that day, Tristan and I sat in the near darkness in his tattered living room, a place that had become a source of comfort to me like a broken-in pillow. My cup of tea sat cold on the coffee table. In the corner, a grandfather clock ticked away the hour, another portion of life relentlessly passing, the sands in the hourglass slipping through my fingers. My parents and Chucky slipping away...slipped away.

"I'm glad I didn't opt to have a dinner afterward," I said hollowly. "I don't think I could've managed to spend any more time with all those people."

"You'd rather subject yourself to my attempts at cooking?"

A dry laugh escaped my lips. I turned to Tristan, who leaned against the other arm of the sofa. The sofa arm that bore my weight was missing a large chunk out of it, like a dog had bitten through it. My legs were pulled up to my chest like I used to sit as a child.

"You looked nice today," I said. Tristan had since removed his suit coat and tie and untucked his shirt.

His lips quirked into a small smile. "This is what you want to talk about?"

"Maybe. Maybe not. Anything but today."

"All right, then. For the record, you didn't look too bad yourself." His smile widened.

I laughed, shaking my head. "What was your favorite part of my look? The raccoon eyes with the smeared makeup or my drawn mouth?"

Tristan sobered and drew closer. "Your eyes and your mouth are always beautiful."

As soon as the words left his mouth, my heart completely, inappropriately skipped a beat.

"I'm sorry. I shouldn't have—" His Adam's apple bobbed.

I drew closer, and Tristan's breath touched my cheek. I was reminded of our first time together, down in that cellar, his earthy scent permeating my nose, his presence my reassurance. Since then, he had become my rock, as grounded and immovable as all the rocks in his yard.

I lifted my hand to his cheek. His beard was softer than it looked. My fingers raked through his facial hair, pushing tendrils of hair behind his ear. I closed my eyes, and our lips met—tentative at first, but then with deeper passion. Tristan's hands cupped my face. I poured every ounce of my heartache into that kiss, and for a time, we were somewhere else, anywhere but this sad world. When we broke apart, I blinked away tears, shocked to see his expression mirroring mine. My breath caught in my throat.

"I-I'm sorry," Tristan whispered, recoiling as if he'd been struck by a snake's venomous fangs instead of kissed. He removed his glasses, placed them on the table, and wiped his eyes. He stood and made a hasty retreat toward his bedroom.

With the remnant of tears on my cheeks, I stared into the darkness toward his room. I wiped my face. My head was spinning. We'd kissed! For those few seeming-forever moments, everything seemed right. Everything that had gone wrong in my life was overcome by the feeling that with Tristan, I could find completion. This broken vessel of Lorna was the whole pot of Laura again. She knew love. She found love. She could still love. Even after everything bad, love seemed to have won.

But as I sat there, it was like someone had turned off the light inside me, and I was becoming one with the darkness in Tristan's house. Confusing, desolate, heartbreaking darkness. *Oh, Tristan...*

When I finally withdrew my eyes from the darkness and gazed at the close surroundings in the weak light coming through the parting in the drapes, I saw them. He had left his glasses. Never had Tristan been without them for more than a few seconds since I'd known him. I picked them up and looked through the lenses, as if I could somehow see the world he saw.

But the lenses were just plain glass, not a prescription to correct ruined vision.

My eyes focused through the false lenses on a small stack of books on Tristan's coffee table—three titles by B.R. Stevenson. Two I had heard of, *Forlorn for Love* and *A Travesty of Torn Souls.* After all, they were my favorites, but the other was foreign—*Cure for the Cries.* I made to reach for the unfamiliar title but withdrew my hand instead. Hadn't Tristan claimed to have never heard of this author?

Frowning, I replaced the glasses, my already tired mind unable to process much more that day, and stood. A few seconds later, the front door clicked shut behind me.

Chapter 13

I went to bed early that night. When I woke to find my bedroom shrouded in darkness, I fumbled for the chain on the light next to my bed and picked up the small alarm clock. It was just after three o'clock. My stomach growled, hating its owner for not feeding it dinner.

As I replaced the clock, I felt wide awake. My eyes roamed over B.R. Stevenson's books stacked on my night table, but I opted to leave them in peace. The humidity and heat from the day hadn't lessened much in the night, so I was comfortable wearing only a thin nightgown on my way to the kitchen.

When I reached the fridge, I opened it and stood there, staring at its contents for too long. If my mother were here, she would've lectured me about wasting energy by leaving the door open. But she wasn't here. No more than Chucky.

I finally settled on the remainder of the spaghetti Macy had brought over three days ago. Too hungry to want to take the time heating it on the stove, I sat at the table and ate it directly out of the casserole dish.

When my annoying hunger was satisfied, I wandered into the living room and looked out the picture window. Tristan's house was dark.

What did I expect? That he would be up all odd hours of the night like me?

But I didn't know what to expect regarding Tristan or myself.

We'd kissed. I'd loved it. I'd feared it.

And then those glasses and books. What did they mean, if anything?

I was about to return to bed when a light came on next door. The small slit in the drapes of Tristan's room didn't allow much light through, but it was clear he was awake. I deliberated at the window for a moment, listening to the crickets.

I finally withdrew, deciding to try out my new old couch instead of returning to bed. I was still wide awake, and since my thoughts weren't giving me a reprieve, I grabbed *A Travesty of Torn Souls* and began at the first chapter again, balling myself into the corner of the cushions.

Macy had found this beauty of a sofa at an estate sale on her street last week, and with some nudging on her part, Tristan had hauled it here in his truck, unloading it with the help of John, Macy's husband. Besides the old-lady couch, I had acquired an equally dated coffee table and a floor lamp that let off a strange odor whenever I turned it on.

Still, I had some furniture, and my house was beginning to feel like a home.

After three chapters of B.R. Stevenson's gem, my eyelids drooped. I closed the book and set it on the coffee table, unable to help the recollection that Tristan had a copy of my favorite author's third book. Finding it in a bookstore would be a challenge, as it was several years old. Maybe the library would have it. I'd rather try there first instead of asking Tristan for his copy.

I couldn't understand Tristan. I left the living room and headed for my bedroom. Maybe it was the drowsiness that was causing my head to spin all topsy-turvy, but as I climbed into bed and turned off the light, I reminded myself that we'd known each other a mere three weeks.

Three weeks. That was all. Yet we'd spent hours together every day during that time. There was no denying this strange man had become someone special to me, but for all his secrets, a part of me couldn't reconcile my growing affection for him with the fear he was hiding something big.

Deciding I was simply too spent from the previous day and too exhausted to contemplate much more, I drifted to sleep.

∞ ∞ ∞

"Are you absolutely sure you're okay with this?" Angela asked over the phone.

"For the third time, yes, Angela. It's fine. Really."

"It's just— Well, when we planned this, we didn't know—"

"Yes, we didn't know my brother's funeral would be the day before. Can we please just drop it?"

"You don't sound too happy."

"I'm sorry." I sighed. "It's not you, Angela. I'm just... Look, don't worry about me, all right? This will be good for me. It'll take my mind off...things."

"Well, all right. Thanks again for driving. You're a real friend, Lorna."

I smiled tightly into the phone, glad Angela couldn't see my face. After hanging up, I grabbed my purse and went to the garage to start up Ol' Bessie. The engine had been cantankerous for some time now, and I hadn't driven it much since school had let out. Muttering under my breath that I should have had the foresight to take the thing into a repair shop earlier, I finally gave up trying to start the car. I got out of the car and threw my keys down as I slammed the door closed.

I growled. Yes, actually growled. Like a rabid dog.

Then tears of frustration escaped from their cages. My eyes were leaking my messed-up emotions.

I was about to go inside when I heard his voice.

"Is something the matter?"

I stopped in my tracks, embarrassed to be seen blubbering like one of my first graders having a tantrum because things didn't go her way. But things really weren't going my way.

"Does something look the matter?" I asked.

Tristan held up his hands in front of him and took a step back. "Sorry to ask if it's just gonna make things worse."

I sighed, my shoulders slumping in defeat. When I could finally meet Tristan's eyes, I stared at those fake glasses, and a hundred questions surfaced. Instead, I said, "I'm sorry. I was supposed to meet Angela...well, actually pick her up since she doesn't drive and take her to the bridal shop. It's her gown fitting, and I still need to pick out a dress to wear as a bridesmaid. Her wedding is only a month away, and— and my stupid car won't start! And Chucky's dead. And—" I stopped, out of breath as the rage left me. "And I just don't know how much more I can take, Tristan." I stared at him and blinked, trying to keep my tears at bay.

"I can fix your car. I offered before. Or at least drive you there." His voice was gentle.

"No, it's...it's fine. Really, Tristan. You don't have to. After everything you've already done for me, it's too much to ask. I just— I don't understand you sometimes. You've been so kind. We've spent every day together these past few weeks, and I'd be lying if I said I haven't grown to, um..." *Love you.* "...care about you deeply. And then we kissed, and you left. What happened?"

He frowned. "Look, about last night, I'm sorry for what happened. You were vulnerable, and I took advantage of that."

"What are you saying? Do you regret kissing me?" I whispered.

"I— Oh, this is ridiculous," Tristan growled. "Yes and no. No, because I'm crazy, okay? Crazy about you and I shouldn't be. So yes, because I'm just crazy. You weren't supposed to come into my life like this. You don't— You couldn't possibly understand—"

"I think I do." My voice was so quiet, I could have been a mouse. Every moment I grew smaller.

"No, listen... Lorna, I —"

"I get it. You love your wife, and you should. I'm sorry."

"You shouldn't be sorry. Please, Lorna, if you'll give me a chance to explain..."

"I'll just, um, figure out another way to meet up with Angela."

"You're sure?"

"Yes. Maybe we need to take a break from seeing so much of each other." *Maybe it hasn't been healthy for either of us, despite my heart telling me the opposite.* I hated myself for saying those words as I watched his face close. He seemed to be reverting to the man I'd first met.

"Are you... Are you sure you don't want me to look at your car?"

I shook my head, all fight gone out of me.

"Well, if that's what you want, okay. You know where to find me." Tristan leaned down, tucked my hair behind my ear, and kissed me softly on the cheek. Then he turned and left.

For a while, I stood there, Tristan's touch lingering. I should have followed him and told him what I fool I was to let him leave. How hard could it be to say three simple words? "I love you." But it was far from simple. Tristan had been nothing short of a miracle in my life, and I had turned him away. What idiot does that? A broken woman named Lorna, that's who.

After a minute of stunned silence, I went back inside and called Macy, sobbing into the phone. When she could finally make sense of me, she offered to drive over to pick me up and then Angela.

"You're a lifesaver," I said. "Are you sure?"

"Of course, darling. I knew you had feelings for Tristan. I just knew it."

"Am I that obvious?"

"You are to me, Lorna. You know that. Besides, how could you not come to love him? He's been everything you've needed in a man."

Not everything, I thought. "There's a lot you don't know about him...a lot I don't know about him, Mace. And I never said I loved him."

I could see the quirked lips on her face when Macy spoke. "You don't have to say it, darling. Again, obvious."

"I don't want to talk about Tristan anymore."

"Come on, let's have a day out. Luck's on our side with it being a Saturday. John's home with the kids. Angela is a fun person. I'd like to get to know her better. She seems like a sweetie from the couple of times I've met her."

"Okay, Mace. See you soon."

After hanging up, I debated on whether to call Angela. At the risk of another volcano of emotion, I decided to tell her only what was necessary when I saw her.

A little while later when we pulled into the parking lot of the apartment where Angela lived, she approached the car, perplexed.

"I was beginning to think you'd chickened out on me, Lorna," she said. "I see you've come with a friend."

"I'm sorry. Remember Macy?"

Angela got into the car and smiled. "Of course. Hello, Macy."

"And hello to you, Angela."

"I ran into some car trouble," I told Angela, "and Macy was kind enough to drive us."

I purposefully left out any mention of Tristan. This day was about Angela. Besides, I wasn't ready to sort through my thoughts about him, let alone discuss him with others.

My two blond, sunshiny friends instantly became friends. I followed behind, listening to them chat. The next hour passed in a whirlwind. I picked a sensible light pink dress that met Angela's approval and would match her flowers. As I watched her try on her gown, I couldn't help but envy her. Until recently, I'd never considered marrying, especially since my parents' deaths. Taking care of Chucky and going to work had been my life for so long, I'd already become like a parent. And I'd done it on my own. I was used to being alone.

But then Tristan came into my life.

"Well, what do you think, Lorna?" Angela asked.

I noted the slight impatience in her tone and blinked, shaking myself out of my reverie. I hoped she hadn't been trying to get my attention too long, for I was too divided to know how to function appropriately right now.

"You look beautiful."

"Thank you. I thought you looked lovely in your dress, too."

I smiled. "Thanks, but no one should outshine the bride on her wedding day."

"Maybe your day isn't far off," Angela said.

My smile died. "Just curious—where are the other girls? Surely, I'm not your only bridesmaid?"

Angela blushed. "Actually, you are, and before this goes any further, I wanted to tell you—you're my maid of honor, Lorna."

My eyes must have looked like saucers. "W—what?"

"I hope that's okay." Angela gave a small smile, her voice just as tiny.

"Of course." Warmth flooded my body as I gazed at Angela. "Thank you. I didn't realize— I mean—" I glanced at Macy, who took my cue.

"Hey, let's all go out for lunch. My treat," Macy said.

"Really?" Angela asked, and I knew that she hadn't noticed my downcast expression.

Although the prospect of forcing down food and engaging in light-hearted conversation the next couple of hours held about as much appeal as swimming naked in Lake Erie in January, neither did I wish to go home and have only my miserable self as company. So, I painted on a smile I hoped looked better than my attempts at art and went along.

∞ ∞ ∞

"Remember," Macy said as she dropped me off a few hours later, "I'll have John stop by either this evening or tomorrow and take a look at your car. Maybe you won't need to take it into a shop, after all."

"Thanks, Mace. I really appreciate it. And thanks again for today."

Macy waved me off with a chuckle. "I like Angela, but I'm glad you and I are as thick as thieves plotting their next big heist."

I laughed. "Okay, Mrs. Thief, I'll see you later."

I stepped out of the car and waved until Macy was out of sight. Standing in my driveway, my eyes tracked toward Tristan's yard. It sat empty. Only the rocks greeted me, and they weren't much company.

I began walking toward my side door, wondering if I should check in on him.

No. I shook my head. The damage had already been done. Tristan had fixed my house and probably could have fixed my car, but I didn't think he could fix me.

Chapter 14

I spent the better part of the next week dressed in self-sorrow like a well-worn pair of shoes. My grass was now halfway up my calves. My house, filled with more things, collected dust as memories of Tristan collected in much the same manner in my mind. Even though I wanted nothing more than to talk to him, I kept away. Looking out the picture window elicited nothing more than staring at rocks, my neighbor apparently choosing to hide away in his house.

I filled my days as much as I could with walks, whether with Macy or alone. John fixed my troublesome car, so at least a trip to the grocery store wasn't any trouble.

I'd had enough trouble on my plate to feed a starving country.

A little over a week after Chucky's funeral, I opened the front door to check the mailbox. Nestled between the storm door and the front door was a small package. I frowned and picked it up, then retrieved the mail: envelopes of bills and no doubt the occasional sympathy card from a well-meaning stranger that still managed to creep its way into my house. I returned to the kitchen, absentmindedly setting the mail aside. My eyes roamed over the package, surprised to see no address on it. Rather, it simply said, "For Lorna." I didn't recognize the handwriting, so as curiosity got the better of me, I undid the brown paper wrapping and found B.R. Stevenson's *Cure for the Cries.*

The book looked new, despite being published fourteen years ago. I opened it, and my heart almost stopped when I found a piece of paper inside with a note:

Dear Lorna,

You like B.R. Stevenson's novels if I recall correctly. I've had this copy of his first novel for years, and it seemed ridiculous to keep it when I knew you would benefit from having it more than I would. You asked me if I'd ever read any of his books, and I said I hadn't. The truth is that yes, I have. I know his work better than I should, but that's beside the point.

Sincerely,

Tristan

P.S. You might want to get someone to mow your lawn.

I folded the paper and looked at the book in awe, both for the man who'd given it to me and for the work itself. I flipped past the title page and read the dedication: *For Julie.*

My breath choked me as my heartbeat increased. I closed the book and set it on the table, picking up the letter again. *I know his work better than I should...*

It couldn't be...

Tristan had said he was a published author.

Could it be?

I placed the book on the table with the mail and darted out the side door, making short work of crossing my front yard and into Tristan's rocky territory. I knocked several times on the front door, each one more insistent than the one before. Just when I was about to turn away, the door opened. Tristan stood there, a bemused expression on his hairy face.

"You're B.R. Stevenson," I said breathlessly.

"Well, hello, Lorna. I may not be an expert on greetings, but a person usually says hello first before making far-fetched assumptions."

I half-smiled and raised an eyebrow. "Come on, Tristan. Don't deny it."

Tristan twisted his mouth and sighed, stepping aside. "Will you come in?"

I was already inside his house before I knew what I was doing. "Why didn't you just tell me?"

"I like my anonymity. I don't want the public bothering me. I enjoy living a quiet life."

I dropped into the armchair. The faded flowers on it were like some washed-out happiness that had died ages ago, yet still tried to persist. I met Tristan's eyes across the room, and he took a couple of steps toward me. "Your books are beautiful."

"As are your paintings."

I laughed a little. "It might sound crazy, but it's like I've known you for years. Your books have always reverberated deep inside, to a level I can't explain. And then I met you, and you're the same way. You make no sense to me, yet you make all the sense in the world."

Tristan was now standing directly in front of me. "Let me cut your grass, Lorna."

"So, who are you really? B.R. Stevenson or Tristan Blake?"

"B.R. Stevenson is just a pen name. Lots of authors use them. Mark Twain, for instance, was really Samuel Clemens." He paused. "I could get my mower now." Tristan's eyes were shining behind his false lenses, dancing in the low light.

"Please take your glasses off." I stood and slowly raised my hands to his face, cupping it as my fingers slipped under the earpieces. Before he could protest, I slid them down his nose and into my hands, setting them aside.

Tristan's hands encircled me, pulling me toward him until there was no space between us. When we kissed that time, that inexplicable warmth that was Tristan Blake and B.R. Stevenson flooded me. When the kiss ended, I smiled slightly. "I suppose you'll want me to cook you dinner in exchange for mowing my lawn?"

Tristan chuckled, that deep rumble that started in his chest and worked its way up. "You'll hear no objections."

"Good. Are you hungry now?"

"I will be after mowing that jungle out there." The smile slid from his face as he gently withdrew his glasses from my fingers and replaced them.

The moment of passion ebbing, I stepped back enough to see his face better. "I know your glasses aren't real. When you left them sitting on your coffee table, curiosity got the better of me, and I picked them up. So why do you wear them?"

Tristan looked to be considering his answer. "They're part of the change I made after Julie died."

"I understand that. You heard what the Western Union boy called me when he came to inform me of Chucky's death, didn't you?"

Tristan nodded. "Laura."

"Yeah, I guess we've both been hiding things from each other, huh? I changed my name after my parents died, well, because I no longer felt like Laura. She was the girl with a family. Laura means victory. Lorna means forlorn. It seemed much more fitting, so I understand why you'd want to hide. I've done enough of it myself. Tristan, I'm so sorry I didn't stop by sooner this week. I guess after everything that's happened, I didn't know how to deal with it all." While this wasn't the first time we'd shared our secrets, something was different now. "Would you think it crazy if I said I missed you?"

"I understand that feeling because I know it too well. Lorna, I never... I didn't expect to feel like this again."

I claimed his lips, and Tristan pulled me to him with such fervor and desperation I thought I might melt into him.

By the time we ended our second kiss that day, I was breathless. “Maybe I should work on dinner. If we keep this up, we’ll be starving.”

“Depends on what you’re hungry for.” The wicked gleam in his eyes was like a drug.

I laughed him off. “One thing at a time, Tristan.” I reached for his hand, and we left that dreary living room and stepped into the light.

While Tristan spent the next hour wrestling with his mower through my foot-long grass, I prepared dinner. When the chicken was ready, I opened the back window in the kitchen and called, “Give yourself a break!”

Tristan tossed the mower aside and entered through the side door a minute later. As he cleaned his hands, I said, “I can’t believe you still use a manual push mower. How old is that thing?”

He shrugged. “I bought it used. Without a blade of grass in my yard, I hardly saw the need for a gas-powered one.”

I smiled. “Yeah, but a gas one might make short work of the mess you’re dealing with in my yard.”

Tristan smiled lopsidedly and wiped his hands on his jeans. “Why waste the gas with the restrictions on it these days?” He made to grab one of my newly acquired chairs but stood there awkwardly and asked, “Can I help with anything?”

“No, everything’s on the table. It’s just chicken and rice and some homegrown green beans. Even when rationing is over one day, I’m afraid I’ll never cook anything fancy. I was glad to get some chicken.”

Tristan took a seat and surveyed the measly spread. “Smells great.”

“Don’t get your hopes up. My mom used to spend hours in the kitchen every day. She had a bunch of old family recipes and knew how to use spices to make even the blandest of dishes taste like it was fit for a king. I did, however, think that we could indulge a little." I grabbed a bottle of white wine from my counter and held it up. "I don't know if it's any good, but when I went to the store a couple of days ago, something compelled me to buy it. Maybe I was hoping I'd have a reason to celebrate, you know, just us."

The truth was I'd been thinking more along the lines of drowning my sorrows with the cheap alcohol if I was feeling particularly low, but standing here now, such thoughts seemed bizarre and foreign.

"I'm sorry, but I don't drink," Tristan said, a deep frown etched into his beard.

"Oh." I stopped in my tracks, suddenly feeling stupid, and set the bottle down.

"Don't let that stop you if you want a glass of wine with your meal." The frown was gone. Now he seemed almost apologetic.

"I'm not going to drink alone. It seems rude."

"It's your house. Please."

"Forget the wine. The last time I had a bottle of the stuff, I went overboard and woke up the next day with a mammoth headache. Not worth it, alcohol."

"It never is."

I began dishing out the food onto Tristan's plate until he was satisfied with the portion. Once we began eating, silence fell between us.

"Do you believe in God?" I asked quietly, my eyes on a stray bean. I wasn't sure why I asked the question or where this was coming from. Some deep ache that had been empty inside so long had finally been filled by Tristan. Maybe coming to know love again was surfacing thoughts about God.

"I have to believe there's something better than this life. Sometimes that hope was the only comfort I had after Julie died."

"It was the opposite for me. My parents died suddenly, you see. A car crash. Where was God when that happened?"

Tristan set aside his fork and swallowed. "I'm not the right person to answer those kinds of questions, Lorna. I'm sorry." His eyes were glassy. Even his glasses couldn't hide that.

"I'm sorry, too. This conversation hasn't gone at all the way I intended." I reached across the table and took his hand. "Maybe having you here is comfort enough for me."

Tristan's smile was almost wistful as he said, "I wish I could be enough."

Chapter 15

We finished our dinner and cleaned up, subdued into silence. I didn't mind the quiet. Tristan's presence at my side, as always, kept me grounded. Afterward, we went into the living room.

I flipped the lights witch, even though the sun was still out. My old-lady lamp bathed its companions, the sofa and the coffee table, in a golden glow.

"It's nice to have a couch," I said. "Thanks for your help with that."

Tristan waved me off and smiled. "It was worth getting it to have somewhere to sit in here." He chuckled.

I laughed. "True, although I don't know about much else in that poor woman's house. Most of her things seemed a bit too nineteenth century."

"Careful, I was born only eight years after the turn of the century. You might consider me a relic, too."

I shook my head. "Hardly. Can I be honest about something?"

"What's that?"

"If you were clean-cut, you'd look younger. I'd even say late twenties." I tried my best to charm him into agreeing with me by smiling.

Tristan laughed. "You really don't like the beard, do you?"

"Sorry, no. It hides too much of your face, and I want to be able to see you."

"As much as I'd love to stand here discussing the merits of my looks, maybe we can spend our time better engaged?"

"Whatever you like."

Tristan turned on the radio, and news of the war blared into the room. He made a face and spun the dial until slow, soft music filled the space. He flipped the light off, and only the evening sunlight illuminated the room, the perfect lighting. Tristan took me by the hand and gently pulled me to him, wrapping his arms around me. I rested my head on his sturdy chest, his steady heartbeat partnered to the music. Closing my eyes, I leaned into him, my arms loosely around him. The warmth from earlier when we had kissed returned, filling every fiber of my being. If there was someplace where heaven met earth, we were caressing it with our feet as we moved to music that became otherworldly. Time stood still. Nothing else existed or mattered. Everything was only the moment.

And that was beautiful, sacred.

When the song ended, Tristan and I slowed to a stop. I opened my eyes and smiled up at him as he gazed down at me, just before his lips crashed into mine in sweet oblivion.

∞ ∞ ∞

After Tristan left that night, I readied myself for bed. It was the end of a day that had become one of the best of my life. As I pulled the sheet over me and turned off the light, for once, I had a thankful heart.

"Thank you," I whispered.

Maybe, for the first time in six years, I was talking to God again. Maybe it was "thank You."

∞ ∞ ∞

Six years earlier...

It was a rare occurrence when my parents went out on a date. Despite the fact Chucky and I were old enough to look after ourselves for a few hours, Mom always had an excuse about why they couldn't get away. Their twenty-fifth anniversary had just passed, and if that wasn't reason enough to celebrate, I didn't know what would be.

I had even agreed to do Mom's hair for the occasion. On the day of their big date, I stood behind my mom as she sat on the bench at her vanity, a heavy oak thing she'd inherited from her own mother ten years earlier.

"What do you think?" Mom asked. "Should I just leave it down and let the curls do their thing?"

Holding the still-hot curling iron in my right hand, I sighed. "Whatever you want, Mom. I'm sure Dad won't complain either way."

"I just don't want to make a bigger deal of this than we already are, dear. Those tickets to the Cleveland Orchestra you and your brother got us were too much, and with Charles insisting on dinner as well...it's just an awful lot of money that could be put to better use."

"Like what?" I raised my eyebrows. I'd saved money from watching neighborhood children, and Chucky had saved money from his paper route for over a year to get those tickets. When Mom didn't reply with a good comeback, I continued, "Mom, when's the last time you went out? Do you even remember? Was it this decade?"

Mom laughed, a nervous titter. "Oh, Laura, don't be silly. Of course—" By the wrinkled forehead and the crease between her eyebrows deepening, I knew Mom was trying to recall the last time my dad and she had gone out on the town. "Oh, fine. So it's been a while. There's the Depression on, you know."

I shook my head and pinned back the sides of her long-bobbed hair, the decorative clips nestled right behind her ears. "What do you think?"

Mom's face glowed as her lips formed a smile akin to the one she'd worn on her wedding day. I glanced at the wedding picture of my parents hanging above their bed and smiled as well.

"Good." I leaned down and kissed her cheek. "Now, get dressed and knock Dad's socks off."

Mom stood and hugged me. "You're the best daughter a mother could ask for, Laura."

I blushed and stared at my feet. "Well, I don't know about that, but I'd better get out of here and let you finish up. I'll see how Dad's holding up."

After going down the stairs, I found my dad pacing in the living room like a teenager waiting for his first date to start.

"She'll be down in a few minutes," I said. I'd never seen him so nervous. Dad had always been the calm one in the family, leaving Mom to fret and worry over every little thing.

Dad stopped and chuckled in his usual deep rumble. "You might think I'm being ridiculous, Laura, but twenty-five years! Can you believe it? I still don't know what Elaine saw in me, but I'm the luckiest guy alive."

"It's odd for you two to refer to each other by your first names around me, you know?" I teased. "But seriously, I hope you have a great time, Dad. Hey, have you seen Chucky?"

"I think he's outside shooting some baskets."

I nodded, going into the kitchen to check on the roast. Mom had still insisted on starting dinner for us, even though I'd tried to tell her that I could handle it. That was my good old mom for you—looking after us kids, even though I was twenty-one and Chucky was thirteen. From the rear-facing kitchen window, I saw my brother dribbling the basketball with a couple of friends.

By the time I returned to the living room, Mom was entering. She was wearing a light blue summer dress that stopped mid-calf, belted around the high waist, with a V-neck hugged by a pointed collar. I stepped back into the doorway that led to the kitchen, not wishing to intrude on this private moment, but neither could I keep my eyes off them as my dad crossed the room and took my mom by the hand like she was a young bride again. He kissed her hand and then intertwined his fingers with hers, pulling her to him as he kissed her on the lips. At that point, I turned my head away and smiled, the warmth of a blush on my cheeks and on the back of my neck.

My parents must have known they had an audience, for my dad chuckled and said, "It's all right, Laura. We'll be on our way now."

"Don't do anything too wild," I said, stepping into the room, guilty as charged.

"Wild? Us?" Mom asked, waving me off. She pecked my cheek and waved goodbye, my dad taking her by the arm as they exited through the side door.

I watched them say goodbye to Chucky and then pull out of the driveway. Satisfied they were out of my hair for the next few hours, and hopefully would be having the cliché "time of their lives," I returned to the kitchen and took the roast out of the oven to cool for a few minutes. As I watched Chucky and his friends play basketball, I thought of extending the offer of dinner to the other boys. As my eyes fell on the smallish pot roast with its vegetables, however, I decided against it. Mom probably wanted to stretch the leftovers for another meal for all of us. Ravenous teenage boys would make short work of the meager food I had.

I opened the window and called, "Hey, Chucky! It's time to take a break and eat dinner!"

Chucky said something to his friends and waved goodbye to them. Once he was inside, he grumbled, "First Mom and Dad embarrass me by kissing me when they left, and now you call me 'Chucky' in front of my buddies. Laura, I'm not a little kid anymore."

I smirked. "You'll always be my little brother."

"Can't you call me 'Chuck,' at least?"

"Not on your life. Now, wash up. You can go back outside after you're done if you want."

Chucky beamed at my words. "Really? You're the best, Laura! Mom hardly ever lets me go back out after dinner. She always comes up with a million chores for me to do."

I handed him a plate. "Fill it up, silly boy. I'm not Mom, but I'm sure I can find something for you to do if you'd rather scrub pots or clean out the garage."

Chucky wrinkled his freckled nose as he heaped food onto his plate. "Dad said something about cleaning out the garage this weekend. Ugh, it's too hot."

After I was content with my own portion, I joined Chucky at the table. He was about to dig in, but I reminded him to pray. After our short prayer, I said, "Not too hot to get all sweaty playing basketball, though, huh? You'll need a good shower tonight, little brother. I could smell you before you came in."

Chucky laughed. "Well, Mitch and Joe were really puttin' up a good game. No point in showering 'til I'm done for the evening."

I just rolled my eyes good-naturedly as I chewed, the meat juicy and tender. As I ate, I realized I was glad Mom had insisted on cooking the meal, as I didn't think I could have pulled off this feat.

Chucky, who had started with much more food than me, finished before I was halfway done and wiped his hand on his shorts.

"See that white thing right there on the table?" I asked.

"Oh, this?" he asked smartly, holding up the napkin.

"Yes, it's good for wiping your messy mouth."

Chucky shrugged and stood. "I'm savin' Mom some work on laundry by keeping it clean."

"Not your own clothes, apparently."

"Can I go back outside now?"

"Yeah, just put your plate in the sink. I'll get it."

"Thanks, Laura! You really are the best!"

"Sure, sure..." I waved him off as he ran out the door.

I spent the next hour cleaning up the kitchen, wiping down every surface. Part of me wanted to have the house in perfect order when my parents returned, not wishing for Mom to fret come tomorrow that she had more work to do because she'd taken a few hours to enjoy herself. As the sun drew toward the horizon, I called Chucky in again, even going so far as to call him "Chuck."

"Thanks," he said when he entered. "Mom would've never agreed."

"Anything to save you further embarrassment in front of your friends."

Chucky made a show of lifting his arms, one by one, and sniffing his pits. The disgusted look on his face couldn't have been an exaggeration. I laughed as he said, "I think I'll take that shower," and then he left the kitchen.

Shaking my head again at my brother's antics, I went to my room, intent to curl up with a good book. While I wasn't usually one to spend money on unnecessary luxuries, books were the exception. Ever since I could read, I'd been an avid collector of books. Libraries were a close second to bookstores, but if I loved a book, I wanted my own copy. In the corner of my small bedroom, a narrow white bookshelf stood, nearly filled. I withdrew my newest addition, B.R. Stevenson's *A Travesty of Torn Souls*. The book had come out last year, and I'd been lucky to get a copy from the library. This would be my second time reading this author who I'd never heard of previously, but his book had been on the bestseller's list for weeks now.

As I lay down on my bed, I positioned myself until I was comfortable. Everything in my room had belonged to someone else —either my mother or one of my grandmothers. Even my quilt had been made by my maternal grandmother, a lovely work of pastel roses.

I opened the book and spent the next hour lost in another world. I was interrupted by a knock from the door and closed the book, setting it on the night table.

"It's not locked," I said, sitting up as I swung my legs over the side of the bed.

The knob turned, and Chucky entered. "I wondered if you were still up. It was so quiet in here."

"I thought maybe you'd gone to sleep."

"Nah, I had the radio turned down low, but I was listening to the Indians game."

"Are they winning?"

"You betcha."

"You boys and your sports." I smiled and shook my head, yawning. "Maybe it's time you turn in."

"Yeah, that's what I came to tell you. I'm hitting the sack."

"Goodnight, Chuck...y."

"So close. Maybe it'll catch on yet."

"Don't bet on it."

"'Night, Laura."

Chucky left, not bothering to shut the door. I stood and decided a quick bath might be a nice way to end the day, as I wasn't about to wait up for my parents. The hallway was dark beyond my bedroom, so I flipped on the overhead light and proceeded to the bathroom. I turned the hot and cold knobs until I found a comfortable temperature. I remembered using copious amounts of Mom's lavender-scented shampoo when I was a kid and wished for a bubble bath, but our shampoo, like a lot of things in the house, was watered down these days. Just as I was about to begin taking my clothes off, I thought I heard a noise beyond the water filling the tub. I turned off the water and listened, surprised to hear the kitchen phone ringing.

Although it was probably just a wrong number at this hour, my heartbeat increased as I ran for the phone. I picked it up and asked, "H-hello?"

"Is this the Ashford residence?" The voice was unfamiliar and urgent.

"It is. May I ask who's calling?"

"This is the Cleveland Police. We need to speak with Laura Ashford."

My brow creased. The police? And I'd been expecting the man to ask for my father. "This is she."

"Miss Ashford, we need you to come down to the precinct six station at 57 Broad Street. There's been an accident."

My heart, which had been beating more and more furiously since I'd picked up the phone, threatened to burst through my chest. "What?"

There must have been a mistake. I looked toward the entrance to the living room to find Chucky standing there in his pajamas, his hair sticking up in all directions.

"Please, Miss Ashford, we can explain everything in person."

"Okay. I'll be there in a few minutes."

I hung up the phone, realizing I didn't have a car. The police officer could have given me something more to go on, but as he wanted to speak to me in person, whatever news he had to share couldn't be good.

"We need to go to the police station," I told Chucky. "I'll...I'll ask Mr. Evans next door if he can drive us."

"What happened?"

"All I know is Mom and Dad were in an accident."

"Are they okay?" Chucky sounded like a terrified five-year-old.

"I don't know. Change your clothes and meet me outside in two minutes."

When Chucky joined me in the driveway, I took his hand as we ran to the neighbor's house. While the urge to pound frantically was overwhelming, I settled on a steady knock. Mr. Evans tended to stay up later than his wife. A man in his early sixties, he was gruff and hard of hearing, but had a heart of gold. The light was on in the living room, and beyond the thin curtains, I saw his silhouette sitting in an armchair. When he didn't move, I knocked more loudly. The window was open a bit, and I heard Mr. Evans grumbling under his breath.

"Who could that be knockin' at my door at this hour?" he asked. A moment later, he opened the door, and his eyes widened behind his glasses. He pulled his pipe from his mouth and said, "Miss Ashford. Everything all right?"

"No. Mr. Evans, I'm so sorry to ask this of you, but could you please give my brother and me a lift to the sixth precinct police station? Our parents have been in a car accident."

"Car accident? Do you know what happened? Are they…?"

"I don't know anything else. Please, Mr. Evans, can you? You know how to get there?"

"'Course, 'course." He fumbled for his keys as he grabbed them from a peg on the wall near the front door. Stepping out into the warm summer night, he remarked, "C'mon, kids. Let's get you to your folks."

"Thanks a million, Mr. Evans," I said, my shoes clicking on the pavement as I rushed by his side to his garage.

He nodded, opening the passenger door for me, ever the old-fashioned gentleman. Chucky remained quiet as he dropped into the back seat. As I got in, I cursed myself for putting on my heels, but they'd been the closest shoes as I'd raced out of the house. As Mr. Evans pulled out of the driveway, I hoped I'd locked up.

"Will your wife be okay if she wakes up and finds you missing?" I asked.

"Don't worry about Betty. She could sleep through a tornado. Besides, you've got more pressing matters, young lady."

I nodded weakly, my stomach flipflopping. Every foot we traveled was one closer to our destination: the place I couldn't wait to arrive at and the place I dreaded. Five minutes later, we pulled into a parking spot right outside the main entrance.

I was out of the car before either Mr. Evans or Chucky could catch up. Barreling into the atrium, I said, "I'm here. I'm Laura Ashford. Where are my parents?"

An officer who didn't look a day over my own age said, "Just a moment, Miss Ashford. Let me get the captain. Please have a seat."

I paced. Mr. Evans and Chucky entered and looked around, bewildered.

"Did you hear what he asked me to do?" I nearly cried, as if that young officer's words had been a personal insult. "He told me to sit. Like I can just sit here at a time like this!"

"Do you want me to stay?" Mr. Evans asked.

"Could you? That'd be great. Thank you." I paced a bit, but when Chucky and Mr. Evans took up seats, I decided to try to sit after all.

So I picked a chair—a hard, unyielding thing that hurt my backside—but something to fall into nonetheless. Resting my elbows on my knees, my head fell into my hands as I worked my fingers through my hair. The movement wasn't comforting, but rather agitating.

"How long is this gonna take?" I begged, looking up to find a much older police officer entering the lobby area.

"Miss Ashford?"

I immediately straightened and stood. "That's me."

"Come with me, please."

I tried to discern his tone but came away with only more questions. Chucky followed in silence, and from behind, Mr. Evans called, "I'll wait here."

When the officer arrived at his office, the name "Captain James A. Shafer, Cleveland Police Department, Precinct Six" was written in black letters on the glass part of his door. He motioned us in and closed the door behind us. The stale smell of the old building mixed with the aroma of a fresh cup of coffee resting on the captain's desk, which was covered with a mess of papers and stained with rings from numerous previous coffee cups. He bid us to sit in two wooden straight-backed chairs.

"I'm sorry to call you here at such a late hour, but let me assure you, I wouldn't have done so unless absolutely necessary." The captain frowned, the corner of his mouth moving in what looked like a nervous twitch.

"Please, Captain, just tell us. What happened to our parents?"

"I'm terribly, terribly sorry, Miss Ashford, Master Ashford, but Charles and Elaine Ashford were killed the moment of impact."

Chapter 16

Six years earlier, continued...

I stared at a large crack running up the wall behind the captain's head and followed it as it made its way across the ceiling and stopped halfway into the room. I wondered how the plaster didn't fall in on us. Beside me, Chucky sniffled loudly. I turned toward him to find him sobbing into his hands, his shoulders shaking.

"Wait, what did you say?" I asked the captain. "I must have heard you wrong."

The older man's forehead creased, and he removed his cap, wiping perspiration from his bald head. Replacing his cap, he shook his head slowly, frowning under his mustache. "No, I'm afraid not, Miss Ashford. I hate to be the bearer of bad news, but it's true. Your parents were found dead at the scene of the crime."

His words seemed to come at me as if I were underwater. I opened my mouth and closed it again, blinking several times to try to understand what I was hearing.

"I'm sorry—scene of the crime?" I asked instead.

"They weren't at fault; that much is obvious. Now isn't the time to go into further details, Miss Ashford. I shouldn't have mentioned we suspect it's a crime. I am sorry."

"Maybe you're mistaken. Maybe it's not really them."

"That's what I must ask now of you, Miss Ashford. Please come with me. As for your brother, as he is underage, it's your choice whether he should come along."

"My choice? But where are we going?"

The captain's face was grim and pale, like a corpse. "The morgue. You are twenty-one, correct?"

"I am. But—the morgue?"

"You will need to confirm their identities. Don't worry. You'll be looking at pictures, nothing beyond that."

I stood and took Chucky's hand, squeezing it—the only sure thing I had at the moment. "My brother is coming with me."

"Very well. I'll drive you."

We followed. There was nothing but lifeless, uncaring brick walls around me. When we exited through a set of double doors, the captain led us to his patrol car. He held the back door open for us. The drive was made in silence, the streetlights shining into the car every so often.

When we arrived at the hospital, the captain led the way to the morgue. We entered the mostly dark building and took seats in the lobby.

"There's no easy way to prepare for this," the captain said quietly, "so just know that I'm only doing this because it's necessary. As much as it will pain you, this is for the best. I'm going to get the morgue attendant. We'll be back shortly."

I nodded, numb. Beside me, Chucky was shaking, so I pulled him to my side, hoping this small bit of comfort would help. As he stilled under my half-hug, I took a deep breath and closed my eyes.

My mind was unable to process much of anything. I kept hoping I'd wake up from this nightmare.

The captain returned with a man in his forties wearing a white coat.

"My condolences," the man said in a soft voice. "If you'll please come with me."

The morgue attendant opened a door, and after a short walk down a hallway, he ushered us into a bland room with a few armchairs and tables with handkerchiefs on them. The lighting was warm, but bright enough to see clearly.

"Please, sit," he said, indicating a pair of chairs.

He took a seat across from Chucky and me, while the captain held back. "I am sorry to ask this of you, but I will need you to look at these photographs and confirm the identities of Charles and Elaine Ashford, Miss Ashford."

He slowly removed a photograph from his pocket and handed it to me. A face covered in dark, dried blood stared up at me, a huge gash in his forehead. For a moment, I was about to tell the morgue attendant and the captain that this man wasn't my father. But his dark curls gave him away.

I nodded, tears beginning to form in the corners of my eyes. When the attendant revealed the second photograph, I saw my mother. Her once-beautiful face, twisted and swollen, greeted me like a horror film monster. I nodded again, covering my mouth with my hand.

I turned away, and Chucky and I clutched each other, both sobbing into handkerchiefs.

"Come, let's go," the captain said softly. He looked like he was about to place an arm around my brother, but he stepped away and held the door open for us.

I pulled Chucky to me again, wishing he were smaller, so he could nestle his face in my chest like he had when he was little.

Now, he was nearly as tall as me, so we leaned on each other for support.

After the drive back to the police station, the captain offered us fresh handkerchiefs and said, "Again, my apologies, but now that we're sure it's them, we can move forward."

Through my tears, I asked, "Now what?"

"Since you are of age, Miss Ashford, you will have guardianship of your brother. That is, unless—"

"Unless what?"

"Unless there is someone else you wish for me to contact."

"There's no one else," I said, anger conquering sadness for the moment. "My grandparents are all dead, and neither of my parents had any siblings. The rest of my family are practically strangers, so it's just Chucky and me now. I'll take care of him. It's what my parents would've wanted."

"Very well. I believe that is enough for tonight. I'll be in touch in a couple of days to discuss our findings further and will let you know if this goes to trial."

"Thank you, Captain, but I don't think I can even think about sitting in a courtroom. I just want to mourn my mom and dad. I don't want to think about anything else right now."

I didn't know how I was so calm right then, but all I could chalk it up to was pure and utter shock. Or was this denial?

"Understood. Go home and try to get some rest."

"Goodnight, Captain."

"One more thing."

I stopped as I was about to take my first step out the door. "What?"

"Do you need a ride home?"

"No, we've got one. Thanks."

We returned to the lobby, and Mr. Evans stood, gripping his hat. His wrinkled face broke into a knowing frown when he saw us. I shook my head.

"Please take us home, Mr. Evans. Just take us home."

For the small miracle it was, I was grateful Mr. Evans didn't ask any questions or offer any sort of platitudes on the way home. He pulled into our driveway and bade us good night, saying, "If there's anything you need, please don't hesitate to ask either me or the missus."

"Yeah, thanks, Mr. Evans," I replied softly, my eyes meeting his for a moment before they returned to staring at my heeled shoes.

He tipped his hat and nodded at me and then my brother. He got back into his car and pulled out of our driveway, only to pull into his next door. I held the door for Chucky, who entered without saying a thing and was lost in the darkness seconds later. It was like he'd been eaten by the house, swallowed into his own world.

I glared at the phone that had been the bearer of the bad news that had started this living nightmare. While tempted to yank it from the wall, I knew the police and others, like the coroner, would need to reach me. My head spun, and I decided not to think about the next few days, let alone the rest of my life without my parents.

I jerked off my shoes and chucked them across the kitchen. One of them hit my mom's cookie jar and shattered it. Immediately regretting my actions, I knelt on the hard tiled floor and began picking up the pieces, my tears mixing with the shards. One by one, I collected them and placed them on the table, hoping to salvage what was broken. When I realized my one thoughtless action couldn't be undone—that some things, no matter how much I might wish otherwise, couldn't be fixed—I gave up.

Surprised Chucky hadn't heard the commotion and come to see what was going on, I left the kitchen in blackness, the remaining smell of Mom's last roast clinging to the room. When I entered the living room, I dropped into Dad's tattered armchair. Even though the air was mild, I pulled one of Mom's afghans around me, somehow cold.

I hadn't realized I'd fallen asleep until I awoke sometime later. I pulled the afghan tighter and turned on the lamp next to the armchair. On the small table was a stack of newspapers Dad had read, and Mom hadn't yet collected them for the trash. They rested beside a few books and our family Bible. I picked up the Bible and thumbed through the pages, well-worn from Mom's daily readings. For as long as I could remember, she'd read the holy book in its entirety every year, starting with Genesis's "In the beginning" every January 1 and ending with Revelation's "Amen" on December 31. She was right in the middle of the Psalms that first day of summer.

I tried reading a few verses, but the text kept blurring, whether from my fatigue or my tears, I couldn't tell. I snapped the book shut and stood, letting the afghan fall to the floor. Above the radio, the cross stared at me. I glared at it and took it down.

"You aren't looking over me any more than You were looking out for them," I whispered, stroking the cross before stuffing it under a cushion on the sofa.

I walked through the house, so familiar, so foreign, with my arms crossed over my chest as I rubbed them with the opposite hands. Wandering up the stairs to my parents' bedroom, I turned on the overhead light, gingerly sitting at the vanity. Had it only been hours ago when my mom had been perched here with me doing her hair? A few bobby pins still rested on the vanity's surface, her hairbrush at the center of them. Mom had left the closet door open. Two other dresses were left lying on the bed.

She'd been so excited. Now she was dead. Dad, too. The man who had been like a boy taking the most beautiful girl to the prom was now forever at her side, but they weren't dancing, laughing, talking, or holding hands. They would lie motionless, hearts stopped, cold and lifeless.

Suddenly, Chucky's face appeared in the mirror, and I jumped, turning around.

"What are you doing?" he asked, walking into the room and sitting on the end of the bed.

The way we were hanging out in our parents' bedroom would have never been acceptable before. I half-expected my mom to come around the corner and tell us to go to our rooms.

"I slept, but now I can't."

"Same here. Laura, what are we gonna do?"

"I don't know. We have each other, at least." I wiped the last vestiges of tears from my eyes and smiled weakly.

"I was thinkin' about what the captain said. If someone's responsible for this, they oughta pay, Laura."

I sighed. I didn't want to hear about crimes. Wasn't it enough that our parents were dead? What more did we need to go through? "It was an accident. I don't feel like fighting. We don't even know all the details."

"But he said it might have been a crime. What d'you think that means? Whoever hit them—maybe they wanted to hurt them." Chucky was visibly shaking, his hands balled into fists at his sides.

"Who would want to hurt them? Everyone loved them."

"I don't know, but— but—"

"If you're looking for a reason for why this happened, Chucky, there isn't one, okay? It was an accident. God looked the other way and let it happen, just like everything else that's bad that happens in the world."

"God? You can't blame God for this, Laura."

"Oh, but I can. I am."

"I'll tell you whose fault it is—the bum who smashed into them!" Chucky was now standing and pacing in the small space between the bed and the wall. "He should rot in jail for what he did!"

I stood and said, "Shush, Chucky. Please..." I pulled him to me as he began to cry. He rested his head in the crook of my neck, and when he finally withdrew, my skin and shirt were damp.

"I just... Laura, it's not fair."

"No, no, it's not. There's nothing we can do but be here for each other."

Chucky nodded, although I suspected he wasn't convinced. I wasn't sure I was. I had nothing to offer my brother but my broken self. I sat down on the bed and patted the spot next to me. He sat.

"Look, I have no idea what the road ahead looks like," I said. "I can't see or think clearly right now, let alone try to figure out tomorrow or the next day, but I know one thing."

"What's that?" Chucky wiped his eyes.

"We've got each other." I repeated my earlier words. Maybe we both needed to hear them, like an affirmation. I opened my arms, and Chucky allowed me to hold him like he was a little kid again.

We'd done a lot of crying on each other's shoulders that night. Now, Chucky and I sat in silence for several moments. I slowly rocked him, the motion comforting for me and hopefully for him. Holding my brother, he was the one sure thing I had.

"Won't you fight for them, Laura?" Chucky finally whispered. He gazed up at me with hollow eyes.

"What do you mean?"

"If this goes to trial like the captain said."

"I don't know. The only thing I care about now is looking after you. We'll worry about it as it comes. The police will be in touch."

"I miss them already."

"I know, little brother, I know." My voice broke as fresh tears fell. "I won't be a replacement for Mom, but I'll try my best, okay?"

Chucky tried to smile, but his innocent face crumbled. "O-okay." He buried his face in my shirt.

I rubbed his back. We were through talking. None of this was fair. Chucky was a kid. When I was thirteen, my biggest care was probably finishing my homework or trying to get my chores done so I could play with my friends. No thirteen-year-old should have to carry the weight of losing both of his parents. No justice in a courtroom could undo the damage. What was the point? For me, I had to be Chucky's rock. My sole concern was him.

Sometime deep into the night, we fell asleep, side by side on our parents' bed. I woke before Chucky to the dim sunrise and replayed our conversation from hours before. Every word seemed to carry the weight of a thousand coffins with it.

I also realized I had gone to bed that night without praying for the first time since I could remember.

∞ ∞ ∞

When I woke that late July morning of 1943, I had a prayer and a smile on my lips. I floated through my routine of dressing and eating breakfast, grateful I had nowhere I needed to be at any time. With the now-cool cup of coffee in my hands, I ventured into the living room and saw my paintings as if for the first time, remembering anew that these were my heart's creations.

Why had I ever been ashamed of them, especially in front of Tristan?

Tristan.

I knew what I had to do.

Twenty minutes later, Tristan was standing at my side in my living room.

"I needed to show you something," I said.

"Okay." His smile seemed to indulge me as he looked around the room, probably confused because there was nothing new here.

"I've decided to name my paintings. This one is 'Dad.'" I motioned toward the largest one that hung over the couch. I then pointed to the next largest one and finally to another that was my newest. "These are 'Mom' and 'Chucky.'"

Tristan squeezed my hand. For the hundredth time, I wished he'd remove his glasses, for his eyes glittered strangely behind them. "Thank you," he whispered.

"For what?"

"Just thank you."

He kissed me and held me, two once-broken hearts beating as one, healing.

Chapter 17

That evening, I called Macy and told her about my day with Tristan. We'd walked for hours on the beach as we held hands and watched children as they ran into the waves. For dinner, we had packed a picnic and gone to a park, where we sat under a willow tree near the pond, mesmerized by the ripples on the surface as the ducks swam by.

"Wow, darling," Macy said at the end of my lengthy story, "it sounds like you had quite the storybook romance day."

My mind's eye could see her teasing smile, the right side of her mouth hitched slightly higher than the left. "Oh, Mace, I don't know the last time I was this happy."

"Maybe the day you met me?"

We laughed. "I don't even remember that day," I said. "Weren't we, what, six months old or something?"

"Something. Hey, listen, do you think Tristan might be open to a double date with John and me?"

"Well, maybe. That was a few weeks ago when we bumped into Angela and her beau at the cafe. I thought Tristan was going to have kittens, but he surprised me. He didn't think much of Mr. Darling, but then again, everyone thinks Mr. Darling would do well to deflate his head enough to get it out of the clouds."

"I'm glad I've never had the misfortune of meeting this Mr. Darling. Anyway, I think John and Tristan would get along just fine. They're both men's men, if you know what I mean."

"Hmm, well, I know Tristan is handy with his tools, but I've never heard him talk about sports."

"John's been tinkering with that old Model T in the garage for years now, darling. Maybe Tristan could give him some pointers. Honestly, I wish he'd just get rid of the darn thing."

"Well, it was John who fixed my old Caddy, not Tristan. But why get rid of the car? Didn't it belong to his dad?"

"Yeah." Macy sighed heavily. "I can't really make him haul it to the junkyard. His dad hasn't been able to drive in years. He's not doing so well."

"I'm sorry, Macy. You know, John should keep that car as long as he can to remind him of his dad."

"Are you— Lorna, are you saying you regret—?"

"Yes," I whispered. "For so long, all I could see was my anger, my sadness, my grief. That's changed. Even though...even though Chucky is gone now, too, something is different. I'm not so alone anymore."

"I hoped you'd realize that one day. That's Laura I hear."

I smiled wanly. "Maybe."

"What's holding you back?"

"I've been Lorna for so long. As happy as I am, a part of me wonders if it's meant to last."

"Nothing lasts forever, darling. We both know that, but that's why life is precious."

"Yeah, yeah, it is." I paused. "Macy, I hope one day that I can get back to where I was, to who I was. I'm getting there, but it's going to take some time."

"Take as much time as you need. Don't rush it. You've got Tristan now, too. Remember, think about that dinner, okay?"

"Will do, Mace. Thanks for everything."

∞ ∞ ∞

July gave way to August. With Macy by my side, we made a long-overdue trip to the beautician's. I came out of the hair salon feeling like a new woman, even though I only had a trim. Spending more time with others prompted me to care enough to leave the house looking like the young woman I was instead of an old spinster.

Speaking of hair, I grew relentless in teasing Tristan about going to the barber shop. With Angela's wedding a couple of weeks away, I hoped he would, as my date, entertain my suggestions. What had once been another sore topic for him had become a joke, but Tristan still managed to evade my question about his hairy appearance every time.

"But, Tristan, not only would I be able to see your handsome face, but you'd be so much cooler!"

He chuckled. "I admire your persistence. I trimmed my beard last month, remember?"

"Which means it's grown back." I smoothed down my hair. "This humidity is awful for my hair, but even I got a trim."

"Can we talk about something else?"

"Angela's wedding is coming up..." I teased.

"Yes, and?"

"I'd like you to come with me."

"Of course." He smiled.

"And think about trimming your beard again."

"Now, that's enough of that," he playfully growled and pulled me to him. Laying a kiss on my lips, he said, "What am I gonna do with you?"

"You're going to keep me...and if you want to kiss me again, trim that beard!"

He growled again and picked me up, twirling me around. We were in my backyard, and my giggles soared as high as I was.

∞ ∞ ∞

When Angela's big day arrived, I drove the bride to the church. Thankfully, it wasn't the same one I had attended all those years.

"You've been a godsend," Angela said as we were readying ourselves in the dressing room.

I waved her off, smiling. "I'm happy to help, Angela. But why didn't you ask any other girls to be your bridesmaids?"

Angela blushed. "I thought of asking some of the other teachers, but I didn't want to give them the impression I had no friends."

"But you talked to many of them more than me. I still am puzzled why you picked me, Angela—not that I mind." I smiled at her reflection in the mirror as I helped her into her gown. "I'm glad we've become friends."

Angela smiled, but it didn't reach her eyes. "I gossiped with those other women, but that's all it ever was. We never did anything socially. But you, Lorna, whenever I saw you, I wanted to get to know you better. I just had this feeling that, I don't know, you were worth getting to know—worth ten of those other silly ninnies any day of the week."

I was trying to place the veil on Angela's head, but my eyes were tearing up. "Darn you," I whispered, choking back a sob. "Well, thank God you thought to speak to me. You're a rare jewel, Angela. I just hope Mr. Darling realizes what a beauty, inside and out, he's marrying."

Angela's eyes filled with tears, too. She fanned herself with her hand and took a deep breath. "Oh, don't make the bride cry on her wedding day, Lorna. Isn't that bad luck?"

"Depends on the tears, I think. I'm no expert on marriage, Angela. My parents would've been married over thirty years now if they were still alive."

Angela turned away from the mirror and gazed directly into my face. "You never told me they were gone. I'm sorry, Lorna."

"It's not something I've told many people, only those I trust. Enough about me. It's your big day, and I want you to be married at least thirty years. I will tell you that when my parents were alive, their marriage seemed like one of the happiest ones I'd ever witnessed. I wish the same for you."

Angela hugged me. "Thank you, Lorna. I picked the right woman to be my maid of honor."

"Thank *you*. Well, I hope I've done a good enough job."

"You've done more than you know." Angela checked the clock on the wall and exclaimed, "Oh, my goodness! We'd better get going. The ceremony starts in five minutes."

As we walked down the hallway to the narthex at the back of the sanctuary, I asked, "Just curious, but why isn't anyone giving you away?" I thought back to the rehearsal the night before.

"You remember what I told you about my family? About how I'm not close to any of them? Well, long story short, that's why. I'm walking down that aisle with my head held high and proud."

We entered the vestibule as I said, "Good for you. I'm glad you're doing this your way."

"Tom tried to talk me into having one of his brothers walk me down the aisle, but I finally told him last week, 'Do you want to marry me or not, Tom? Because if you keep trying to force me to do something I don't want, you can forget it. I'm not going to be forced into anything in this marriage, do you hear me?'"

"It sounds like you have your priorities right. I hope Tom treats you like a queen."

Just then, the organ started. Angela jumped and clutched her bouquet. I opened one of the doors and peeked into the sanctuary, unsurprised to find the groom's side fuller than the bride's. Despite my feelings toward Mr. Darling, I wished him well, for he was marrying a woman who was many times his better half.

When the music signaled my entrance, I flashed Angela one last smile and began walking down the aisle. What a strange experience to have all eyes on me! I wondered if this was how the bride felt, but to me, most of these people were strangers. I recognized a few coworkers and even Macy, who Angela invited just a couple of weeks ago. When I spotted Tristan, my heart rate increased, and I smiled at him. He was giving me the strangest look, somewhere between captivated and overwhelmed. Then he smiled. Although he hadn't gone to the barber shop, he was dressed smartly in a black suit, hair combed and beard trimmed. I passed him and refocused my gaze on the front of the sanctuary, taking my spot. Across the short distance, Tom Darling stood there, rocking on his feet.

When Angela entered, the congregation stood. I had the best view of the bride as she came down the aisle, radiating sunshine like her name spoke. She seemed to infect everyone with happiness. As my eyes shifted toward Mr. Darling, he relaxed and had eyes only for her. I smiled softly as Angela came to stand next to her beau, and the music stopped.

All through the ceremony, I glanced between Tristan and the couple. The pastor's words were a blur, a foreign echo in the back of my mind. Standing there, all I could imagine was a day when I might be the woman in white, and the man I would be marrying was no longer some faceless man, but Tristan. I caught myself in my daydream. Where had that thought come from?

When the pastor announced the couple as "Mr. and Mrs. Tom Darling," I snapped out of my reverie of Tristan wading in my sea of dreams. Holding the bouquet under my arm against my body, I clapped with the congregation. I couldn't help that my eyes fell on Tristan again and wondered if his thoughts mirrored mine.

When everyone was gathered outside afterward, I found Tristan.

"You looked lovely up there," he remarked, taking my hand.

"Thank you. You know, you don't look too bad yourself." I stood on my tiptoes and kissed his cheek.

"This is the first wedding I've been to in, well, I can't say how long."

"Did you get a chance to congratulate the newlyweds?"

"Yes, but that Mr. Darling fellow rubs me the wrong way. I hope your friend knows who she's marrying."

I couldn't help but laugh. "You're being awfully frank out in the open. What if someone hears you?"

"Let them. Maybe if Mr. Darling hears a fragment of my thoughts on him, he'll stop worshiping himself enough to worship his wife."

I gazed through the crowd at the new Mr. and Mrs. Darling and remarked, "Oh, I think Angela is the exception. It's true he seemed to think he was a gift to women this whole school year, but he's pretty smitten with Angela."

"Hmm, well, enough about him. I'm not here to talk about that man."

"You brought him up," I teased.

Tristan raised an eyebrow. "Your point?"

I shrugged. "Then why are you here?" I smiled flirtatiously and swung our clasped hands. My palm was starting to sweat, but I could have held onto Tristan all day.

"I think you know the answer," Tristan whispered in my ear. His breath was warm on my lobe as his hair tickled my cheek. A tingle went up my spine, and I wished everyone else would disappear.

"Hmm, should we just skip the reception and go somewhere alone?" I returned.

"Hey, you lovebirds!"

Tristan and I stepped back a couple of feet from each other. My face heated with embarrassment as I turned to find Macy and her family approaching us.

"Hello, Macy," I said, challenging her with what I hoped passed for a look that said: "Do you mind?"

"Hi, Tristan," Macy replied. "You know, I've been trying to get your girlfriend to put a date on the calendar to have dinner with my husband and me. She seems to be stalling, although I can't imagine why."

My face must have looked sunburned by this point, but Tristan saved me the trouble of answering. "We're more of the private sort, Macy, but thank you all the same. I'll leave that up to Lorna to decide."

I shot Tristan a glare and then turned back to Macy. "Don't you think we ought to get to the reception?" My smile was as painted on as a doll's.

"Whatever you say. See you there—or not." Macy winked and sauntered—yes, hips sashaying and all—away.

John cast me an apologetic smile and followed his wife.

"Sorry about that." I groaned. "If anyone knows how to embarrass me, it's Macy."

"We don't have to attend the reception if you'd rather be alone," Tristan said. "I know what my first choice would be."

"At the risk of being unsociable, I really should attend the reception, at least for a bit. I *am* the maid of honor. I have a certain duty to be there." I winked. "Although perhaps we can step out a little early."

"Okay, and there's always the chance to dance."

"Yes, there's that, but I preferred our dance in my living room."

"There's time for that later."

My heart fluttered as warmth coursed through me. A few weeks ago, I never would have imagined I would be the type to swoon over a man like this, but Tristan did things to me that no rational part of my mind could explain. We got into my car and drove to the reception, which was an overdone affair. Mr. Darling's family had money in excess since they were able to spend it on a seven-course meal. The centerpieces were so large that the guests seated on opposite sides of the round tables couldn't see each other. I half-wondered if the Darlings had paid for members of the Cleveland Orchestra to play, for a chamber ensemble took stage, the music old-fashioned and lovely. There was no big band stuff or jazz, but Tristan and I had a lovely time dancing. When the reception was nearly over, I made my excuses and wished Angela and, by extension, Mr. Darling, all the best.

When we returned to my house, it was evening. I sat on the sofa less than ladylike and shrugged out of my shoes. I groaned as I rubbed my feet.

"Ugh, you men have no idea the pain of heels," I said.

"Do you want me to do that?" Tristan asked.

"Ah, you're an angel." I graciously offered my feet to Tristan, who worked his magic on them like some voodoo doctor.

After a few moments of silence, Tristan said, "I'm really not an angel, Lorna."

I frowned at his tone, lifting my head from its reclined position. "What?"

He shook his shaggy head, his hair long since messy from its earlier neatness. "Haven't you ever done something you regret?"

"Well, sure. We all do. But that's part of life."

"Yeah." His eyes were deep and introspective as he removed his glasses. He stopped massaging my feet, slumped into the cushions next to me, and stared at the ceiling in the darkening room.

"You know, if you'd have asked me a couple of months ago about regrets, I could have filled your ears with basketfuls of them. Now, you know what I regret the most?"

Tristan turned toward me, his face almost begging. "What's that?"

"I regret the time I wasted on anger and hurt over something that can't be undone."

Tristan's gaze was intense. "I know that feeling all too well. You know what the crazy thing is?"

I took his hand and waited for him to continue.

"I feel guilty that I don't feel as guilty as I should—if that makes any sense."

"Guilty?"

"I thought I'd feel a whole lot guiltier about coming to love someone else after my wife, and because I don't feel that guilty, it's making me feel guilty."

I couldn't help but laugh softly. "Leave it to you to feel guilty over not feeling guilty enough. Jeez, that's gotta be a tongue-twister or something. Anyway, maybe you just need to allow yourself to be happy." In all my babbling, it struck me what Tristan had said in all those tangled words. I sat up straighter, a jolt shooting through my body. "Wait. Y-you *love* me?"

"I do. Lorna, I love you in my guilty, messy, you-drive-me-crazy way." Tristan didn't give me a second to reply, for the next thing I knew, he was kissing me with such passion I thought we might melt into each other.

Our bodies radiated heat. Tristan removed his tie and suit jacket, and I fumbled with the top couple of buttons on his shirt, exposing his undershirt. My hair tumbled out of its fancy twist, grazing my shoulders as I leaned into Tristan. Our hands worked their way up and down each other's sides, exploring.

When we broke apart, our foreheads still touching, I whispered, "And I love you, Tristan, in all my guilty, messy, you-drive-me-crazy way."

Tristan smiled, kissing me almost reverently this time. We collapsed side by side into the couch and talked long into the night.

Several hours later, my head rested on Tristan's shoulder and his arm wrapped around me. In the last moments of coherence, I thought he might have said, "Lorna, if only..."

Chapter 18

Tristan was gone by the time I awoke, but he left a note on the coffee table, telling me that he thought it would be best if we each got some sleep in our own beds that night.

After a quick morning routine, I was looking forward to seeing the man who was foremost in my thoughts. Not wasting a beat, I went next door.

When the door opened, I nearly asked the stranger standing there where Tristan was, but then I recognized him.

"Oh, my goodness," I said, stepping back as I lifted my hand to my mouth.

Ten years could have fallen away. The face looking back at me was clean of any beard and was framed by much less hair, combed neatly behind his ears. Gone were those hideous glasses, and Tristan's eyes were on display in all their amazing blue.

I blinked, still taking in his transformation, and an image flashed through my mind. Those eyes. That striking, unmistakable blue, unhidden by spectacles or hair. A man walking past me, looking at me with those same eyes...in a courtroom. Eyes etched in guilt for what he had done.

"Oh...my...goodness." I took another step back and tripped down the concrete steps. Contact with each step reverberated through my body on the way to the bottom, stabbing me like a knife. Upon reaching the walkway, the physical pain mingled with my mental anguish, twisting into a sickening mess. I tried to stand, but my left ankle cried out in protest, and I winced. "Ouch!" I held onto my betraying ankle.

Despite all this, I crawled on my stomach, using my arms to propel me forward. The gravel scraped across my forearms and exposed lower legs. The rocks pushed against my chest and stomach as rasping breaths tore at my lungs. I was determined to escape. I had to... But then Tristan scooped me up like I weighed nothing and took me inside. All the while, I writhed in his arms.

"Put me down! Put me down!" I cried, hammering his chest.

He set me gently on his sofa and stepped back.

"So, you've figured it out, then," he said.

I swung my legs over the front of the couch and tried to stand, resolved to leave faster than a rabbit about to be a fox's dinner. Instead, I buckled into the cushions, doubling back in pain.

"When were you planning on telling me?" I demanded, hot tears coursing down my cheeks, every second spent with this man a betrayal to my parents' memory.

"Today. That's why— That's why I finally stopped hiding. I couldn't keep fooling you...or myself. You deserved to know much sooner, Lorna. I-I'm so sorry."

"I don't care if you're sorry!" I yelled. "This whole time, Tristan, this *whole time*! A lie, just one big lie! And that's not even your real name, is it?"

Tristan knelt beside the couch and tried to take hold of my foot. It was hard to believe that we had been in a similar position only hours earlier, where I had let him massage my aching feet. Now, I was trying to pull away from this man I both loved and hated. "Let me see your ankle. You may have broken it, but hopefully it's just sprained."

"Are you *serious*? You've been deceiving me for months—*months*, Tristan, and you expect me to just take this lying down?"

Tristan frowned and stepped away, as if slapped. "Lorna, please stop yelling. If you'd let me explain— "

"I've heard enough. I've seen enough. Tristan, you made me fall in love with you! I thought you loved me?"

Tristan dropped to the floor on his knees again, his face inches from mine. "I *do* love you, Lorna! And that's been like a dagger to the heart every time I've been with you because I know what I am, what I did, okay? I was the last person who should've grown to love you, but you showed up one day, and you didn't leave."

"Oh, so it's *my* fault you're a liar, a drunk, and a killer?"

Tristan covered his face with his large hands, rubbing furiously. "A liar, yes, and you have no idea how much I wish I could've told you sooner. But I swear on Julie's grave that I haven't touched alcohol since that night six years ago. I'll forever regret stepping into that car. The pain I've caused you has been mirrored in myself. After Julie died, I never expected to fall in love again—with you, of all people—but it happened, and I don't regret it."

"You're the reason my parents are dead." Then I remembered his name, a name I'd been told by the police and then had heard spoken on the prosecutor's lips years ago. "*Stephen Richardson.*"

Tristan—or Stephen—whoever he was, stood and said in a shaky voice, "Let me call an ambulance."

"I don't need or want any more help from you, *Stephen*. You've done enough damage. Just take me home, and I'll call Macy."

"As you wish."

Tristan picked me up again, and I kept my eyes on the floor and then on the rocky ground, anywhere but on him. Once I was inside my house, he left me sitting in a chair in the kitchen by the phone. He stood there for a moment, shifting from side to side, and I detested him for it.

"You can leave."

"Lorna, please—" His voice broke.

"Tristan, just go. I can't—" I loathed every traitorous tear that forced itself from my eyes as I watched him turn, shoulders hunched like a man who had lived a hundred years of agony, and walk out the door.

For some time—I couldn't say how long—I sobbed into my crossed arms as they rested on my good knee, which was pulled up to my chest. The pain from my ankle was meager in comparison to what Tristan had inflicted on me. How could he? How could he have knowingly and willingly spent all those weeks with me, helping me, getting to know me, pretending to tell me about who he was, and then fall in love with me? I never imagined it possible to love and hate the same person so much, but the line between the two seeming opposites was a thin membrane penetrated by the truth.

When the man responsible for my parents' deaths had been some faceless person, I couldn't hate him the way my heart filled with condemnation now. I hadn't even wanted to go to court over their deaths, wishing to bury them in peace and get on with my life. But I hadn't really been living for years, had I? Instead, I had chosen to dig my own grave and bury myself in my grief. The pain had been greater than my will to live. But for caring for Chucky, I had been an automaton, who was finally broken when my brother was taken away overseas. Long before that, when the trial had occurred, the police captain had convinced me to show up, to sit in the back of the courtroom, telling me that it might bring me some closure if I knew the man who had caused the accident would be doled out his portion of justice. Nothing could have been more wrong.

∞ ∞ ∞

Six years earlier...

The humidity was high that late August day. Breathing was already difficult enough as I stood on the steps to the Cuyahoga County Courthouse and stared at the imposing granite building with its deeply recessed arched windows and doors. Streetcars passed behind me on Lakeside Avenue, the hustle and bustle of the city going about its day. I didn't want to be there. Chucky was at a friend's house, leaving me the afternoon free to attend the hearing of the man responsible for my parents' deaths.

I could still turn away. As hard as most would find it to believe, I'd kept away from any information about my parents' killer. I avoided reading the newspaper, and my friends knew it wasn't something I wanted to discuss. Even poor Chucky had to put up with my ignorance. It was the one thing I refused to talk about with him. I only knew a name—Stephen Richardson. A couple of days after the tragedy of losing my parents, the captain had called to inform me that they had the man in custody whose reckless driving had killed my parents. The captain had told me the man's name, but I didn't want to see his face. Maybe it would have only been further confirmation of what I already knew, the loss of my parents quivering deep in my bones. Putting a face to that name would have been nothing but another nail in my coffin buried in depression.

In the past several weeks, Macy remained the only steadfast friend I had. I couldn't really blame the others for pulling away, as my frame of mind had gone to a dismal place. At first, my friends' calls and letters had been overwhelming, but as each day passed, those old friends dropped like flies scorched by the hot sun.

I took a deep breath and focused my mind on the double doors, finding my resolve to take each step. When I entered the building, someone directed me to the appropriate courtroom when I gave my name. I slid into a seat somewhere in the back, hoping to remain inconspicuous, and stared at my lap as I twiddled with my purse strap.

During the trial, I kept replaying the night of my parents' death. The words spoken around me were lost in a sea of disorientation, my mind incapable of wrapping itself around being present, my denial so deep it engulfed me in unawareness.

Hours passed in this vein. A few times, I gazed in the general direction of the accused. The back of an unremarkable head of sandy hair stared back, the man's shoulders slumped, his head bowed. He never once tried to defend himself, at least from what I recalled with my limited attention. I heard his name as the prosecutor stood and mentioned driving drunk and killing three people because of it. I must admit I was shocked to hear of a third death and felt a bit guilty for not listening earlier. Who else had died because of this selfish man's actions?

By the end of the trial, I perked up enough to listen to the judge's sentence: two years for being guilty of three cases of manslaughter while under the influence of alcohol. It seemed a small price to pay for his crimes, and being there to hear it brought me no peace or closure.

As the man, Stephen Richardson, was escorted out, he glanced in my direction. Our eyes met for a couple of seconds, and his face was written in remorse, his vibrant blue eyes seeming to beg me to forgive him. I blinked and looked away. Could he know who I was?

I left the courtroom, disappearing in the crowd and stepping into a rainy Cleveland afternoon. By the time I reached the bus stop, I was soaked. The temperature had dropped twenty degrees during the day. As I waited for the bus, I tried to focus on the future without my parents. I would need to learn how to drive and finish my last year of college. I would have to take care of my brother. Money wasn't an issue, as my parents had left us plenty to take care of ourselves, but it wouldn't last forever. I would find a job as soon as college was finished.

And I would no longer be Laura Ashford.

That day she died.

Hello, Lorna.

∞ ∞ ∞

When I managed by some small miracle to turn off the waterworks, I straightened in the chair and reached for the phone. As my index finger dialed each number, waiting for the rotary to click back in place seemed to take an eternity. The last number finally dialed, I cradled the earpiece to my cheek. After two rings, the only voice I could abide in this lonely world answered.

I tried to speak, but my breaths came short and labored as I lost control and began crying again.

"Hello?" Macy asked. "Lorna, darling, is that you?"

"Y-yes. Macy, I—"

"What is it? Did something happen? Are you okay?"

"Macy, I need you."

"Okay, I'll be right there, darling. John is home, so I'll be right over, okay?"

"Yeah. Okay."

My hands shaking, I hung up and waited. I didn't try to stand, knowing that I couldn't even manage that. Staring at my swollen, discolored ankle, I thought about how pathetic I was. I had trusted Tristan when all he had done was lie to me.

When Macy arrived, she came through the side door without knocking. She rushed to my side, her green eyes large as she took in my injury.

"Your ankle... What happened, darling?"

"I fell down the stairs, the front ones at Tristan's house." My voice wavered like an out-of-tune violin with every word.

Macy knelt at my side and took my hands, her brow creased. "That's not really the problem here, is it?" she whispered.

I shook my head. "Tristan isn't who I thought he was."

Macy stood. "Do you want me to go next door and give him a piece of my mind for breaking your heart?"

"No! It's way more complicated than that. Oh, Mace. I don't even know where to start."

"Look, I think the first thing we need to do is get you to the hospital and have your ankle checked out. We'll have plenty of time to talk while waiting. You can fill me in on every detail."

"I don't think I can walk."

"Here, lean on me. I've got you."

∞ ∞ ∞

And Macy had me. She took me to the hospital and listened as I told her all about Tristan. At first, Macy had been shocked to learn the truth, but as my words sank in, a mixture of feelings covered her face. Even though I knew his real name, he would always be Tristan to me. As much as I wanted to hate him, my heart ached for the man who had come to mean the stars and the sun to me.

By that evening, Macy and I were sitting in my living room, my ankle wrapped. Crutches leaned against the arm of the sofa. If you could call it luck, I had only mildly sprained my ankle, and it would feel better in a few days' time.

Despite it still being August, the late-summer evening sent a chill through the window. We were each nursing a cup of tea made from peppermint in Macy's garden, mostly to calm my frayed nerves. I shivered and glared at the picture window.

"Do you mind closing it?" I asked, nodding toward the window.

"Not a problem, darling." Macy stood and closed the window with more force than necessary. "Do you want me to draw the curtains shut as well?"

"Please. I don't want to see anything out that window." Every damning memory of Tristan-watching surfaced, although they blended. How many days had I wasted surveying him through that window?

Macy took her seat again in my dad's old armchair. "I'm really sorry Tristan didn't turn out to be the man we thought he was, Laura. You deserved some happiness after everything awful that's happened."

"Maybe I'm just not meant to be happy, Macy." My voice was tired, dull. I set the cold tea down, unable to finish it.

"That's not true."

"How do you know? There aren't any guarantees in life, Macy! There's no rhyme or reason for any of it. There are good people who suffer, and then there are horrible people who seem to get everything they want."

"I don't think things are always what they seem. As much as I don't wish to defend Tristan, he has suffered, too. Greatly. I think he loved you the best he could."

"He still lied to me, Macy. He had two months to tell me the truth."

"I know, darling, I know." Macy sighed, setting her cup of tea down. "Maybe he just didn't know how to tell you."

"Then he shouldn't have fallen in love with me."

"But you fell in love with him, too."

"What's your point?"

"Could you help it, falling in love?"

"Well, no. I remember thinking he was the last sort of man I'd ever want to be with when we first met, but even then, there was something about him that drew me to him. I was drawn to him before we even spoke, but that was all a huge error in judgment on my part."

"You'll drive yourself crazy if you keep replaying the same thoughts through your head, Laura. You've been through enough for one day, and I think it's time you rested. Do you want me to stay the night?"

"No." I yawned, quite done in. "You've already done so much for me, Macy. I don't know how I'd have survived the last six years without you. You should go home and be with your family."

Macy came to my side, placing a hand on my shoulder. "Please call in the morning, darling. Do you need help getting to bed?"

I was able to stand with Macy's assistance and then took up the crutches. "I'll manage, thanks. No jumping jacks or cartwheels from me, I promise." I smiled ruefully.

Macy half-hugged me and kissed my cheek. "Good night, Laura. I'll see myself out."

"Yeah, good night."

I stood there, forcing my weight on the crutches to hold me up, but once I was alone in that house, the walls seemed to cave in on me. I had to get out of here.

Chapter 19

By the time school started, my ankle had healed. I didn't wish to regale a new batch of wide-eyed students with tales of my tragedy. Maybe I could have come up with something interesting, like I had tripped on a banana peel as I was racing into the street to save an innocent kitten from certain doom. As it stood, I was standing fine. My tall tales would have to wait for another occasion.

Angela and Mr. Darling were back from their honeymoon. With school back in session, it was almost like the summer hadn't happened. Everyone was in full swing with keeping their noses to the grindstone, which was satisfactory to me, as I didn't need their noses in my business.

Grindstone. Rock. Why did so many thoughts throughout the day have to remind me of Tristan? I'd kept my picture window's drapes closed ever since Macy had done the deed for me. When I left for work in the mornings, I drove the other direction, away from Tristan's house, going around the block. It may have been the long way around, but I was willing to take any measure to avoid him.

Work was a useful daytime distraction, but the evenings were difficult to abide. I couldn't risk stepping outside to take a walk without worrying about spotting Tristan. My grass was overgrown again, and while I could have asked John to mow it, the thought of cutting it drew me back to Tristan and his old manual mower. Heck, my own house, with its patched roof, echoed Tristan's footsteps when I thought I was alone.

I began searching the newspaper in earnest for apartments. I needed to sell this burdensome house and be free of yards and neighbors in them. When I told Macy of my plans to put the house on the market, she said, "But you just moved less than a year ago, Lorna! Aren't you jumping the gun just a little bit here?"

"No. I've had plenty of time to think about it, and moving here was a mistake. I don't even need a whole house. When I first moved, I thought Chucky would one day return, but now I know I'm going to be alone for the rest of my life. What do I need all that space for?"

Macy perked her eyebrows at me from across her kitchen table. Her curly hair had grown enough to pull back into a short ponytail, giving her face more power to stare me down. "Maybe, but still, don't do anything hasty, darling. I know it's hard, but you shouldn't let your emotions make big decisions for you."

"I'm being perfectly logical about this." If that wasn't denial, I didn't know what was.

"Right." Macy harrumphed, shoving a plate of cookies toward me. "Eat. It'll help you think more clearly. You look drawn, Lorna, like you've been losing weight."

"I hardly think cookies are the right source of nourishment for me, but fine." I picked a cookie up and took a mechanical bite. "My point is, why should I stay somewhere where I'm just going to be reminded of the past?"

"Wasn't that why you moved from your parents' house?"

"That's different."

"How?"

"I had no control over losing my parents, Mace. I had control over choosing to spend so much time with a man I really didn't know. Tristan kept stuff from me from the beginning. Getting answers out of him was like doing some sort of complicated dance and messing up at every step."

"Yeah, he wasn't honest. We've established that, but you were always telling me that he was your—what did you call it?—your rock." Macy laughed. "Funny."

I glared. "Rocks, yeah, ha, ha. I don't really want to talk about Tristan anymore, okay?"

"Fine with me." Macy spoke like she didn't believe me.

"How's school going for Johnny?"

"He groaned about it when they first went back. I think he wasn't ready to give up summer yet."

"I was glad to go back to work."

"I'm sure." Macy stood and walked to the fridge, rifling through it. "I need to figure out dinner. Do you want to stay?"

"I don't want to be a bother." Why did I feel like an overgrown rosebush among a manicured garden of daisies?

Macy pulled a handful of vegetables out of the refrigerator and slammed the door shut with her foot. She dropped the load onto the countertop and then turned toward me. "Help me out here, will you?"

I sighed and joined her. She pushed a bunch of carrots in my direction and handed me a knife. Without arguing, I set to chopping. The next hour passed in this manner, Macy giving me directions and me following them. At the end of it all, we had dinner in the oven and on the stove. As we set the table, Macy passed off four regular-sized plates and one baby plate to me. I knew I'd be staying for dinner.

John and the kids joined us a little while later. Throughout the meal, I remained quiet, glad to listen to John talk about work or Johnny about school. The young boy boasted about his new basketball he'd gotten for his birthday and how he'd been practicing every day. His little sister, Annie, banged her spoon and fork on her highchair, squealing in delight at her brother's excitement.

When the meal was over, I helped Macy clean up. I was shocked to see how late it had gotten as I put away the last of the dishes.

"It's dark out," I remarked. "I've taken up enough of your time, Mace."

"Nonsense, Laura."

"I'm not—"

"We're not arguing about that again. I've obliged you until now, darling. I'm glad you had the sense to stay and not return to that house you can't wait to get rid of."

"Thank you, Macy." My heart warmed for the amazing woman in front of me.

Macy hugged me, and I returned the hug. Before she let me go, she said, "You're Laura, no matter how much you've been hurt. You're strong, a fighter. Don't let anyone tell you otherwise...Laura."

I smiled wistfully and wished her good night, stepping out into the cool evening. When I started up my car, tears of gratitude prickled in my eyes. On the short drive home, I thought of how Macy had never given up on me all those long years, even when I had tried to push her away. Once I was on my street, I didn't realize I was going past Tristan's house until it was too late. I slowed the car as I stared at the largest tombstone among many—his house. The home was shrouded in darkness. I shook my head, in the vain hope I might stop caring about the man who lived in that coffin.

∞ ∞ ∞

When I returned to work the next day, Angela searched me out in the staff room first thing. I was one of the first to arrive and sat in the corner, nursing a cup of strong, bitter coffee.

"Good morning, Lorna!"

"Hi, Angela. How are you?" I smiled like a Kewpie doll, wondering if it was more of a grimace.

"I've been meaning to catch up with you. I haven't gotten a chance to talk with you since we got back." Angela wrinkled her pert little nose on her smooth face. "Ugh, how can you drink that sludge?"

"The coffee?" I shrugged. "My dad used to say the blacker, the better. My mom said it was what put hair on his chest."

Angela giggled. "I hope you aren't hoping for that to happen."

I couldn't help but laugh a bit. "No, I doubt I have to worry about that. So, how was your honeymoon?"

"It was a dream, Lorna, purely and simply a dream come true!" She went on to entertain me with every detail of her trip.

"I can only imagine," I said.

Angela went on as if she hadn't heard me. "Oh, and let me tell you about a little boat cruise we made around one of the islands one evening. It was a sunset cruise with dinner..."

For the next several minutes, I continued to listen to Angela. Other teachers started to filter into the staff room, most of them making the wise choice to steer clear of the coffee. Mr. Darling made a brief appearance, like an actor obliging his fans. I glanced at the clock, noting classes would start in five minutes.

Angela, noticing my distracted move, said, "Oh, I'm sorry, Lorna. I've been talking your ear off and haven't asked how you're doing. Any news about your beau? Maybe you have some of your own wedding bells in the not-too-distant future?"

Everyone's eyes seemed to be on me, their ears trained in my direction, waiting for me to spew the awful truth in an emotional vomit. Instead, I said softly, "That's a story for another time, Angela. We need to get to class."

Angela gazed at me as I walked away. If it weren't for the classroom of hopeful youngsters, I would have run into the bathroom and bawled my eyes out.

∞ ∞ ∞

At the end of the day, I jogged out to my car. As I was about to open the door, Angela stepped into view. I jumped. "What are you trying to do? Give me a heart attack?"

"Sorry, Lorna. I didn't mean to startle you."

"It's fine." Withdrawing my hand from the latch, I motioned for Angela to follow me. "Probably better if we're on the grass instead of standing in the parking lot. Have you seen the way some of these people drive around here? Plain madness."

Angela wasn't biting my baited distraction. "I was hoping to talk to you."

"Won't Tom be waiting?"

"Oh, he has a meeting with the principal."

"I hope everything's okay."

Angela waved me off. "Nothing to worry about. He's just hoping to get moved to the junior or senior high. I think he wants to coach, too."

"Is working together awkward now that you're married?"

"I don't know. It's too soon to know, but anyway, you told me this morning you would tell me about you and Tristan later. Is everything okay?"

I sighed and pursed my lips. "Tristan and I aren't together anymore. That's the short version of the story."

"Oh, no! I'm so sorry to hear that, Lorna."

"Shh, keep your voice down, will you?" I hissed. At Angela's hurt expression, I continued, "Sorry. It's just a mess. I'm not interested in everyone at work knowing about my love life or the lack of it."

"So, you really were in love? I'm sorry. I don't understand. What happened? You two seemed so happy together at my wedding. I seem to recall you two leaving early, and I couldn't help but wonder if..."

"What? That we went off somewhere and did the dirty?"

Angela blushed. "Lorna!"

"Sorry. I'm fine, Angela. We just weren't a good match. We both had too much from our pasts that got in the way of moving forward. He isn't the man I thought."

"Hmm. You're sure you don't wanna talk more about it? I have some time. We could take a walk or go down the street for some coffee."

I shook my head. "I need to get home, Angela. Maybe another day."

"Yeah, sure. Another day. Bye, Lorna."

I wished Angela a good day and returned to my Cadillac. I was beginning to become the Queen of Bad Excuses. As I drove home, I wondered why I was in such a rush to get back to nothing at all.

Chapter 20

Some places are forever etched in our minds and on our hearts, no matter how much time has passed. I dreamt of my childhood home that night.

My old bedroom, with its secondhand bookshelf filled with novels and textbooks. The dining room with my grandma's lace tablecloth and a fresh vase of lilies, Mom's favorites. Dad used to get them for her every Friday after work and would visit every florist until he found some.

I stepped into the kitchen, where Mom was busy making pork chops, seasoned just right. The smells permeated my nostrils, giving my stomach cause to growl. I smiled at her back as she worked and withdrew into the living room, where Dad sat in his worn armchair, tendrils of smoke drifting up from his pipe as he read the paper.

As I turned toward the window, I spotted Chucky, thirteen years old again, playing basketball with his neighborhood friends in the driveway, their timeless laughter now an echo.

I awoke with a start, realizing as my eyes adjusted to the darkness that I was alone in my new house. Sighing, I pushed away the covers and slid my feet into my slippers. I pulled my robe on, shivering slightly in the early-autumn air.

My bookshelf was no longer an accessory in my bedroom, but as I flipped on the light, my eyes roamed to B.R. Stevenson's three novels stacked beside the bed on the nightstand. As much as it pained me to know who the author was, or who he wasn't, I couldn't part with them. Neither had I picked any of them up in the weeks since my last encounter with Tristan.

I left the room and sought out my dad's old armchair, no longer at its place beside the picture window. I folded into its cushions, drawing my knees up to my chest. Toying with Chucky's dog tag on its chain around my neck, my mom's wedding ring molded into my right index finger, I marveled at these ghosts from a former life. A chair, a ring, and a dog tag.

I wiped away an errant tear, grateful the lights were off, and I couldn't see the paintings I'd named after my family.

Standing, I whispered, "Good night, Dad, Mom, Chucky..."

Then I returned to bed, my sleep restless the remainder of the night.

∞ ∞ ∞

In the morning, I did something I'd never done. Good girl Laura never would have lied and called into work sick. Maybe I was sick in some way, but I doubted any doctor would write a note for a broken heart. As it was, the principal didn't question my claim.

I dressed and ate breakfast with the usual vigor to leave that house as quickly as possible. After arguing with my car and nearly losing, I was questioning my decision fifteen minutes later as I turned onto Emerson Street.

About halfway down stood a narrow, light blue house built shortly after the turn of the century. The steep roof hugged a single window on the third story, which held the attic Chucky and I had played in as kids. The front porch with its white spindles had a new rocking chair. Red tinged the tips of the two ancient maples in the small front yard. I parked my car on the street and stepped out.

Not wishing to draw too close, I stood on the sidewalk on the opposite side of the street and stared for several minutes at my childhood home. This was the first time I had returned since leaving.

The left window on the second floor had the same light yellow curtains as when I'd slept in that room. All in all, the place hadn't changed much.

Then, a woman about my age stepped out the front door with a baby and a little girl. Our eyes met for a moment, but I averted my gaze and got back into my car. As I drove away, I realized the place had changed completely.

What had I expected to find by returning there? Comfort and peace? Part of what I'd found had been those things, if only for a little while. Still, seeing a stranger walk out of the house that had belonged to my family for so many years had reopened the wound on my heart. For the next hour, I drove without purpose. I considered stopping by Macy's to see if she was home but decided I had burdened her enough. Like that young mother in my old house, Macy had her own family. I couldn't keep taking her away from that.

Of all places, I pulled into the parking lot of my old church. I eyed the imposing building warily and chose to head for the cemetery. Chucky's grave was still fresh, no grass on the mound of dirt. A small cross marked his empty spot, since I hadn't yet picked out a headstone for him. The one final act seemed like it would bury him forever. Several small American flags decorated what would one day be his final resting spot when this war was over, and he was brought home. As I knelt on the damp earth, tears threatened to fall. Touched anew by the kindness of strangers who paid their respects to Chucky, I inwardly chastised myself for not returning to his grave sooner. Selfishness had kept me away. Even if it had been grief, when would enough time pass before I was willing to accept what had happened?

But wasn't that what I had been trying to do by being with Tristan? Choosing to open my heart and love again after years of closing myself off?

Not far from Chucky's grave, I found my parents' double headstone. I visited here seldom, but seeing their names etched in stone, I was no longer sure what I felt. While standing there, I sensed someone behind me and turned to find Pastor Wilson shuffling across the lawn toward me. He was leaning heavily on a cane, and I wondered why he didn't retire.

"Good morning, Laura," he said.

"Pastor." I nodded, not bothering to correct him.

"I feel fall will be early this year." He motioned toward the golden leaves above us.

"Yes. I noticed that, too. The trees at my house are already turned. That is, my old house."

"You visited your childhood home?"

"Yes. Although I don't know why. Or why I'm here."

That was the question, wasn't it? Why was I here, as in on earth, when my family was in heaven?

"Would you mind stepping inside with me for a little while?" the pastor asked. "I'm afraid my legs aren't what they used to be."

"Of course." I frowned at the back of the pastor's white head as he dragged his feet through the grass. This man had dedicated his life to serving God, and he was still at it. He was even so kind as to invite me into the church.

Once we were seated in his office, Pastor Wilson asked, "Would you care for something to drink? Tea? Coffee? Annette can bring you something."

Annette must have been the secretary. We had passed a middle-aged, dark-haired woman on the way to the pastor's office. The lady had smiled at me and wished me a good morning, and her warmth had prompted me to do so in return.

"I'm fine, thank you." I fiddled with my purse strap, keeping my eyes on my lap.

"I'm glad to see you, Laura. Did visiting your family bring you here today?"

I looked up and sighed, glancing around an office that hadn't changed since I was a child. The dark-paneled walls, the small cross hanging on the wall behind the pastor's desk, his mismatched chairs, and his numerous books were frozen in time. I felt like a child again in Pastor Wilson's presence as he gazed at me behind thick glasses. His eyes were understanding, however. I took a breath and nodded.

"You know, child, few are aware that I was once married."

My eyes were drawn to his face. "I never knew that."

"It's not something I share in my sermons or Bible studies, Laura. There are a few people who I tell because they are the ones who need to hear it—that I understand firsthand their pain."

"What happened to your wife?"

"It's well over fifty years now, but Laura—yes, that was also her name—died giving birth to our daughter. Both Laura and our girl were lost."

My insides felt empty, from my chest down to my stomach. It was like someone had removed all my vital organs, and I stopped breathing. No words came for a long time. When I could speak, I whispered, "I'm so sorry. I had no idea."

I had the courage to keep my gaze on Pastor Wilson, and he looked back at me from two feet away. "Even all these years later, I think about it. The pain isn't as fresh as it was when it first happened, but I can never forget. How could I?"

"But how do you do it? I mean, how do you keep living when the ones you loved the most were taken from you?" I was sure I was begging like a woman in need of a single drop of water after going days without drinking.

"That's no easy thing, child. As a pastor, my parishioners expect me to have answers. I'm the one who helps comfort them during difficulty. I don't like to ask it of others to return the favor, but you know what?"

"What's that?"

"I'm a hypocrite if I don't allow my brothers and sisters to be the same source of comfort for me as I am for them. You see, Laura, I'm an old man now. I know plenty about the painful ways of life and the unfairness of it all. There are times when, in my anger, I still want to yell at the Good Lord."

"Really?" I couldn't believe that this man, who seemed to have the faith of one of the biblical giants, would rail and rant at God.

"Oh, yes, child. Yes. But God puts others in our lives to help us through the tough times. I have realized too late that I should have leaned more on others when I was younger, much the way I lean on this cane, and it helps me to walk. When I cannot carry myself, God is carrying me through the help of others."

I blinked away tears. "Pastor, I've spent six years being angry and blaming God. I'm so tired. I'm...worn out. I thought I was healing not so long ago, even when Chucky died, because I finally had someone. But then, everything I'd been working so hard to rebuild shattered."

"It's never too late, Laura. You're young yet."

"I just don't know. What if the damage is irreparable?"

"Do you believe that with God, all things are possible?"

"I don't think God likes me a whole lot right now."

Pastor Wilson's brow furrowed, his bushy eyebrows drawing together, as he frowned. "God loves you, Laura."

I shook my head, crying silently. "Then why do I feel like He's punishing me? That's what this has to be: punishment for blaming

Him all these years. When I thought I'd finally found happiness, it was taken away from me."

"Then let me ask you a question, child. When your parents were killed in that awful, awful accident, do you think God was punishing you then?"

"I-I don't know. I didn't think I'd done anything to deserve that, and that's why I was so upset at Him. He could have stopped it, but He let it happen. He doesn't care. He doesn't love me. How could He? I've even turned all this talk to being about me when you were just telling me about your own sufferings. I'm a selfish, horrible person."

"No, Laura." Pastor Wilson's words were gentle but firm, insistent that I listen to him.

"No?"

"You are not a horrible person. You're a person who has been put through an inordinate amount of pain in a short period of time. I don't have the answers for why, but I do know that you shouldn't feel so lonely. If you let Him, God will comfort you. But you have to open yourself up first. I believe you came here today because you wished for healing, but that's up to you to decide."

For several minutes, I wept in that broken-in chair in Pastor Wilson's office. I didn't try to understand every reason for my tears, but I let them fall and tell their stories by the heartache they revealed. It was a pain too great, too deep for words. Finally, I wiped the last of my tears away. "Thank you, Pastor."

"Why do you thank me? I've done nothing."

"Oh, but you have. If what you say is true, about God working through people, then I'm certain He's just worked through you to get to thick-headed me." I laughed back a sob.

The old pastor's lips spread into a smile, the wrinkles around his eyes and mouth crinkling deeper—a beautiful sight to behold. "Then go and be well, Laura. Please come back again soon."

I stood and nodded. "I will. I promise." I stopped at the doorway, my hand on the threshold. "Oh and, Pastor?"

He looked up. "Yes, child?"

"It's not too late for you either."

He smiled, although it didn't quite reach his eyes. I remembered his words. *I have realized too late that I should have leaned more on others when I was younger...*

I left Pastor Wilson's office that day with the sense of a fragile scab forming over a long-opened wound.

Chapter 21

The next morning, my car won the war. In my final battle with my car, Ol' Bessie rattled and wheezed and then died. Even John couldn't fix her. Was this punishment for taking a day off work and pretending to be sick?

I'd been healing. I'd been doing what I need to do, and now this? It was like God was laughing by throwing one more wrench into the works of this busted clockwork of a life. My faith was as brittle as my junk car.

But in all this, ever-dependable Macy was my angel. I remembered Pastor Wilson's wise words about God choosing to work through others. Macy was living proof of that, and so, with my faith holding on by a thread, I took John's word that he knew of a garage that charged honest and fair prices. My car was towed, and I took the bus to work the rest of the week.

On Saturday morning, Macy turned her car onto a street that was half-lined with dilapidated houses, and unsavory individuals walked on the sidewalks. I frowned at her from the passenger seat.

"You're sure this is where John had my car towed?"

"That's what he said, darling. He's taken our car here before. The neighborhood may not look like much, but the guy who has a garage here is a good and decent fellow. His prices are low, and he does quality work."

I tried not to wrinkle my nose at the stench wafting up from the Cuyahoga River, where a few dockworkers called out to each other. "Hmm, well, if you say so..."

Macy smiled. "You know the best things are usually hidden in the oddest places."

My mind went to Tristan. My eyes fell on my lap. "Yeah, but it's not easy, Mace. What if we never talk again?"

"Give it a little more time, Laura. Now, here we are."

In the middle of what remained of the Haymarket district, Macy parked in front of an ancient brick dwelling, its garage behind it. I stepped out of the car and stood there, looking for the owner.

"Do you want me to stay with you?" Macy asked.

"You can go. I trust what you said about this guy being honest and whatnot. I'm hardly going to be murdered, Mace." I smiled ruefully, remembering my misplaced opinion of Tristan being an ax murderer...only to find out he had killed, albeit by accident.

Just then, a young man exited the garage and asked, "Are you Lorna Ashford?"

"I got this, Mace," I said, waving.

Macy honked the horn and was off.

I turned back toward the man. "Yes, I'm Miss Ashford. You're the owner?"

"That's me, in a nutshell." When he smiled, the slight wrinkles around his eyes deepened. He must have been older than I realized, but with the glare of the sunlight and the grime on his face, it was hard to tell. His brown hair was messy. Something about him reminded me of Chucky. "I'm Harry Rechthart, proud owner of Dawson's Garage."

He reached out his hand to shake mine, but then retracted it, laughing. "Just kiddin'. I mean, I'm Harry Rechthart, but you don't really wanna shake my hand. Dirty and all."

I laughed at his easygoing manner. "Is my car fixed?" I followed him to the garage.

"Good as new, Miss Ashford. It's in the back. Let me show her to you. Real beauty. Reminds me of my parents' old Caddy."

I smiled. "I'm afraid my car and I always had a bit of a complicated relationship."

"What relationship ain't complicated?" He chuckled. When we reached my car, Mr. Rechthart went on to explain what he fixed, but my head spun.

"If you say so," I said, "but you might as well be speaking a foreign language."

"I felt the same way when I first began learnin' cars."

"You weren't always a mechanic?"

"Me? No way." He laughed. "Notice it's called 'Dawson's Garage' and not 'Rechthart's Garage'?"

I nodded. Boy, this man could really talk my ear off, but something about him kept me captivated. I watched as a woman and two kids, a boy and a girl, joined Mr. Rechthart in the lot.

"You're not going on about the details of fixing cars again, are you, Harry?" the woman asked.

"No, Kathy. Actually, I was just about to tell Miss Ashford here why it's called 'Dawson's.' That's Kathy's dad, a great man—taught me everything I know about cars, including how to do business right. I'd never change the name of the place."

"And my husband makes sure every customer knows it," Mrs. Rechthart added, holding her husband's upper arm as she looked up at him.

I saw admiration in her eyes for the man she no doubt loved deeply. My heart ached. This couple was the perfect example of what I wanted: just to be happy. I didn't know their story, but from what they'd shared, I was certain they were genuine.

"That's a beautiful tribute," I said. "Is he still alive, Mr. Dawson?" But as I asked the question, I knew the answer.

Both Mr. and Mrs. Rechthart's faces took on a somber quality as they watched their children chase each other in a game of tag.

"Sadly, no," Mr. Rechthart said, meeting my eyes, "but I've done my best to make sure his memory lives on. It's all we can do, right? Make the best of what's been given to us, count our blessings, and be thankful."

I considered his words. He seemed much older than he probably was. His was a strange face—an odd mixture of mischievous boy and wise old man. Mr. Rechthart kept his eyes on me a bit too long, as if he could read every page of my sad story. I forced a smile and blinked, looking from him to his wife.

"You're right, of course, but I-I must be going. Thank you for fixing my car and all. How much do I owe you?"

"You know what? Nothin'. It's on the house."

I gaped at Mr. Rechthart and then at his wife, but she was smiling. "He's taken pity on you...or a liking to you," she said. "It's a compliment."

"But— surely... I'm afraid I can't accept that, Mr. Rechthart. You can't very well keep your business running if you don't charge a thing."

"Business is fine." He waved me off and took a step away from his wife. In a low voice, he said, "I know a thing or two about goin' through tough times, Miss Ashford."

"But how could you possibly—? John or Macy Wells didn't put you up to this, did they?" As much as I loved Macy and her husband, I couldn't accept this charity. It was too much.

"No, no, not to worry. Don't blame them, Miss Ashford. I've lived long enough to know when a person's been down and out. The last thing you need is more trouble. Dawson, God rest his old soul, taught me more than just fixin' cars. He fixed me. I'm just tryin' to live on in that spirit—not that I think I can fix anyone, mind you. I just wanna do my small part to help a fellow woman or man."

"Thank you, truly, but you still didn't answer my question. How could you know?"

"It's written all over you, Miss Ashford, from the way you hold your gaze on the ground, to that shiny look in your eyes like you're about to cry, to the slight hunch in your shoulders. You're a woman who's known tough times, am I right?"

I stepped away. "You presume an awful lot, Mr. Rechthart. I'm a complete stranger."

"Sorry. I didn't mean to offend. Look, if it's your pride, pay me what you will. I get that. I've got my pride, too." He winked.

"Well, fine, then." I withdrew some money from my wallet without bothering to count it and shoved it at him. Realizing how ridiculous I must have looked, I lost some of my resolve and sighed. Then I smiled and laughed. "Okay, so you win. I'm sorry for taking offense, but you're, uh..."

"I say whatever I want without thinking? I probably think too much. Maybe I've read too much into something that's not there, but people've told me I'm pretty good at reading, um, people. I just wanted to say, you know, good luck and all. If you need someone to fix your car, I'm your guy."

"Thank you, Mr. Rechthart, for— just thanks."

I got into my car, and Ol' Bessie started up without protest. For once. Mr. Rechthart half-smiled and waved as I nodded and waved back. I pulled out of the small parking lot behind his garage, wondering about the encounter.

Okay, I get it, God. First Pastor Wilson and now a perfect stranger.

Chapter 22

I left the Haymarket district and returned to the church cemetery with some flowers to place on both my parents' and Chucky's graves. I sat in the soft grass under the shade of a maple that was older than any of the surrounding buildings. For once, my mind was still. I stared at the branches overhead as the wind rocked them, the sound of thousands of leaves rustling as nature's symphony. While there, I ate a simple lunch.

For the first time in that cemetery, I found peace. When I felt it was time to depart, I said a prayer and returned to my car. I wasn't sure what propelled me, but my next stop was a secondhand shop. My parents had owned many old pieces of furniture, and since my own house was still sparse, I thought I might find something with that old creature-comfort to add to my collection.

Before I entered, several rocking chairs lined up in front of the store window caught my attention. I sat in the closest one and gave it a few rocks. It was comfortable enough, but it didn't have the feel I was seeking. One by one, I tried each chair, only to come away disappointed. When I came to the last one, I regarded it. It seemed so familiar. I took a seat and rocked. The left side was slightly lower than the right. I could tell by the movement of the rockers that it was an old friend. I stood and examined it thoroughly, certain this rocking chair was the very one that had belonged to my family for generations.

I beamed. There was no price on it, but what price could I place on something that was part of precious history? It was Providence.

I entered the shop and sought out the woman who was working there, finding her buried in the back among lamps and chests of drawers.

"Excuse me, ma'am?"

The woman jumped, standing ramrod straight as her glasses rested askew on her aquiline nose. "Pardon me, I didn't hear you come back here. May I help you with something?"

"I'm interested in one of the rocking chairs out front."

"Oh, lovely. Which one?"

I led her to the door, and once outside, I pointed to the one on the end. "How much for that one?"

"Oh, that's a rare beauty. Fifteen dollars, miss."

"Fifteen dollars!" For a second, my heart sank. "I have to have that chair. Very well."

The lady smiled.

"I don't have the money with me, but would you take a check?" I did some mental math to ensure that I'd still have enough money in my bank account.

"That would be just lovely. You do understand, of course, that if the check bounces, there is a fee."

I sighed. "Yes, I'm quite aware of that. Just let me get my checkbook." I rummaged through my purse until I found it and followed the lady back inside. As I wrote a large portion of my paltry savings away, I remembered how happy I had been five minutes earlier upon rediscovering that chair. Yes, it was worth fifteen dollars.

The chair was too big to fit inside my car, so with the help of the shop owner, we laid it on its back and secured it to the roof of the car with ropes. It reminded me of the times my parents had done likewise with our Christmas tree when I was a child. My mind couldn't help but think that if I had Tristan and his pickup truck, this task would have been much easier. Once home, I hailed the mailman as he was passing by to help me take the rocking chair down from the car, and then I took it inside. My front porch in this house amounted to two feet on either side of the door and a half-dozen steps leading up to it. Not the type of place I wanted to put a rocking chair.

While I hemmed and hawed about where to put my new-old acquisition, I finally decided on my own bedroom. For the next hour, I sat in that chair and rocked, my eyes drifting closed until I fell asleep.

Upon waking, I checked the time, surprised to find half of the afternoon had passed. I wandered into the living room and studied my paintings. It had been months since I'd painted, and seeing as I had time to kill, I got out my only fresh canvas and my painting supplies. Careful not to get too close to any of my furniture, I laid newspaper on the floor and set to work. This canvas was about two feet by two feet. For the next hour, I worked, dripping, smudging, and wiping paint this way and that.

When I finished, I stood and admired my creation. The edges were dark, the colors blending into an ugly greenish-brown. The center, however, was light yellow, even white in places where I had left the canvas pure.

I thought about my conversation with Pastor Wilson, about how it was never too late to rebuild a life. The old pastor had, in his pain, comforted others. He had reminded me of something I had known deep down but seemed to have forgotten when I needed it the most: to let other people help me and carry me through the hard times. Wasn't that what Tristan had tried to do? What I had also done for him? We had been building a life, a beautiful work of art. We had been potters molding clay into function and form.

I smiled sadly at my painting and whispered, "I'm calling you 'Tristan.'"

While I left the painting to dry, I went to the picture window. The drapes had remained shut for weeks now, cutting me off from a view I had once been so drawn to that I couldn't stop myself. I'd been like an alcoholic with her liquor. Frowning, I opened the curtains just enough to peek through.

Alcohol had been Tristan's vice, a horrific secret he had kept swept under a rug. In all our time together, he had never touched alcohol. He had even avoided it when I'd offered him some wine on one occasion. Sure, he had lied to me, but the burden he had carried for so long had to weigh on him.

In all my anguish, I had forgotten Tristan had also suffered. My goodness, his wife had died because of his actions! Here was a man who had lost the one he loved, yet he had chosen to love again. Of that I was certain. I hadn't wanted to believe it when I'd first found out the truth, but when I remembered all he had done for me, who he had been toward me, who he had become for me, there was no denying the deeper truth. Love covered a multitude of sins, according to the Bible.

I silenced my thoughts as I surveyed Tristan's rock garden. He was nowhere. Beyond the rocks, his house was as sealed tight as a casket underground. I pulled the curtain shut and stepped outside. The flowers were still in bloom in some places, but the effects of fall were evident. In my front garden, overgrown orange mums smiled at me.

Going to my garage, I found a shovel left there from Tristan the last time he'd worked in my yard. I carried it to the front of the house and began to dig in earnest. Even though it wasn't hot outside, sweat beaded on my brow. By the time I was done, my face was covered in perspiration. I wiped my forehead and carried the plant to Tristan's yard.

If I thought digging through hard dirt and roots was a challenge in my yard, working my way through the rocks in Tristan's yard would test my endurance to see my task through to the end. I kept looking up, half-expecting him to gaze out the window or walk out the door. If he did confront me, I wasn't sure what I would say. *I'm sorry? I'm digging in your rocks for fun? I still love you?*

I was spared having to humiliate myself, for I finished planting the mums without Tristan making an appearance. Stepping back to admire my work, I smiled at the color among the drab grey. *Like it or not, you're stuck with them, Tristan.*

Chapter 23: Tristan

1929

July in Cleveland. I hated that month. Heat and humidity. Humidity and heat.

I lifted another beam, carrying it on my shoulder as the sun beat down on me. Much like Father used to beat down on me. I muttered something less than Christian about my old man as I dropped the beam onto the ground.

"Watch it with that, will ya?" old Mr. Jenkins growled, like I had the choice to gently set it down. He was the foreman and did more sitting than any of us sorry louses.

"Yeah, sure." I turned my back. Without my muscles, I'd love to see him get half the work done around this dump. This was another job, another means to bring in enough money to pay the bills. In a few weeks, I'd move on to another construction site and heave, hammer, and haul until the job was done.

I smirked at Ben, who stood off to the side with his smokes. Joining him, I said, "Give one over, pal."

Ben held out a cigarette.

I lit up."

"What's up his?" Ben jerked his head toward our boss.

I snorted, taking a long drag. "Lord knows."

We chuckled. Just then, a group of young dolls sauntered past. Those hips of theirs worked magic.

Ben wolf whistled. "Hey, good-lookin'!" He waved.

The dames stopped and giggled.

"Yeah, and what's it to ya, big boy?" a redhead asked.

"What're you doin' in this neighborhood?" Ben left my side to make a fool of himself.

I followed but held back some. One of the girls, a pretty, dark-haired one, smiled at me. I smiled back and raised an eyebrow. While Ben was busy sweet-talking the other two, I stepped closer to her. Maybe this was the opportunity I needed. *Time to stop being an idiot and get serious.*

"Hi." She looked at me, then at her feet.

"Hi to you. Is there something interesting about your shoes that you wanna tell me about?"

She snapped her eyes to me and laughed nervously. "What? Oh, no. I'm not as good at this"—she waved—"as my friends."

"Do you have a name?"

"Of course I have a name. What kind of a question is that? Don't you usually ask, 'What's your name?'"

I chuckled. "Okay, then. What's your name?"

"Anna Julie. Although no one calls me that. Just Julie to my friends."

"Are you Julie to me?" I quirked my lips. "I'm Stephen, by the way."

"I can be Julie to you, Stephen."

"Great."

Pretty girls rarely noticed me, and I'd made that simple by mostly avoiding them. Not that I looked like something the garbage man pulled out of the bottom of a pile of rotting, dirty, mangled who-knows-what, but girls and I didn't speak the same language. This Julie doll seemed willing to give me the time of day. I'd kept my hair trimmed and sometimes had sported a short beard the past couple of years, but seeing as it was the middle of summer now, I was clean-shaven.

While guys like Ben could talk their way into the underthings of anything with boobs and legs, I couldn't even ask a girl her name without tripping over my words. And here I was, a writer! Words on the page were friends. Words from my mouth, enemies.

As luck would have it, Julie, this attractive, sweet girl, agreed to see me again. And again. And again.

The only thing was, she wasn't my only addiction. Ben introduced me to the bottle. At first, I refused, never wanting to be the monster my old man had been. But then the tug grew too strong, and I gave in. Julie never liked my drinking, but she tolerated it when we went out with Ben and his girl, Bea, to speakeasies. Julie had no idea how serious my drinking was at home, however.

By Christmas, I couldn't get enough of her. When Julie, all dressed up like she was going out on the town in the Big Apple, showed up at my door on Christmas Eve, I second-guessed my plan. We'd never gone to her place to meet her parents, but Julie had told me many times she didn't need anyone's approval.

For the first time, my life was becoming something I only dreamed about. For whatever crazy reason, Julie loved me. I sure loved her. So seeing her on my doorstep, all beautiful like some sort of angel here to take me to heaven, turned me into a fumbling mess.

"Well, are you just gonna stand there, or are we going out on a date?" She smiled, the right side of her mouth a bit higher.

Tempted to kiss her, I stepped aside, and motioned her to come in.

"I see you've tidied up." She glanced around my small apartment. "Where did you hide all the undergarments?"

I laughed. "Those were mostly Ben's. He's out for the night, so we don't need to worry about him. Some new girl and some big party."

Julie raised a thin eyebrow as she took a seat on the lumpy sofa. "Drinking, I suppose?"

The mention of alcohol churned my stomach as I imagined my old man downing a few pints that night by the Christmas tree, singing raucously and ruining any semblance of holiness a carol might have. If the papers were anything to go by, my father, like thousands of others, had suffered a terrible blow from the stock market crash. The auto industry, where he'd worked so hard to move up the ranks, had laid off hundreds. His precious funds may have slipped from his grasp. If so, he'd likely be drinking away his sorrows instead of celebrating.

"Stephen, are you listening?"

"What? Oh, sorry." I dropped onto the couch next to her. Why couldn't I get myself under control? "Um, I thought we could just, you know, have dinner here. Stay in for the night." I gestured toward a simple meal laid out on the small table.

"That's fine. It would be hard to find a restaurant open tonight, anyway." Julie's eyes shifted as she locked and unlocked her hands.

"You're missing spending time with your family for this, aren't you?"

She sighed. "Yes, but I don't regret it. This is just... Okay, it's hard. I do feel guilty about missing church and Mom's dinner. It's always been a tradition, but I'm through. I wouldn't want to be anywhere else."

"Really?"

Julie nodded. The low light danced in her eyes. Here we were, two young people in love in a moldy, dim apartment. The world was in shambles beyond those dirty brick walls—walls that had seen the rise and fall of the American Dream. In homes throughout the country, families were together to celebrate Christmas, but their tables wouldn't be as full this year. Under Christmas trees, if they even had one, would seem barren compared to the preceding decade of prosperity But Julie and I, alone as we were, weren't lonely. We would make our own family. We would fill our hearts with love and our minds with memories, those precious gifts money couldn't buy. So, when I gazed upon this beauty shining in my dump-heap dwelling, I'd found gold among garbage.

"Why me?" I whispered.

"Because you're kind, and you listen." She frowned, then giggled. "Well, most of the time."

"I know I don't have much, but I..." I reached into my pocket for the ring. My fingers shook as they searched. For a second, I panicked, unable to find it, but then, in the depths of that infernal pocket, I clutched that life-saving ring box. Withdrawing it, I took her hand. "Julie, will you be my wife?"

She began crying.

Oh, no. "Julie? I'm sorry. Did I—?"

"No, you silly man. Be quiet. Of course not! I mean—" She laughed. "These are happy tears."

"So, is that yes?"

"Yes!" She fell into my arms and threw hers around me.

I laughed, unable to comprehend the happiness filling my heart. The feeling was so foreign, I almost didn't believe it.

When the embrace ended, Julie studied the ring for several moments, turning her hand this way and that. "It's beautiful," she said in awe.

I took her hand in mine and kissed it. "Not as beautiful as you."

She laughed. "Stephen, stop it. You're such a romantic."

"Funny you should say that. I—"

"Oh, I can't wait to tell Bea."

I smiled. "What about your parents?"

Julie's face dropped. "Well, yes, I'll have to tell them, but that can wait. I don't care about anything but us. I meant what I said. I don't regret missing my family for this, right here, right now, with you."

"Then our future will be ours alone. No interfering families. Just you and me."

"That sounds perfect."

I held Julie's hands in mine and faced her. "I have something else to tell you."

"All right." She sobered, perhaps shocked by my sudden seriousness.

"Nothing bad." I half-smiled. What I was about to tell Julie was huge, but I had decided to ask for her hand first because I had to know if she would marry me. Then, when I told her about my writing, I would know if she didn't want to marry a poor man. "I, uh... How do I say this? I never told anyone besides Ben, but I've been writing things for years. Anyway, I finished a book...yeah, an actual book, earlier this year and decided, what the heck, why not try to get it published?" Of course I wanted to get it published! That had been my dream forever and forever, so why was I downplaying it?

Maybe because I wasn't in the clear yet.

I plowed onward. "I never expected it would be good enough, but I got an agent to represent me. Someone out there thought my attempts weren't half-bad, I guess."

Julie beamed and hugged me for the second time in a matter of a few minutes. "Oh, Stephen, that's wonderful! The bee's knees! Why didn't you ever tell me you wrote?"

As the hug ended, I laughed and shrugged. "I never thought I was any good at it. I rarely shared anything I'd written with anyone, even Ben. He isn't much of a reader, and when he saw me use my typewriter, he made fun of me and said I was wasting my time."

"It's not a waste of time. In fact, I'd love to read your book. Few people get to live their dreams, and now with the dubious future, who knows what to expect?"

"You're right. The last few months have been the best in my life. I've told you what growing up was like for me. I learned years ago to keep to myself what I wrote. My family never supported me. Never in my wildest dreams..."

Julie took my hands in hers and squeezed. "Believe it. Forget all that. This here, right now, is the promise of a better future."

I kissed her with every ounce of passion I had, this wholly beautiful woman.

"Nothing's guaranteed yet. The agent is trying to find a publisher."

"I'm sure someone will want to publish your book!"

I chuckled. "Well, thanks for the vote of confidence, but time will tell."

Although much was uncertain, from that defining moment, I knew I understood love...or so I thought.

1931

Married life was like entering a foreign country and not speaking the language, even more so than talking to girls. As much as I loved Julie and she loved me, as time passed, I sometimes wondered if our love was enough. Just as visiting another country could prove fun and entertaining at first, so was being a newlywed. We wasted not a moment after our engagement and got married in Julie's church in April 1930. Neither of us cared about a big wedding or involving our families. We had each other, and that was more than enough.

I also had my book deal. My romance novel, *Cure for the Cries*, was the sort of story people were looking to lose themselves in during that time. While money was tight for many, my book proved a popular Christmas gift a year after its release. We were doing well financially while others suffered.

But our time of excitement in the territory of marriage soon drew to a close. While money could solve many problems, there were some things it couldn't buy. Julie and I were young and wanted nothing more than to start a family. But she miscarried, again and again. My drinking grew worse as well, and rather than comfort my wife, I turned to the bottle and my writing. As another year died, the hope we'd once had died a little more every month Julie didn't become pregnant.

"Are you sure you don't wanna have the Carsons or the Garrisons over for the New Year?" I asked, referring to our neighbors on both sides. "You just want to stay home? Or what about Ben and Bea? Ben said he has big news to share."

Julie sat in the floral armchair in the living room. Next to her on a small table, a dozen red roses were drooping and dropping their petals. I'd bought them for Christmas, in the hopes of cheering her up.

"Why, Stephen? What's there to celebrate?"

I knelt on the floor in front of my wife and took her small hand in mine. "A new year. You know what that means—hope of things to come."

She wiped at her red eyes. Even though she wasn't crying, she had been, and my heart lurched into my throat. "Oh, sure. More like another month of disappointment. We've been to the doctor, but no one can help us. It's likely we can't have children."

"You don't know that. Maybe having some friends over will give us the distraction we need."

"And that's all it will be—a distraction. When the morning comes, we'll still face the same problems. Besides, they have kids, in case you forgot."

"I didn't forget. I just—"

Julie stood, shrugging out of my grasp. "You should get back to your writing."

And the unspoken: Back to your drinking.

I stood as well and followed her into the kitchen. While she busied herself with some dirty dishes, I asked, "What's that supposed to mean?"

The dishes clanged as Julie dropped them into the sink and turned toward me, her eyebrows furrowed. "Isn't that what you always do? Write? To escape from the reality of our situation?"

"Wait a minute. That's not fair."

"So, when will you be done with your next best seller, Mr. B.R. Stevenson?" Julie stomped toward me, arms crossed over her chest.

"I can't force it. My inspiration to write anything good hasn't exactly come easy lately."

"Oh? So sorry to be the source of your lack of inspiration."

"Julie, please don't do this. I didn't mean it like that."

"Then how did you mean it, Stephen?"

"I..." For a guy who could find ten different ways to describe falling in love in a story, I had no words for the woman I loved. Sighing, I dropped my gaze, turned, and walked out the door.

Stepping into the frigid outdoors, I got into my car and drove in circles. Stopping beside an old storefront rumor said was a speakeasy, I turned off the ignition and frowned at my white knuckles gripping the wheel. I glared at the back of a man staggering out the door into the snow.

"What are you doing?" Shaking my head, I started the vehicle and headed home.

Julie was asleep. At least I assumed she was because the house was dark. Careful not to make a sound, I crept through the house until arriving at our bedroom door. When my hand tried the knob, it was locked. Frowning, assuming it had to be sticking, I jiggled it again. And again. *Yes, definitely locked.*

I considered rapping on the door but decided I'd already hurt Julie enough for one day, let alone the past few months. Turning away, I headed for the door to the upstairs, where my writing room and the spare bedroom were. On the landing, my mind wavered between forcing myself to write and surrendering to the single bed in the room at the end of the hallway.

Go to bed. You've done enough damage.

For once, I listened to my better self, suppressed too long. As I kicked off my shoes and shrugged off my coat, I dropped into the bed and rolled onto my side. A glance at the bedside clock showed it was one minute before midnight.

The second hand roved around the clock's face. Time seemed so slow when staring at the instrument that marked it. When it struck twelve, the minute hand eased to join the hour hand. It was midnight, a new year.

"Happy New Year," I muttered.

I sat upright and slid over the side of the bed until I knelt on the unforgiving floor. Under the bed rested a box labelled "writing." I withdrew and opened it, then stared at several notebooks. Nestled between those and the box's side was a single bottle of moonshine. Ben had brought it two weeks ago when he'd showed up with the usual beer, and he'd said it was a real treasure.

"The guy who makes this stuff swears it's solid gold, old sport," he'd said.

I'd laughed. "Whatever you say. I'll save it for a special occasion."

This was a special occasion. A new year. Alone.

I snorted, opened the bottle, and took a hefty swig. It was nearly at its end after a fortnight of daily kisses to my lips. With a shrug, I thought, *What the heck?* and drained it. Returning the empty bottle to its home, I replaced the box and crawled into bed, killing the light and closing my eyes.

And wishing 1931 would be a better year.

Chapter 24: Tristan

1931-1937

If I had any hope left, it had to be false. Ben and his fiancée, Bea, died in a car crash on New Year's Eve. So much for 1931 being a better year when attending my best friend's funeral was how it started. Now, my spirits had sagged since a couple of years earlier, and Julie had given up all together that she would ever have a child. My drinking ebbed and flowed. I tried to quit, begged Julie to give me another chance—to try to have a child. Begged her to give us another chance. Of course, this dirge played on a never-ending broken record. At one point, we tried getting a dog, hoping that having a pet to care for would help with the loneliness. While the puppy had been cute at first, the mutt had grown into an unruly hound with a desire to chew up anything it could get its teeth on.

"It has to go," Julie said finally. She wiped her sudsy hands on a towel as she stood at the sink. "If that— that thing ruins one more pair of my shoes—"

Part of me wanted to say, "The shoes you never wear since you don't leave the house?" Instead, I sighed and gave in. "All right. I'll see if I can get a neighbor to take him."

"You'd better, Stephen. The dog destroyed the arm on the couch last night. Now it looks like that meatloaf you tried cooking last week."

"Hey, I was just trying to help." My face heated. "You're always going on about how you have to cook all the time. I thought I'd do something nice for you."

"Enough is enough."

A heavy sigh escaped my mouth. So much for doing something nice.

So, poor Samson had not been a suitable substitute for a child, nor had he saved our marriage. When I dropped him off at the pound the following week, having failed to find him a home, even the mutt looked at me like I'd betrayed him.

"Hey, don't blame me, pal." I rubbed his shaggy head. "It wasn't my idea."

With that, I said goodbye to what I thought could've been a good pet under better circumstances.

Months passed. In 1936, work was still scarce, and Julie remained locked in a home devolving into an asylum. With my writing suffering and my book several years old, I found work where I could once spring arrived.

Then a small miracle of miracles happened. My oldest brother, George, called. Mind you, that wasn't the miracle.

"How'd you find this number?" I demanded.

"Wasn't hard. You think you ain't in the phone book? Always thought you were special, but we knew better."

"Cut it out. Why are you calling?"

"Dad's dead." To the point, like always. His clipped voice hadn't changed. "Now he can join our mother."

"I doubt he's in heaven if such a place exists. Hell's more fitting."

"That's it? You don't even wanna know how he died?"

"Fine, fill me in on all the details. Maybe I'll write about it."

"Heart attack."

"So, he didn't blow out his brains from losing all his money?"

Silence. I thought George hung up, but no such luck. "You're... I don't know what to say. Have you no remorse?" He was incredulous. I almost wanted to laugh because this was the most emotion I'd heard from the guy.

"Ha. Remorse? That's a funny word. What do I have to be remorseful about? I didn't do anything to regret. Is your memory that short? Oh, wait. He never hit you, and you hightailed it out of that dung heap when I was a kid. You turned a blind eye when he was beating me."

"Are you at least coming to the funeral?"

"Why? I never respected the old man; that hasn't changed."

"You're unbelievable, Stephen." Now, disgust coated his tone like puke-green paint.

"Hey, I'm just holding up my end of the deal of being the family's biggest blunder."

"Have a good life."

Click. The line went dead, and I smiled grimly into the receiver before hanging up.

"Who was that?" Julie asked as she stepped into the kitchen.

"No one important."

"It sounded like you were talking to someone you know."

I sighed and rubbed my face. "It was my brother. My father's dead."

"Oh, I'm so sorry, Stephen." Julie's face softened in the way it used to when we first knew each other before time had undone her happiness.

"Don't be." I hardened, making to turn away, but Julie's small hand on my arm stilled me. I stopped and looked at her hand, then into her eyes. "Please, it's nothing," I said more gently.

"Okay, if you're sure..."

"I am." I studied her. "You haven't looked at me like this in a long time. What is it?"

Julie took my hand and led me into the living room. We sat on the couch. Julie's lovely face morphed into a beacon of hope. "I think I'm pregnant again. I'm over a month late. This is the longest I've gone. I think it might actually take this time."

My mind drifted to a night several weeks ago when, for once, we hadn't been arguing. Those moments had been rare over the years, but every so often, we reminisced about our early days and connected physically and emotionally. Pulling myself from my thoughts, I said, "You're...really? You're pregnant?" My heart leapt as visions of a child running around the yard filled my mind. Yet, I couldn't quell all the previous loss—miscarriage after miscarriage, until we'd given up all together.

"Yes. I'm going to the doctor to be sure, but I'm awfully sure it's real this time. All the signs are there—nausea, the tiredness..."

"That's why you've been especially moody lately."

"You're hilarious." She glared.

"Just kidding. A bad joke."

A smile crept onto her lips. "Well, all right..."

I pulled her to me. "This is wonderful! Can you imagine it? We're going to be parents."

For the first time in I'd forgotten how long, I dared to be happy. To dream. To have hope.

After Julie went to bed that night, I couldn't sleep. My whole body was ablaze with excitement, inspiration to write coursing through my veins. I paced my writing room, sat, and scribbled some ideas in my notebook. Then I paced again, imagining I might wear through the floorboards. At about two in the morning, I took a seat and typed. When the sun rose, I woke with a start, shocked to find drool on the desk.

I wiped my mouth and smiled, shaking my head. "I'm going to be a father," I said, mesmerized. Yes, for certain, we would be parents this time. Years of disappointment had evaporated. Wasn't it high time something went right?

On my desk, I'd reimagined *A Travesty of Torn Souls.* My second novel would be born, along with our child.

I smiled at a desk that held nothing but papers, my typewriter, pens, and a horde of possibilities. Well, there was the overflowing ashtray...but no alcohol in the open. I'd stopped going to the bars after getting rid of Samson and had halted stocking beers in the fridge. But I couldn't let go of my last stash. What Julie didn't know wouldn't kill her, as they say. As I told myself.

But the condemning, invisible eyes of twenty or more bottles seemed to glare at me from behind the wall. I considered a celebratory drink and crouched near the loose panel. My hand hovered for several seconds, but I withdrew it, telling myself I could stop. Yes, once and for all. I'd lost track of how many times I'd said I wouldn't drink over the years, but now, now I meant it.

I'd become so good at lying to myself, I believed it.

Righting myself, I stretched away the stiffness from sitting in a chair all night and went downstairs.

When I opened the bedroom door, Julie was still sleeping. I joined her under the covers, and she didn't stir. Since there was no reason to wake her, I let my eyelids grow heavy and drifted to sleep.

When I woke, it was to the sound of Julie vomiting in the bathroom down the hall. Momentarily alarmed, I rushed to her side, but she had already flushed.

"Everything okay?"

Julie laughed. "Everything's fine. This is normal."

"Right." I smiled. "It'll still take some getting used to."

"Well, good afternoon, sleepyhead. It's after lunch."

"Sorry, I was up late. I was writing."

"That's wonderful. About what?" She glanced over her shoulder as she walked to the kitchen.

She had to be in an excellent mood to acknowledge my writing.

I followed her.

"Are you sure you want to know? You haven't asked about my writing in years." I spoke with gentle shock as I took a seat at the table.

Julie placed a cup of coffee in front of me. Her hand lingered on my shoulder. She kissed my cheek, then brushed a lock behind my ear. "I wouldn't ask if I didn't." She sat, mirroring me as she clutched her own cup.

I took a long, steady gulp. "Um, it's about a young guy named Jason. He's working through whether he believes in God."

"Sounds familiar." Her gaze met mine. "And where do you stand with that these days, darling?"

"Darling?" Smiling, I placed my hand on Julie's. "You are happy."

"I am."

"Well, to be completely honest, I'd say…I'm on the better side of things now. Maybe we had to go through all that hell to get here. That's how it's going for Jason…or will go once I figure out how to connect the beginning to the end. That's the thing with writing. You can know the end, even write it, before the middle."

"Do you ever wish real life was like that?"

"Sometimes. I mean, not that I want to be at the end of my life, but to be happy, yeah. I'd like to avoid all the bad stuff and just arrive."

She entwined her fingers with mine. "Yet you just said you thought we had to go through hell to be…here. Maybe." Her mouth hitched up on one side.

"Come here, you." I stood, still holding her hand, and pulled her to me. "Things are going to be better from now on, I promise."

So, for the next several weeks, we lived some of the best in our marriage. In some ways, we were like newlyweds again. Only now we had another person on the way. My inspiration was back in full force as I cranked out another manuscript.

By July, I was nearly done with the first draft of my next book.

∞ ∞ ∞

"Julie?"

My wife lay on her side, her back to me. I stood by the door, just beyond the threshold, but out in the hall, nonetheless.

"Julie, please..."

She made a noise but didn't speak.

"You're not alone in this. Let me—"

"Just go, Stephen. I can't..." The pillow swallowed her words, her sobs.

"Fine. I'll sleep upstairs."

The words were a familiar phrase, their tune a lament. How many times did we need to relive this circular narrative?

I withdrew, angry at myself. I couldn't comfort my wife and was angry at Julie for pushing me away. But my wrath was directed mostly at some ethereal force for letting this happen, again and again and again. Yes, at that point, I believed enough to blame God. Julie, however, was different. Her faith had always been strong, until it wasn't. Her words from a previous loss struck me like a brick to the head.

It's like I'm being punished.

Maybe you're right. Maybe there is no God.

And in that moment, that brick shattered her window of faith.

What else was new? I should've been used to this dirge that was my life's song.

I sat in the darkness for several hours. I'd cried to the point of draining my reservoir of tears hours ago. Now, I was an empty vessel, perhaps waiting for something to fill me besides hopelessness.

I had no words. No words for Julie. No words for what had happened. No words to write.

My dreams were dashed on the rocks, where I was the rock at the bottom.

I stood from the sofa and wandered outside. My old friends beckoned as I went to the garage. The bottles upstairs were empty, so these good old fellows would have to do.

I pushed aside cans of motor oil, filthy rags, and a watering can on the shelf. When my fumbling fingers found purchase with the wine bottle's smooth, familiar contours, I grasped the neck and withdrew it. Despite not drinking for months, it was like not a day had passed. Images of my father, in violent fits or cruelly laughing as he raised the rod, flashed through my mind. Nevertheless, I stepped into the sultry summer night air, hit the top of the bottle just right on the pavement, and the glass broke off below the cork. I cradled the bottle with both hands and brought it to my lips, the jagged glass cutting into the skin. Blood and alcohol mixed, but I drank it all down...until it was gone.

Let it hurt. Let it burn. Let it cut me into shards and throw me into oblivion.

Anything to forget I wasn't going to be a father. Somehow, this time, I knew this fact was final. But maybe it was for the best, for I knew what sort of man my father had been. Now, as I held the empty bottle to the stars and gave drunken cheers to an indifferent God, I was, without a shred of doubt, cut from my father's cloth.

This was it, the culmination of years and years of trying to fight a losing battle.

I laughed at the raw, agonizing irony that I had become the monster I had tried for years not to be.

Then I dropped to the ground and sobbed anew, holding that bottle like a baby to my chest, then letting it fall and break. My knees gave out, and I buckled to the ground, a mixture of fatigue and drunken stupor.

Then darkness.

∞ ∞ ∞

When I woke with the sunlight glaring in my eyes and the unyielding surface of the pavement beneath me, I sat up and groaned. If a man could survive falling from a skyscraper and having a train run over him and then back up, I suppose this was what it would feel like. Leaning on the side of the house, I managed to stand.

"What was I thinking?" I muttered, shaking my head. And here I thought I'd been doing better, that maybe I was finally past all the drinking.

Yeah, right.

I entered the house and searched for Julie. She was wrapped in a blanket on the couch, staring vacantly out the window.

I joined her and waited for her to speak. When no words came, I asked, "Aren't you warm with that on?" I pointed toward the blanket.

Julie shrugged.

"I..."

"You don't have to explain, Stephen. I saw you passed out in the driveway. If that's your way of dealing with this, who am I to change you? Anything I said all these years hasn't mattered. You've turned to the drink so many times, I'm not surprised it's any different this time." Julie's voice was distant and raw, her throat parched from too much emotion wailing through it in the past day.

"Julie, it was stupid. That's not what I...I mean, that's not the type of husband I want to be. Not anymore. This doesn't have to be the end." I grasped at words, knowing how pathetic I sounded.

Julie glared. "But it's been the end for years. Just a long, drawn-out end. This conversation should sound familiar, or have you numbed your mind to remembering? How many times can we continue on this path before it's finally over?"

"But...but...I'm still your husband. You're still my wife. Whether we have kids or not, that won't change. I've been doing better, haven't I? I've been making an honest day's wage, providing for you. I've loved you the best way I know how."

"The best way you know how?" Tears tracked steadily down her cheeks.

She flung my hollow words back, but they hit me with the force of a locomotive.

Desperation seized me. I wondered how I ever could have wrecked her. Wrecked us. "We're in this together. I know it's too soon to have a kid, but we can still try—" What was I even saying? Did I even hear myself anymore?

A crease appeared between Julie's thin eyebrows, and she recoiled, as if my words had lashed her. "How can you even suggest—?" With muffled sobs, she ran from the room and slammed the bedroom door.

Yes, how could I even suggest? I had no right.

∞ ∞ ∞

For Julie's sake, I kept alcohol out of the house and hoped she wouldn't find the evidence that lingered from days gone by. Was this easy?

Is asking a leopard to change his spots easy?

This leopard grew more ferocious without his old enemies disguised as friends, but then he simply grew weary. Anger took too much energy, and hollowness replaced it. Julie and I became strangers living in the same house. We barely noticed each other, and while tempted to ask why she didn't return to her parents, I never did.

I never asked her how she was doing, what she was thinking, or what she thought about us.

How do dead people talk to each other?

For that was what we had become.

Dead to each other. Dead to the world.

The one small light was the completion of my second novel. Since my first book had been a success, my agent was more than happy to work with me again. Before I knew it, *A Travesty of Torn Souls* was off to the publisher, and several months later, it became another literary triumph.

"Let me take you and the wife out to celebrate," Mr. Riggs, my agent, boomed over the phone in early June 1937.

"I don't know." I gazed at Julie in the other room, in her usual spot on the couch with the worn blanket around her shoulders. "We don't really go out much these days." That was the understatement of the decade. "Besides, should we really celebrate when so many people have lost what little they already had?"

Maybe I'd become so used to wallowing in bitterness that the suffering economy and hard times were extensions of my worldview. Nineteen thirty-seven was a deep valley for America, so why should I be on a mountaintop?

"Come on, old boy! It'll be fun. Not getting out much is all the more reason why you should. My treat."

"Well, okay." I sighed, unsure how I would convince Julie to leave the house. I didn't much favor going out and pretending to have a good ol' time.

"Great! Clear your busy schedule for June 21, B.R. It's a date."

I hung up and frowned at the empty calendar next to the phone.

I left the kitchen and stood a few feet from Julie. "That was Riggs."

She turned toward me and raised her eyebrows. "Your agent?"

"Yeah, him. Do you know another Riggs?"

"What do you want to tell me, Stephen?" She sighed with the weary slump in her shoulders of a woman who had long ago given up.

"He wants to take us out to celebrate in a few weeks."

"Fine," she said with exaggerated calm. "You did write and publish another book. That's one thing you've managed to do. If there's something worth celebrating, that might as well be it."

"You don't sound enthusiastic."

"Should I be?"

"Look, we don't have to go—"

Julie stood. "Let's go. It might be nice, for once, to pretend we're a normal couple with friends who go out to eat from time to time." She brushed past me with all the iciness of winter, leaving a frost in her wake.

∞ ∞ ∞

A couple of weeks later, I looked myself over in the mirror. I had put on my best suit for dinner with Riggs and his wife. Grinning, I found Julie sitting at her vanity in our bedroom. She placed the finishing touches on her look with diamond earrings as I stood behind her.

My heart skipped a beat as my stomach dropped inside. "You look...gorgeous."

Julie smiled, her reflection giving the twinkle in her eye away as she gazed at me. She turned. "You shaved."

I quirked my lips into a small smile. "I haven't forgotten how."

She stood and touched the side of my head, brushing her fingers through my hair. "When did you go to the barber's?"

"I skipped out this afternoon while you were taking a bath and getting ready."

"You look...like you did the first time I saw you." Julie's mind seemed elsewhere.

I took her hand and kissed it. "You've always been beautiful. I'm sorry..." I cleared my throat. "I'm sorry I haven't taken the time to tell you lately." My shoulders slumped, but I held fast to her hand, afraid to release. "And I know there's nothing I can say to undo what's happened, but maybe...maybe this night is what we need. Maybe it's a step in the right direction. Julie, I love you."

"For what it's worth, I'm sorry, too. And you're right; going out tonight will be what we need. I wasn't looking forward to it at first, but as I got ready today, I realized how much I've missed spending time with you." She placed her hand over my heart. "This you. No alcohol-altered version. Just the real you."

I squeezed her hand and pulled her to me. We kissed, and in that moment, years of hardship melted away. We were twenty-one again, dreamers with our whole lives ahead, not a care in the world. Together, we could conquer anything. We forged our bond with our everlasting love, a promise made to never part. When we withdrew, we remained lost in each other's gaze for what could have been seconds or hours.

I cupped her chin and tucked a stray lock behind her ear. Bringing my face to hers, I kissed her again. When I pulled away, I smiled. "We probably should get going, or Riggs will wonder what's held us up."

Shortly thereafter, we were driving downtown to some fancy French restaurant whose name I couldn't pronounce. Julie and I were in better moods than we'd been in years. Caught up in the atmosphere's glamor and Riggs's infectious big personality, the wine and conversation flowed easily that night. At the end of it all, we wished my agent and his wife well and were on our way.

"What a night!" I exclaimed, feeling free and young again.

"How many glasses of wine did you have?" Julie pulled at my arm.

"I'm fine." I calmed and smirked. "I'm high on the excitement of celebrating. Another book published! At this rate, we'll make it big when so many others have it hard."

Julie frowned. "Hmm, well, I'm not so sure I'd go about bragging."

"But I wasn't bragging." I scowled, hating how deflated her comment made me feel. "Can't you just be happy for me?"

Julie curled her arm through mine and leaned into me. "I am happy for you, darling."

As soon as my joy-filled balloon had begun to lose air, it inflated. I swept Julie up in my arms, spun her around, and kissed her. She giggled.

"Oh, Julie, everything's turning around, don't you see? I know it right here." I thumped my chest.

"Seeing you smile makes me smile. Tonight was lovely. Thank you for suggesting we go out. It was long overdue."

"Yes, yes, it was." I drifted along in a daze, heady with pleasure from the wine.

We reached the car, and I opened the door for Julie. I fell behind the wheel and started her up. Julie and I lapsed into silence as we left the city's lights and drove onto darker streets.

I smiled and glanced at Julie. Out of the corner of my eye, the glare of oncoming headlights hit me. As I turned my head, the steering wheel pivoted also, tied with an invisible cord. And that was all I knew.

When I opened my eyes to more brightness, I thought those headlights were still coming at me. With a flinch, I cried out in pain. After I adjusted, my surroundings gave way to a hospital ward. Only one eye could see. I tried to move my arms, but they lay paralyzed at my sides. I panicked.

Finding my voice, I called out hoarsely, "What's going on?"

A frowning nurse came to the bedside. After studying me, she left, only to return with a police officer.

"Mr. Richardson, you've been in an automobile accident. Are you aware you were driving under the influence of alcohol?"

"I... Where's my wife?"

"Mr. Richardson—"

"My wife. Where is she?" I tried to sit up, but my body wouldn't budge. Every bandage restrained me. Why wasn't this clown answering me?

"What you need to understand, sir, is that—"

"No, where is Julie Richardson? Anna Julie. She was with me. Tell me—" I couldn't finish. When I gazed into that young cop's eyes, I knew. I just knew.

"Your wife was pronounced dead on the scene."

"No, no..." I muttered, trying to shake my head.

"I'm afraid so, Mr. Richardson, and unfortunately, you are responsible—"

"Go away."

"I'm afraid that I must insist—"

"Go away!"

For a moment, the cop hovered, then left. I glared to the right—the eye I could see out of—to see four beds parallel to my own and occupied by people. Other patients. They flinched as if by looking at me, I would infect them with this vile life of mine. A few others gazed at me, and I wished I had the strength to bolt and punch every one of them for condemning me with their eyes for something they couldn't understand.

"Julie, no... It can't be."

I killed my wife. Because of me. I was just like my old man. Just. Like. My. Old. Man.

Staring, glaring at the ceiling, it blurred as tears overtook my vision. I tried to fist my hands, to pound into the mattress, but my stupid body wouldn't cooperate. My liquid shame poured down my face as I was forced to stare at a crack in the ceiling. Cracked. I was cracked. Broken. I'd broken Julie, my everything, the one who'd chosen to be with me. Now, there was nothing. No point. I wept for all I was, for what I had done, for who I was.

The bed was a rock beneath me, pressing against my body. I was buried with Julie. Around me, whispers from nurses and patients went up as judgment against me, but those people could've been demons in hell for all I knew. Yet my idiot lungs kept working, every breath stabbing me. In and out. Out and in. Why, oh why, wouldn't it just stop? Stop! Just. Stop.

Because Julie was stopped. Yet time kept moving forward, ever forward. No choice. No point or purpose. Was I to live out my days in a seemingly endless impossibility?

I was the unwanted, the forgotten, the one who shouldn't have existed. I was everything my father had instilled in me. That truth rooted inside in the forefront of my mind, and the poisonous plant that grew there instead would branch to every part of my brain for the next several years. I watered it regularly with self-loathing, shame, and guilt. It flourished where hope died.

"They need to take me away," I murmured. "I can't be here. Let me die. Just let me die, so I can see her again. They need to take me away. Julie, Julie... They need to take me away...to you...to you."

But I would not die. My inner tree of hatred made sure of that.

Others continued to stare at me like I was out of my mind. Maybe I was, but in that dizzying, unimaginable, nightmarish moment, what else could I do? My sobs mingled with my words. I'd done the unthinkable.

In my all-encompassing exhaustion, I fell asleep. Don't ask me how. Maybe my mind and body had shut down, despite the pain shooting through my head and down my frayed nerves.

But my escape was short-lived. Upon waking, the fact Julie was dead struck me all over again, like getting hit by a car repeatedly and not dying. That was a horrible analogy, but too true for my situation. Why couldn't I have been the one to die?

An older cop entered the room. His demeanor was much less hesitant than his younger partner, who loitered by the door.

"Mr. Richardson, you already know you're responsible for your wife's death. You can add two more to your count. You will be going to court."

"Wait, what? I killed two more people?"

The room spun. I wanted to hold my head, to stop the movement, but my arms lay worthless on the mattress. Instead, I squeezed my eyes shut, willing to close my ears, too. It was no use.

"That's correct. However, it hasn't been determined whether the next of kin will press charges."

"They should condemn me. It's nothing less than I deserve."

"I'm glad to see you understand the implications of your crime, Mr. Richardson. I don't take kindly to drunks."

I glared at the police officer as my blood boiled. "I don't need your judgment. You think I don't feel guilty enough? Nothing will bring my wife back! Nothing!"

The cop stepped back, holding up his hands. "Keep your voice down, young man. Justice will be served, no matter how you feel. You'll be here until the doctors deem your injuries sufficiently healed, but then it's off to prison with your sorry self."

I was about to retort, but then I saw the man's badge for the first time and realized he was a captain. I didn't know what his beef was with alcoholics, but I didn't care. In my grief, my anger had surfaced and taken hold.

He shook his head at me and left.

∞ ∞ ∞

Left alone, I would continue in that vein for the next six years. Alone in prison for two years. Then alone in my old house, surrounded by dead things. I should have been dead.

"They need to take me away." That was all I believed about my pathetic plight, for without Julie, what was the point of anything?

Until *she* came. Lorna Ashford, the woman who would become my next addiction, who reminded me of the worst night of my life and who was my light for the future. The woman who I never should have touched or tainted with my past and lies, yet the woman who I had come to love.

The second woman who had suffered because of my damaged version of love.

Alone again.

But not for long. They should have taken me away years ago.

Now they would.

The broken bottles surrounded me on the rocky beach near the lake as the water lapped at my feet in the darkness of night. I got into my truck, as beaten and tattered as I was, and drove straight for the concrete barrier that separated land from water, life from death.

Chapter 25: Lorna

A day passed, but not once did I see Tristan outside. The flowers I'd planted in his yard began to wilt. I frowned, wondering if he had noticed them.

The breezy fall afternoon made leaves spiral down from their branches and then swirl around my feet as I went to my garage in search of a watering can. I came away disappointed. Did I expect one to materialize out of thin air?

Standing on the border of my yard, I watched Tristan's house for any sign of movement within. This was ridiculous! If I wanted to water the flowers, I would borrow his can.

I had been looking for an excuse to see him again. Maybe he would see me snooping in his shed and would step outside to demand what I was up to. Instead, I spent the next ten minutes in his shed looking for a blessed watering can, but to no avail. My only other option was Tristan's garage. I tried the door, and it opened.

Tristan's truck was missing. Wondering where he had gone off to, I smiled with relief upon finding a rusty watering can. After wrestling with the spigot for a trickle of water, I managed what should have been an easy task.

While I was watering the mums, the ringing of my phone came through my open kitchen window. I dropped the can, ran inside, and tried to catch my breath as I answered.

"Laura, darling, thank the heavens I reached you."

"Macy, what is it? Is something the matter?"

"Have you read the paper this morning?"

"No, why?"

"It's not front-page news, but turn to the fourth page."

"Macy, what—?" I grabbed the paper off my table and flipped it open, finding a picture of a familiar pickup truck smashed into a concrete wall. My stomach knotted as I scanned the article. "Oh, my—" Tears sprang into my eyes. "Tristan..."

"I didn't want to be the bearer of bad news, darling. I'm so sorry."

"How could he do this?"

"I don't know. Do you want me to come over?"

"Can you? Please."

"See you in ten minutes, darling."

After I hung up, I reread the article, a task made more difficult by my blurry vision. I kept wiping the tears away, but they were relentless. Tristan had driven his truck into the barrier near the lake last night. Several empty bottles had been found near the scene. There was no doubt it had been deliberate. He hadn't wanted to risk hurting or killing anyone else, so he had gone off alone to a place and a time where there would be no one.

"Oh, Tristan, how could you? How could you be so stupid?"

Those next few minutes seemed an eternity, so the moment Macy stepped inside without knocking, I bombarded her with a hug. She was my lifeline. She held me until I let go.

"I'm so sorry, Laura. I never thought he would do something like this."

"Me, neither. I mean, things ended badly between us...but if I'm the reason he—"

"Don't even say it. Come, now. Let me make you a hot drink, and we'll talk or just sit in silence if that's what you need."

I shook my head. "I don't want anything, except things to go back to the way they were between Tristan and me. Macy, why didn't I go to him sooner? I've come to understand these past few weeks why he kept that awful secret. I-I loved him, Mace."

"Then you need to tell him that."

"But who knows what condition he's in. The article didn't say. What if—? Macy, what if he dies?"

"He didn't die, so there's hope. Maybe his injuries aren't life-threatening."

"But I don't know that!"

"Do you want me to drive you to the hospital?"

"Do you think it's too soon?"

"We won't know unless we try."

I took a deep breath, trying to calm myself. With a nod, I grabbed my coat and followed Macy out the door. Fifteen minutes later, we parked at the hospital. I walked at a brisk pace across the pavement, my shoes clicking on the hard surface. Macy tried to keep up with me but fell behind.

I entered and approached the front desk. "Where can I find Tristan Blake?" I asked the nurse.

She raised her eyebrows at my demanding tone. "Are you family?"

"No, but—"

"Please take a seat, miss. I will have to figure out where he is located and if he is allowed visitors."

I exhaled loudly through my nostrils and frowned.

Macy joined me. "Any news?"

"Nothing yet. The nurse is checking his status. I don't even think she knows who he is or where he is in the hospital."

"Well, this is a big hospital, darling. You won't do yourself any good standing and rocking on your feet like that. Let's find seats."

I acquiesced and sat on one of the straight-backed wooden chairs in the lobby. A few people dotted the area, murmuring to each other in hushed voices or lost with their gazes straight ahead. I kept looking at the clock, willing the second hand to move faster. Every agonizing minute when that hand would click to the next dash between the large numbers only fueled my mounting anxiety.

The middle-aged nurse returned and stepped behind desk, motioning me to come to her. I exchanged a glance with Macy and returned to the desk.

"Mr. Blake's condition is stable but serious. He's not yet ready to receive visitors, I'm afraid."

"How much longer?"

"I can't say. Perhaps by this evening if all goes well."

"Can I wait?"

"If you wish, but, Miss—"

"Ashford."

"Miss Ashford, it might not be until tomorrow or the next day. You would be more comfortable returning to your home and coming back at another time."

"But— but..." I squeezed my eyes shut, trying to keep the tears in. I failed. "Darn it."

The nurse's face softened. She leaned across the desk and said, "I can tell he's someone very special to you. I'm sorry."

"I loved him. I l-love him." I sniffled, my bottom lip trembling. "I can't—"

Just then, Macy joined me and placed an arm around me. "Come on, darling. You do yourself no good like this. At least sit back down."

I didn't protest and allowed Macy to guide me back to the seat. "I'm staying, Mace. I don't care if I have to sleep here."

"Okay. If that's what you want. Do you want me to stay with you?"

"You should go back to your family, Mace. Thank you for everything you've done." I faced my best friend straight on and looked at her for the first time in months. If there was a physical manifestation of selflessness, Macy Wells was it. I took her hands in mine and squeezed them. "Thank you for everything you've always done, for every time you've been there, especially when I was horrible to you. But I'm going to be okay, Mace."

Macy's eyes were glassy as she kissed my cheek and stood. "You call me if you need anything, anything at all, Laura. Don't even think of taking the bus home either. I'm always here for you."

"Thank you."

I watched Macy leave through the front doors and sighed. Leaning my head against the paneled wall behind me, I closed my eyes and hoped for some sleep.

I was awakened to the gentle shaking of a hand on my shoulder.

"Miss?"

"Oh, sorry." I saw the same nurse from earlier and then gazed past her at an empty lobby. "What time is it?"

"It's late, but you can go see him if you wish."

Hope fluttered in my heart. "Really?"

"Yes." She smiled, the worry lines around her mouth and forehead softening. "He's on the third floor in room 304."

I stood, thanked that kind nurse, and made my way to the elevator.

Chapter 26

The lights were low as I stepped into the room. A curtain was drawn partway around the bed, and beyond it, the evening sun was shining an orange glow in through a window that overlooked the city. Just past the threshold, I stopped, my left hand on the door frame, my mom's wedding ring still nestled on the index finger.

There he was. Tristan was stretched out on the bed, his lower half covered. From my vantage point, his face was hidden in shadow, but both of his arms rested at his sides, wrapped in casts.

Right now. This was the moment of decision.

Without allowing any thoughts to hold me back, I took another step and then another, until I arrived at Tristan's bedside.

At first, I thought he was sleeping, but through a heavily bruised and discolored face, the right side of which was covered in bandages, his left eye met mine.

"I called you Mr. Rock Garden."

"Lorna," he whispered, his lips barely moving.

"Before I knew you, that's what I called you."

"Am I dreaming?"

"But then we met."

"Is this heaven?"

"And I got to know you."

"Have they finally come to take me away?"

"And then I grew to love you."

Tristan didn't speak, but tears were flowing steadily and silently down his exposed cheek, losing themselves in the new beard that had begun to grow there.

I leaned in until my lips touched his ear. "I love you, Tristan. No one is taking you away. You tried to take yourself away, but it didn't work. You're my rock, Mr. Rock Garden."

Tristan's breaths came short and labored, and his tears turned into sobs. "Are you really real?" He turned his head toward me, which was no small effort, and stared at me with one impossibly vivid blue eye.

"Yes. And don't you dare try to..." My voice gave way to the torrent of emotion that I had been keeping in check. "Tristan, when I heard... You could have died!"

"I wanted to die."

I rubbed at my face, dashing the tears away. "Stop it. Just stop. You've made me so angry already. Don't do it again."

"But...I thought you'd be better off without me. I caused you more than a lifetime of pain. If I'd have died that night when they all did, none of this would've happened. You would have still suffered the loss of your parents, but I wouldn't have been able to inflict more damage on you."

"And I would've never met you, but you know what? As much as I wanted to hate you, I couldn't."

"You should have. You still should, Lorna. If you know what's good for you..."

"Maybe I don't know what's good for me, then. Maybe I've finally, completely, utterly cracked, gone nuts. Put me in the insane asylum and throw away the key. Lock me in a padded cell. Anything but live the rest of my life without you. Tristan, *you're* what's good for me."

"But everything bad I've done..."

I wanted to hold his hand and pull him toward me in an embrace, but his injuries were a poignant reminder of his grief. Instead, I kissed him, gently, so as not to hurt him in any way. His lips responded to mine. When the kiss drew to a close, I said, "Forgive yourself. I forgive you, Tristan. It was an accident. I don't believe you have a malicious bone in your body. I'll say it again at the risk of sounding redundant, but you are my rock."

"But how can you be here like this, so ready to forgive? It's not that easy."

"I've had a long time to think about this. Years and years before I knew you, I chose to be bitter, depressed, and angry...any number of negative emotions. I was starting to fall back into that same pattern after I found out the truth, but you know what? I know better now. I knew life could be something good and worthwhile again, even after all the heartache. I chose the better part. You were, *you are*, that part."

"Why would you risk loving a man like me? My past will be a shadow that follows us everywhere we go. What if I do something reckless again, something that...?"

I pulled a chair up to the bed and placed a hand on either side of Tristan's face, willing him to look at me. "That's a risk I'm willing to take. I choose you, Tristan, because I love you, pure and simple."

He sighed, his brow creasing. It must have pained him physically and emotionally, for he winced. "I love you, Lorna, but is it enough?"

"Listen, Tristan. You're stronger than you think. I'm betting you didn't touch alcohol for years based on your aversion when I offered you a drink all those months ago. The drinking aside, you've shown me your soul. You're selfless, giving, and honorable. You did more for me than you'll ever know. You saw something worthwhile in me when I didn't see it in myself, and I'm telling you, I see how beautiful you are. Your love is like a precious treasure some people spend their whole lives searching for and never find."

"Maybe." He didn't sound convinced. "You're right. I didn't touch alcohol after Julie and your parents died, although the lure of drowning my sorrows after Julie's death was tempting. You know, it wasn't always like that, me drinking. When I first met Julie, it was still Prohibition...if you can believe that. I drank then, but things turned south after we got married."

"What happened?"

"We wanted to start a family, but it seemed Julie couldn't stay pregnant. It was miscarriage after miscarriage. We nearly gave up after years. My drinking became unstoppable. We grew more and more distant. Then, when she finally kept the baby the longest she had, we were overjoyed. I stopped drinking for a time, but..."

"Oh, no." I knew what was coming. My stomach dropped inside, and fresh tears prickled in the corners of my eyes.

"She was about four months along when it happened. After that, our marriage was in shambles. She didn't want to try to have a family anymore, saying it was impossible. I kept pushing her to keep trying, but when she refused, I surrendered to the monster I'd fought all those years. Alcohol was once again a better comfort than my wife."

"I'm sorry. I can't imagine."

Tristan shook his head as much as he could. "Something inside me just broke, cracked. My own father was an alcoholic, so I guess the tendency was already in my family. I hated myself for it, but the more I drank, the further into the pit I got. Until one day, it took her life."

"Where did you two go that night?"

"It had been months since we'd been out of the house to do anything other than go to the store. So much had suffered because of my problem—Julie did, of course, but so did my writing. I didn't publish anything for years."

"That's why there's such a gap between *Cure for the Cries* and *A Travesty of Torn Souls*," I said, everything falling into place like a well-played chess game.

"Exactly. Well, my second book had been out for several months by that point, and my agent wanted to take us out to celebrate its success. Julie and I went downtown, and we met up with my agent and his wife at some overpriced restaurant. Mr. Riggs, my agent, insisted on paying for everything, including drinks. You can guess what happened."

I nodded. "And Mr. Riggs had no idea of your problem?"

"No one knew but Julie."

"So, you were enjoying yourself?"

"Too much. We spent several hours out. I was good at tricking everyone I wasn't as gone as I was. Since Julie couldn't drive, I got behind the wheel. She asked me if it was wise for me to drive, but I insisted I was fine. But I wasn't, was I?"

"No, you couldn't have been. Do you remember what happened?"

"All I know is it was incredibly dark; the road we were on had no streetlights. One second, we were the only ones on the road, and the next, headlights were coming at us. I blacked out and awoke to find myself in a hospital bed much like this."

"When did you find out...about Julie?"

"It doesn't matter anymore. The past is written in stone."

"Is that why the rocks?"

"Yes. Those rocks were my constant reminder, that my past was immovable as they were." He sighed. "I guess I should tell you the rest of the story, seeing as I've told you everything else. I'll never forget when the police officer walked into that hospital room and told me I killed Julie...and your parents. When you came here today, part of me expected a cop to step through that door."

"No, no more police," I said, holding his right hand, careful not to disturb his broken arm as it lay useless at his side. "You may think the only person you hurt this time was yourself, Tristan, but you'd be wrong."

"Lorna, I know I keep saying it, but I never...I never meant to hurt you. In any of this."

"If you'd have died, you would've hurt me more than you can imagine," I said, anger spiking. "Don't you *ever* do something like that again, you hear me? Your life is valuable, precious...if not to you, then to me."

"I thought you were willing to take that risk."

"Don't be foolish. Of course I am willing, but that doesn't give you the right to throw your life away. You've finally told me the whole truth, and you know what? I love you more for it. I want to know you completely, Tristan."

"You know Tristan isn't my real name."

"Perhaps not, but no more than Lorna is for me. Legally, I never changed it."

Tristan laughed weakly. "I changed mine, legally and all, after I got out of prison. I suppose it was my attempt at starting over, like you said with the deliberate changing of your name. Stephen means honor, fame, victory..."

"Much like Laura." I smiled. "And Tristan is like Lorna."

"Sad, sorrowful, forlorn. Yes."

"We both tried changing to escape our pasts," I said. "I tried starting over by destroying everything that belonged to my family. Lorna had already been around for a while by the time I moved."

"Are you going to keep it, the name, I mean?"

"I don't know."

"You're Lorna to me, sorry. I guess if you're really willing to give a messed —up bugger like me a try, then we're stuck with each other, huh?"

"Yes, Tristan, I afraid you're stuck with me, warts and all."

"You don't have any warts!"

I smiled, laughter bubbling up inside me for the first time since I'd entered that hospital room. "It's just a saying, you insufferable man." I sobered, then continued, "But seriously, after all this talk, I really hope you and I are stuck with each other. I don't want it any other way. I love you in my guilty, messy, you-drive-me-crazy way."

"As soon as I'm able, I'm gonna pull you to me and never let you go, Lorna Ashford. You're the most stubborn woman I know and thank God for it. And I love you in my guilty, messy, you-drive-me-crazy way."

I leaned down and kissed Tristan again. While this wasn't the first kiss we had shared, it was the first kiss of many we would share with the promise to be stuck with each other. Just like I was stuck with Laura and Lorna. Just like he was stuck with Stephen and Tristan. We were, neither of us, one persona or the other, but rather some beautiful, messy, complicated version splattered on a canvas, but a masterpiece painting, nonetheless.

When we broke apart, Tristan asked, "Is the beard bothering you, by the way?"

"It's growing on me."

The Story Continues with Book #2 in the Lorna & Tristan Series: Rocks and Flowers in a Box

I stared at my mother's wedding band nestled on my ring finger. A week and two days ago, it had moved from my index finger to its current residence, the significance of that simple act still pulsing through me.

Married.

I, Lorna Ashford, was now Lorna Blake. I, the woman who at the ripe old age of twenty-seven, had resigned herself to the fate of old maid, was married. The tiny wedding had been officiated by my childhood minister, Pastor Wilson, in the Methodist church in my old neighborhood in Cleveland. It was nothing short of a miracle.

A year ago, I didn't believe in miracles. My faith was broken, as shattered as the bottles of booze my husband left on the beach when he tried to kill himself last fall. He wasn't even my husband then, but he was the man I loved, the person I opened my heart to after knowing only loss for so many years.

My husband led me back to God. My husband taught me what it was to forgive the seemingly impossible. My husband healed my heart, renewed my faith, even though his own faith still hung with the light shining on half of it, the other half shrouded in darkness. Like a lot of things, he kept his faith as a closed book.

But I had my husband, my new family. My old family was dead.

Two and a half weeks before my wedding, the United States and the other Allies had invaded Normandy in France. Both my life and the world were moving in a positive direction, yet a pang rang through my heart as I remembered Chucky, my brother, who had died last year in this awful war. Getting married three days after the seventh anniversary of my parents' deaths was also a mixed bag. I hoped to create some new, happy memories.

Stop it, Lorna. Be happy.

As I packed boxes of books, I sneezed from buildup of dust.

"You okay there?"

I looked up from my task and smiled, the warmth overtaking the sadness in my heart. Walking into his tired old living room was the man I loved. Even after all this time, to see him as he really was—blue eyes shining with happiness instead of pent-up heartache—it was like a fairytale dream. I hoped he would open his book and tell me more of his story.

"Just some dust. You really want to keep all of these?" I asked.

He came to me and stilled my hand, removing the tattered book from my grasp, and kissed me. My eyes slid shut for the next several moments, and I let the book fall to the floor, bringing my hands to his face. The usual stubble of not shaving for a week greeted my fingers as I skimmed them over his jawline and cheeks, working into his sandy-colored hair.

"Lorna," Tristan breathed, "the things you do to me."

I giggled. "There's time enough for that later. Let's get these boxes to my place— that is, *our* place. That still feels odd to say."

Tristan picked up one of the larger boxes with a grunt and chuckled. "*Our* place, yes."

As I walked beside him out the door of his bungalow and across his rocky yard, I said, "Are you sure you're okay with living right next door to your old house? Because we can still move. I know it can't be easy."

"I'm sure." Tristan stopped to catch his breath. "As much as I'm glad to be getting rid of that house, it's still part of my history. It wasn't all bad."

I paused beside him. "Are you okay?"

"I'm fine. Just feeling a bit worn out for all this heavy lifting."

"If you're sure..." I studied his flushed face. "This isn't like you, Mr. Tall and Handy."

"Lorna," he groaned, "you worry too much."

"You're right. Don't listen to me. I'm just being a concerned wife." I beamed.

We entered through the side door of our bungalow. Tristan set the box on the kitchen table, his face unreadable.

"What's on your mind?" I asked. "Maybe a break is in order. We've been sorting through your things all morning."

He gave a small smile and a slight nod, wiping sweat from his brow. "That would be welcome."

"I can make some iced tea."

"Anything liquid would be like heaven going down my throat right about now. I hope the whole summer isn't going to be this hot."

I grinned as I put the teapot on the stove and turned on the burner. "Until the tea is ready, you'll have to settle for water."

I filled two glasses and placed them on the table. We drew up mismatched chairs and drank. Tristan finished first and sighed with pleasure.

I eyed him over the top of my glass. He gazed out the back window toward his house, the line between his eyebrows deepening. I put my glass down and asked, "So?"

"So, what?"

"Really, Tristan? Do you enjoy playing these guessing games?" My mouth hitched up on one side.

"Maybe." There was a teasing undertone in his voice, but the crease between his eyebrows was still present.

"We're married now. I think you can tell me anything."

He whisked his eyes away from the window and met mine. "There's nothing I could tell you that you don't know already."

"I find that hard to believe," I joked, then grew serious. "But something's off about you today." As happy as I was, doubt poked at me.

"To be honest, I never thought I'd be married again."

I took his hands in mine. For a moment, I stared at his large, rough hands—hands that could fix anything, from a house to a car, but also had typed and penned thousands of poetic prose, weaving those threads into the fabric of three novels. I met his eyes. "I think this will taking adjusting on both our parts. We weren't exactly social butterflies before we met." I laughed.

The line between Tristan's eyebrows lessened, and crinkles formed around his eyes as he smiled. "That's the understatement of the century."

After the moment of levity passed, I said, "So, enlighten me, O Talkative One."

"Going through all my things, it's like digging through the past." His eyes shifted to the box on the table. "Maybe it would be better if I got rid of most of these things and be more like you. You know, completely start over."

The tea kettle whistled. I stood and went to the stove, turned off the burner, and added a teabag. I gave a little snort. "My house is filling up quickly, but throwing away everything from your past isn't the answer, Tristan. You can see how well that served me." I joined him at the table.

"My stuff is taking over in here. I'm letting go of the house. It's time I let go of other reminders, too."

"Of Julie?" I asked quietly.

"Yes, of Julie." He stared out the window toward his house again, as if his wife's ghost were looking back at him out one of the windows.

"Hey." I placed my hand on his arm.

He slowly turned his head, but his eyes were on the table.

I moved my hand to his cheek. "You wouldn't be forgetting her."

Eyes so empty and so full lifted from staring at the tabletop. "I know that here." He pointed to his head. "But here, well, that's another matter." He gestured toward his chest. "Pain and pleasure mixed."

My lips quirked. "We make quite the pair, don't we? I can hear Macy asking now, 'Why can't you two just be happy? Why do you always have to complicate things?'"

Tristan half-smiled. "Your best friend doesn't know the half of it. Messy people are like that...complicated."

"Complicated," I murmured. I brushed my thumb over his lips and raked my fingers over his stubble. "You should keep the beard this time." I withdrew my hand and walked over to the teapot, added ice, and poured two cups, returning to the table with them. "Here. Drink. You're dehydrated, and it's making you crazier than you already are."

Tristan chuckled, picking up the glass and draining it. He clunked it down. "Crazy about you, maybe."

As I was about to take a sip of iced tea, Tristan left his seat and came from behind, wrapping his arms around me and kissing my cheek.

I nearly spilled my glass and set it down, laughing. "Careful there, crazy guy!"

I stood and allowed him to hold me in his strong arms. We rocked to the music in our heads. My eyes were closed, and I imagined his were, too. My face relaxed into an easy smile. Tristan stopped the gentle movement. I turned in his arms and opened my eyes. He stared at me with such intensity that I almost looked away. He brushed a stray dark curl from my cheek.

"What did I do to deserve you?" he asked in a husky voice. Then he leaned down and claimed my lips with his.

After nearly a year, I marveled how almost every kiss from Tristan could reduce me to feeling like a puddle. I brought my arms around his neck and pulled him closer. The world melted away around us. Like the first time we kissed in his dismal living room of days gone by, our kiss created beauty. When the kiss ended, I caught my breath.

"Keep that up," I said, "and we can forget about getting any work done."

"I can think of better ways to pass our time." He raised an eyebrow and winked.

"Yes, well..." My knees threatened to give out.

Before I could utter another word, Tristan scooped me up and took me to our bedroom. He placed me on the double bed, a new purchase. My old single bed now occupied one of the upstairs bedrooms. The curtains were still closed from that morning, but as I lay on the bed, my head still spinning, Tristan went to the window and shut it. He closed the door and joined me.

"I'm a private man," he murmured, running his fingers along my arm.

A tingle shot through me at his touch. "Mine and mine alone," I whispered.

"Come here."

I moved in closer. Tristan started to undo the buttons on my blouse. I finished for him. He pulled his shirt off over his head, his hair standing on end. He eased me into the embrace of the mattress, bringing his hands to my face and holding me like I was the most precious treasure in the world.

∞ ∞ ∞

I woke as the sun was going down. My stomach rumbled as I turned toward a slumbering Tristan. I smiled.

"How I can manage to sleep through your snoring is a mystery I will never solve," I whispered, kissing his grizzled cheek.

His eyelids fluttered open. "Lorna?" he asked in a gravelly voice.

"Yes, sleepyhead, it's me. It looks like we may have missed dinner."

He groaned as he pushed himself up. He yawned. "What time is it?"

"About nine o'clock, I imagine, at least judging by the sun."

"I guess we won't be getting any more work done today."

I made to leave the bed, but he pulled me toward him, wrapping his arms around me.

Tristan nuzzled my neck, placing kisses along my jawline and using his nose to push my hair out of the way. “It’s almost night. Maybe we should just, you know, stay in bed?” He raised an eyebrow.

I laughed.

“Stay with me, right here.”

“You’re terrible, but still...” Gazing at my husband in the near darkness, the last of the sunlight warming his bare shoulders and chest, I relented. “Oh, okay, you’ve convinced me, but first thing in the morning— ”

“Yes, dear, it’s down to business.”

We chuckled. As the light faded, we lost ourselves in the blankets and each other.

∞ ∞ ∞

I opened my eyes to blinding sunlight. For a moment, I thought the alarm clock was going off beside the bed, as a strange noise had woken me. My brain didn’t register that the sound wasn’t the ring of the clock but rather the wheezing of my husband beside me. I gasped, realization hitting me like ice water as I gazed upon Tristan.

His eyes were shut, but then they flew open. He gazed at me in horror, opening his mouth to try to speak. He grabbed at his chest, as if trying to pull the skin from it.

“Tristan, oh, my gosh! What...what’s happening?” I grabbed at him, tears streaming down my cheeks. “Please, say something. Tell me what I should do!”

“L-Lorna...” The effort to speak my name died on his lips.

Frozen, afraid to leave him to call an ambulance, I watched as his body relaxed. Color returned to his face, and his breathing became normal.

He released a shuddering breath. "I… Lorna, we need to go to the hospital. I think I just had a heart attack."

Illustrations of the Characters

Lorna

Tristan

About the Author

Bestselling author of the Lorna & Tristan Series, Cynthia Hilston is a stay-at-home mom of three young kids, happily married, and lives in the Cleveland, Ohio, area. Writing has always been like another child to her. After twenty years of waltzing in the world of fan fiction, she has stepped away to do her debut dance with original works of fiction, although she still dabbles in fan fiction.

In her spare time–what spare time?–she devours books, shamelessly watches Hallmark movies and *When Calls the Heart,* pets her orange and black kitties, looks at the stars, drinks wine or coffee with good friends, and dreams of what other stories she wishes to tell.

Also by Cynthia Hilston

Hannah's Rainbow: Every Color Beautiful

A Laughing Matter of Pain

Mile Marker 139

Rocks and Flowers in a Box: Lorna & Tristan Series #2

Murder: It's All in Your Head

Arianna

The Rock at the Bottom: Lorna & Tristan Series #3

Short Stories:

Latent Infection & Flushed

Connect with Cynthia Hilston

Did you enjoy this book? Hate it? Whatever your thoughts, please leave a review on Amazon and/or Goodreads! I'd really appreciate it. Reviews help authors. Thank you!

Website: http://www.cynthiahilston.com

Facebook: http://www.facebook.com/cynthiahilstonauthor

Instagram: http://www.instagram.com/authorcynthiahilston

Twitter: http://twitter.com/cynthiahilston

Goodreads: http://www.goodreads.com/cynthiahilstonauthor

Made in the USA
Middletown, DE
24 April 2023